SCC

DYING TO LIVE
LAST RITES

"Delivers a gritty dystopian nightmare that runs a crazy zigzag between the gross, the touching and the carnivalesque. A master of the genre, Paffenroth gives us equal parts horror and social commentary in a tale that crackles with startling insights about the human condition."

—Alden Bell, author of *The Reapers Are the Angels*

"*Last Rites* is Kim Paffenroth at his absolute best. There is intelligence here, and injustice, and heartache, and even love. Paffenroth has made a name for himself by challenging readers' expectations of what the zombie story should be... But this time, he's taken his message not just to our heads, but to our hearts as well, and the result is a haunting book you will not soon forget."

—Joe McKinney, author of *Dead City* and *Apocalypse of the Dead*

"Are the dead still people? A craftsman of the genre, Kim Paffenroth offers his literary take on the zombie apocalypse with *Dying to Live: Last Rites*, combining flesh-ripping gore with a thoughtful view of what it means to be human."

—Craig DiLouie, author of *The Infection*

Also by Kim Paffenroth:
Dying to Live (Permuted Press/Gallery Books)
Dying to Live: Life Sentence (Permuted Press)
Valley of the Dead (Permuted Press)
Gospel of the Living Dead (Baylor University Press)

Edited by Kim Paffenroth:
History Is Dead (Permuted Press)
The World Is Dead (Permuted Press)

DYING TO LIVE
LAST RITES

Kim Paffenroth

Permuted Press
The formula has been changed...
Shifted... Altered... Twisted.
www.permutedpress.com

Acknowledgments

Once again, beta reading duties were ably and generously carried out by Robert Kennedy and Christine Morgan. They were joined this time by Ursula K. Raphael, who brought to the analysis an impressive knowledge of the zombie genre and its permutations. Christine was also the designated replacement writer for this volume: it is a morbid tradition of mine, to choose an author who will finish the manuscript in the event of my untimely death. Christine is an excellent writer whose lean, action-oriented style complements my rather more lumbering, embellished prose and I was thrilled she agreed, and glad she offered her help as the story progressed.

As usual, many people helped with technical questions. On firearms, the experts consulted were again Scott Field, Christopher Iwane, and Doug Wojtowicz, while Alex Parker provided details of the workings and terminology related to boats.

A PERMUTED PRESS book
published by arrangement with the author
ISBN-13: 978-1-934861-71-4
ISBN-10: 1-934861-71-5

Dying to Live: Last Rites copyright © 2011
by Kim Paffenroth.
Edited by D.L. Snell.
All Rights Reserved.

"...for love is strong as death, passion fierce as the grave."
Song of Songs 8:6 (NRSV)

"Let us beware of saying that death is opposed to life. The living is
only a form of what is dead, and a very rare form."
Nietzsche, "The Gay Science," 109
(trans. J. Nauckhoff; Cambridge, UK:
Cambridge University Press, 2001)

"The living are few, but the dead are many."
From the story of the Buddha and Kisagotami
(R. O. Ballou, ed., *The World Bible*; New York:
Penguin Books, 1944; p. 143)

Chapter 1
Lucy

Lucy loved killing. It was the only thing she found exhilarating, the only thing that made her feel vital and real, as though she still mattered and wasn't just a spectator to all the sorry, broken-down things and people—including herself—that surrounded and buffeted her every moment. Every other thing around and within her felt limp and slippery, like you couldn't get a hold of anything and clutch it to yourself, couldn't suck the beauty out of it till your body was filled with warmth and strength. What was that stupid saying she'd heard somewhere a long time ago? "If you love something, let it go." What the fuck was that supposed to mean? If you loved something, you should grab it and make it yours, make it a part of you, or else squeeze yourself into it until you're lost inside and never want to get out. If you love something it should be that kind of wet, warm, dark blanket that envelops you and carries you off to a better place, away from all the stark, glaring, worthless crap around you. Only killing did that for Lucy, really. Everything else, even if it were pleasant, dragged and enmeshed her into the endless network of a miserable, half-dead world of echoes and smoke.

Killing took her out of that, above that: it was an escape, an epiphany, and she missed it badly.

Lucy hadn't killed much since she met Truman. She thought he wouldn't like it, and she'd respected and honored what she thought were his desires, because she was fond of him. It was Truman who had named her "Lucy," since she didn't remember what her name had been when she was alive, and it was useful to have something to call her. Not just useful, but downright nice, like she was more of a person now that she had a name—a pretty one, at that. Truman was good that way—he was gentle and liked pretty things, and she loved him for it, loved him in a way wholly different than she loved killing. Truman was like her music—calming and lovely, to be savored for hours and days; the only bliss she had in this existence was being with him and playing her violin.

Killing, on the other hand, was never blissful, but there was no substitute for the frenzied ecstasy Lucy felt at the solid, searing snap and tear and gush of killing. The drawback was that it wore out—it got more stale and bitter than even the ordinariness and boredom from which she wanted to escape. Lucy remembered a long time ago, long before she met Truman, she used to kill several times a day, every day—people, dogs, cats, mice, insects, anything she could catch. She was faster back then, so she could catch a lot more things. But it was too much.

It got tiresome: her muscles hurt and her head ached and she was hot and sticky all the time from the blood. There was all manner of crap wedged between her teeth and she felt bloated and stretched from the various kinds of flesh she'd eaten. But as full as she felt, she never felt satisfied, not even as she wolfed down more. She'd wallowed in the killing till it had been more like an addiction than an escape. Truman's gentleness—along with her own weakening, uncooperative body, which was slower now and less able to catch and kill—had cured her of that, and she was grateful, even as she felt the pang of regret and longing for something so delicious.

No, killing was a lot like falling in love—it had to be done sparingly, carefully, and with the right objects. Like when she'd picked up a big rock and bashed in the head of that man who had been trying to kill Truman. Even Truman had approved of that afterward, though he seemed a little dismayed at how she'd eaten the man's brain. What was she supposed to do? She'd earned it, and

2

there was all that warm, beautiful pink meat there in a thick, glistening stew of blood, bone, and dirt. She really didn't know how Truman restrained himself, let alone how he could be shocked at her indulging her urgent hunger. But never mind the eating—even Truman had said she was right to kill the man, which was the more satisfying part of the act, anyway. And oh, did that kill feel good—a fact Truman could not realize or sympathize with, but Lucy was pretty sure it didn't diminish the rightness of what she'd done.

The first blow had shuddered up her arm with so much intensity and power it felt as if it would shock her heart into beating. The thrill had caused her to gasp unconsciously and take in a breath, which she never did, normally, and which she found exhilarating, that rush of air. She'd draw strength for weeks afterward from the memory of the look on the man's face: it wasn't primarily the terror—though that was almost overwhelmingly delectable at the time—but the weakness. There she was—a tiny, dead woman who could barely drag herself around without every joint and muscle aching and stiffening, her own body in constant rebellion against her—and this big, strong man with a gun was totally at her mercy. But he neither deserved her mercy, nor would she offer any—and for a moment she could see they both knew that. There was real power coursing through her body and, weeks later, reverberating in her mind. Lucy needed that kind of jolt, at least from time to time.

She heard a long moan from behind her, followed by several seconds of a dry, hacking cough. From the other side of the ship's cabin, she heard Will say something, but his voice was low and she couldn't make out the words. Lucy looked down at the large pot of boiling water she'd been standing by for several minutes. Sometimes she tried to measure the time by counting to herself, but she always got lost somewhere in the seventies. Even if she didn't try to pronounce the words out loud, something in the syllables got her confused and she slipped back into the sixties and then gave up. But Truman had showed her the clock and how it moved—not showed her, really, but reminded her was more like it, though she didn't know from when or where she remembered—and she could tell that the water had been boiling for a long time, almost five minutes. She often lost track of time like that. It was easy to do when you didn't breathe or get hungry or sleep—there really wasn't much to separate one minute from the next, or the previous.

3

Lucy turned off the stove and covered the pot as she heard footsteps behind her.

Truman shuffled over next to her. He looked tired, now more than usual. "Water," he said, drawing the syllables out and not really making the "R" sound clearly. He'd gotten pretty good at speaking, though it was still an obvious effort. It was hard to take in the breath necessary to form words, then expel it just right. And any sound involving much movement of the lips—"V" or "F" sounds, for example—never came out right, since every part of Lucy and him had become so dried up and stiff. Lucy still wasn't that good at it, but Truman continued to help her practice.

Lucy turned to the little refrigerator. She got out a plastic jug of water that she'd boiled and cooled earlier. It was one of her jobs, to keep up the supply of clean water that way. Truman was a lot smarter than she, but he wasn't coordinated enough to do the job. He couldn't bend his fingers enough to grab the jug, and he certainly wouldn't be able to pour the water into it in the first place without spilling it all over. Lucy felt proud that she could do something he couldn't, something useful. She shuffled past Truman and carried the water jug across the cabin, to where Will sat on a stool, just inside the doorway to one of the little sleeping compartments. Truman followed behind her.

Rachel lay on the bunk under a grey blanket. She and Will were different from Lucy and Truman. They were alive and could still breathe and talk and bleed. Lucy would often stare at the sweat glistening on them as they worked, hoisting the sails or doing something else on the boat the four of them lived on now. Seeing how their bodies shone at times like that, she'd think how wondrous and exciting it must be, to have so much moisture and life in you that it kept seeping out all the time, overflowing from you, and you could just make more.

Lucy would watch them, so full of life, and think how they probably screwed, too, when they went to bed and locked the door to their cabin. She had checked the door once when she was sure they were asleep; Truman had tried to stop her. She loved him, but he didn't control her, and he should've known that. Besides, she wasn't going to hurt them, and she thought Truman realized that; he probably found her curiosity rude, in a way, even if he knew she wasn't going to do anything really bad. Lucy just wanted to know if they trusted her now. She wasn't surprised they didn't, and she

4

couldn't blame them. They were smart, and Lucy knew being smart meant being careful. Lucy wasn't that smart, and there was plenty she had to be careful of. Besides, it seemed to her that being alive was quite a bit more difficult and dangerous than being dead, necessitating so many more precautions. There wasn't that much for her and Truman to worry about, especially now they were far away from other people.

Lucy handed the jug to Will. "Thanks, Lucy," he said, smiling. He and Rachel were both nice that way. Not just polite but appreciative, even respectful of her. She was glad to be with them, away from the other people with their guns and cities and various nonsensical rules, along with their sudden violent enforcement of those rules. People like that always thought everything and everyone had to be in a certain place, doing a certain thing, and if things and people went where they weren't supposed to, then out came the guns and somebody ended up dead—not the way she and Truman were, but all the way dead. Will and Rachel weren't like those other people, and Lucy liked them for that. She didn't like them as much as she did Truman, of course, because he really understood and loved her in a way they couldn't; but she liked them as much as you could someone who's alive.

Lucy took a step back as Will wetted a cloth with the cold water and put it on Rachel's forehead, pushing aside the girl's thick, red hair. She'd been sick for several days and had worsened to the point where Will had anchored the boat—again, being careful to secure it a good distance from the riverbank—so he could tend to her all the time.

Seeing the usually robust, laughing girl so drained, pale, and weak made Lucy sad and anxious, for as much as she loved killing, she very much hated pain of any kind, in herself or in others. It was more than hate, really—it felt more like resentment. And it wasn't just the discomfort of pain—that was nothing. The world didn't owe anyone any amount of pleasure, and certainly not an endless supply of it. It was something else, something that Lucy couldn't quite articulate in her mind, but she felt it in her stomach every time she experienced or witnessed suffering like this. Death was natural. Killing was even better than natural—it was elating and fulfilling. But pain wasn't any of that. It just didn't fit. It didn't make sense. Pain wasn't *for* anything, didn't accomplish anything, so Lucy felt resentment and frustration that such a useless, ugly thing existed, especially with such abundance, frequency, and intensity. Sometimes she almost wanted there to be someone responsible for the senselessness of suffering, someone powerful and hateful she could find and hurt for what he had done. But there wasn't such a person, she didn't think, for everyone suffered in their various, random, disconnected ways, and no one knew why, or when it would end or start up again.

No, that was the real problem with pain, and the real source of Lucy's confusion and anger that afternoon—that there was no one to blame for it. All she could do was stand and watch helplessly, swaying slightly with the rocking of the boat, the rhythm of which matched Rachel's wheezing, and also lent Lucy a faint, uncertain sort of comfort.

Chapter 2
Rachel

Rachel closed her eyes and enjoyed the cold cloth on her forehead as much as she could. Her head still pounded and it felt as if acidic muck was sloshing around in her stomach, even though she hadn't eaten in days, and hadn't held down much of the water Will kept patiently forcing on her. He'd opened the portholes and kept the door open, except at night, but the smell of vomit and sweat had soured in the cramped space.

She rocked her head from side to side and tried to count days. If she was right, there'd be the fun of her period to deal with soon, on top of everything else. Making Will clean up her upchuck was at the limit of what Rachel thought she could stand; changing bloody sheets and dragging her to the tiny head to shower her off—that really sounded like the worst it could get. But she couldn't move her arms or legs without the muscles and joints screaming, so she didn't have any plans at the moment on how to avoid that indignity. She'd laugh at the ridiculous unfairness of it all, but the others would think she was going nuts, and it'd probably hurt like hell too.

Rachel rolled her head to the left and opened her eyes to look at Will. God, he was still so gorgeous—tall, big mane of blonde

7

hair, muscled, always tanned, and with those intense but gentle blue eyes of his. She, on the other hand, must look worse than Lucy, covered as she was with all the stink and slime that was supposed to be inside her small, weak body, not oozing out everywhere all the time. Yup, being halfway to dead probably looked and felt worse than the full version. That thought really almost made her laugh out loud, but she just sighed.

Rachel looked past Will, over at Lucy. It was one of the unexpected, charming, and slightly unnerving things Rachel had discovered in their life together, that Truman always helped Lucy dress so nicely, while Rachel and Will had little concern for what they wore. They'd gone ashore a couple times as they drifted downriver, and the dead couple had seemed gladder than their living companions at the prospect of finding new clothes.

At first, it was mostly Truman's idea to prettify his partner, but Lucy had come around quickly and then seemed to enjoy it as much as he. They were always so cute and bashful about it, dressing her at night, since they didn't sleep. Rachel had seen how they both fumbled with things—Truman worse than Lucy, but neither with the dexterity you'd think it would take to button and unbutton clothes—so they probably needed a lot of time to accomplish it. Every few days, Rachel would see Lucy in the morning with a new dress on, and a new kerchief covering the left side of her face and head.

They were so carefully shy in their dressing and redressing that Rachel didn't know what the wound under the scarf looked like. Like someone had taken a bite out of the woman's cheek? Or tore at her with their nails? Or with a weapon? Was her eye completely gone? Or was she burned? Well, it hardly mattered. It was just something you couldn't help being curious about, even though it's embarrassing to wonder about such things.

The rest of Lucy's body was in pretty good shape, from what Rachel could see. She must've died young, with a strong, toned body, a little on the wispy side, not much in her chest or hips. And Lucy's one good eye always overwhelmed Rachel with its beauty— such clarity, so dark blue even now, though always cold. Men must've loved gazing into a pair of them when she was alive. Guys liked that—the Ice Princess kind of look, bitchy and demanding, distant and unattainable. You could sure tell Truman was smitten; he stood behind her now, looking from Rachel to his beloved.

Rachel smiled thinly at them, though it ached to make the effort. It was weird as hell, watching two dead people in love, but it made about as much sense as anything else in this messed-up world, and it was a good deal more peaceful and lovely than a lot of stuff Rachel had seen. So let them make death a little nicer for one another: Rachel always thought it was sweet, even if she'd shake her head at them afterward.

She turned back toward Will and took a second to refocus on him.

"How you doin'?" he asked.

"About the same." She licked her lips. It didn't help much, as her tongue and lips were both covered with the same gummy, sticky crap. "I kind of feel like talking. Maybe just a little."

"Sure." He paused, then seemed to realize what she was implying. "Oh." Will turned toward the two in the doorway. "Um, thanks for the water, guys. You've been a big help. I think Rach and I will sit here for a while. Um, you know—by ourselves."

Rachel looked for Lucy's reaction. There was only a brief pause. Not exactly awkward, but perceptible. Then the dead woman gave a slight nod, and she and Truman turned and shuffled off, climbing up the stairs on to the deck. There wasn't much point denying that Lucy still frightened Rachel. Truman didn't, not at all. He'd come up behind her and she'd never think of flinching or pulling away. Lucy, on the other hand—well, Rachel always knew where all the nearest weapons were when she was around. Weak as she was, the 20-gauge on the wall above the bed was out of the question, but Rachel was pretty sure she could get to the little Kel Tec .380 under her pillow.

She had stopped trying to push down such thoughts: they were just unavoidable when you saw that one beautiful eye; there was still some spark of anger and hate in it, something hurt and broken that waited and longed to lash out. Lucy probably couldn't help it. Most of humanity was out there in a worse frenzy than she was, clawing at anything they could get a hold of. She at least was working really hard to keep it in check, so even if Rachel didn't suppress or ignore her own instincts, she tried to admire the dead woman's resolve and courage. And she tried really hard not to let the other woman notice how careful she was, for Lucy was as observant as she was beautiful.

Will scooted the stool the rest of the way into the space next to Rachel, and pulled the hatch closed. He patted Rachel's hand. "What is it, Rach?" he asked.

She looked at him, then up at the ceiling. "Will, I don't think it's gonna happen. I mean, I don't feel worse. But we have to discuss it. You know—what happens if I don't make it."

She couldn't bear to look at him, but she could feel him shift and tighten his grip on her hand. "You'll get better. The fever will break. You'll be fine."

Rachel sighed. The effort of trying to talk and reason was making the room spin, just a bit—first a little clockwise, then back. That really wasn't helping with the nausea. She just needed to say what had to be said and get it over with. "I might be. I didn't say I was giving up, but I want you to know what to do, okay?"

His grip on her hand slackened. "Okay." Even if Lucy had been hanging right outside the door she wouldn't have been able to hear him.

"I don't know if I—want to be like them."

They paused. "You want to just—be gone? Completely?" Will pulled his hand off hers, and she finally looked at him. He'd turned slightly. He was wiping his face with the back of his hand, though he was trying to hide it. Guys always did that. "What? Bang, and throw you over the side?"

It took all her strength and felt like her back was breaking as Rachel twisted to the side and put her hand on his shoulder. "Will, stop. Just discuss it. Please." She couldn't hold that posture for more than a second and she slumped back onto the bed.

He turned back, chastened and hurt, with red eyes looking down. "All right. I'll do what you want. You know that. I love you."

This time her smile came naturally and without pain. "I love you too. It's just—it was different with them. We found them like they are. And they're beautiful, both of them. Hell, Truman's been dead for probably twelve years, and he's so smart. He just wants to sit and read his books and write stuff. Who knows what he'll come up with? And Lucy—well, she's a little scary, but she plays her violin so beautifully, and she makes him happy." She paused till she'd caught his gaze. "Will, I think that's it: they have each other. If I die, I'll be dead. Even if you kept me around like them, you'd still be alone. You said yourself, when we kept dead people around back in our city—we were treating them like dolls or statues or something, not like real people. I think I'll still be me when I—well, if I die and come back. But we won't be able to still be together. So please, when it happens—if it happens, let me go."

Will didn't try to hide wiping his hand across his face this time. "I could—you know, die too."

"No!" her voice was as strong as she could make it. She raised herself up again and lowered her eyebrows, though all of that put her in agony, especially her head. "No one's going to talk about killing themselves. You stop that. I won't forgive you or talk to you if you say anything like that again."

"Well, I can't just shoot you. What're you thinking of? How could I do that? How could you ask me to do that?"

Rachel's face softened as she let herself back down, keeping her eyes on his. "I know. And I can't think of killing myself before it happens. It's funny, I don't know if I'm just too scared, too much of a coward, and I'd keep hoping that I might get better, or if there's something left of all those years in church and CCD. God— they told us not to commit suicide or get an abortion so often I thought that was all the Bible was about." She couldn't hold back a laugh this time, and it dissolved into a coughing fit, only stopping after Will gave her a sip of water.

They paused as Rachel caught her breath and stared at the ceiling again.

"So what do you want me to do?" Will asked finally.

She turned toward him again. "I'm not sure. I guess all you can do is let me go, let me wander off. If I don't even remember who you are, then you're not losing anything. And if I do—well, I'll think of you and I'll miss you, but it'll be better and safer for both of us if I'm not around." She extended her hand and he took it. "Is that okay? Can we agree to do that?"

He nodded. "I guess. I'll miss you. I'll worry about you."

Again the smile didn't hurt Rachel for some reason. "I know. It's just the best we can do, I think."

"Okay."

Rachel closed her eyes again. "I'm gonna rest now. Maybe I'll feel better when I wake up."

Will's lips pressing against her forehead was Rachel's last conscious impression, before she slipped into a feverish sleep. All that talk had drained her strength. Some of what they'd discussed even worked its way into her dreams, where she found herself an eight-year-old again, sitting in church beside her father. Funny, how it was almost always him in her dreams and not her mother. Funny, too, how she was always about eight or nine, like it was shortly before he died in real life, and that always made the dream so enjoyable, because she knew what was to come and how she'd miss him.

In this dream now it was Easter, for the altar was surrounded by lilies, and she was wearing a white dress with green trim. It was one of those dreams where every sense is heightened, and she could feel the stiffness and newness of the fabric. She rubbed her palms on her thighs, relishing the cool softness of the cotton tights. She looked down at her white shoes—shiny, with brass buckles—then up at the stained glass windows of blue and red. She couldn't make out all the words the priest was saying, but he was making some joke about the "onions and garlic." He repeated that phrase a couple times, and she looked over at her father, who was chuckling as he looked forward, not noticing her.

The next thing she realized in the dream, she was outside the church, though she didn't remember getting up and walking there. Everyone else was still inside, singing, but she was out on the lawn. The grass was wet, and there were puddles on the sidewalk nearby. Sitting next to one of the puddles was a large frog. Rachel had never really been a tomboy, but she also never minded bugs and other things people found gross, so she walked right over to the creature, which hopped away. She pursued it, laughing, and noticed that each time it landed, it got bigger. After several hops, it was about the size of a cat. At that point it didn't hop anymore, but let Rachel approach. She was leaning very close to it, just staring into its large, shiny, bulbous eye, when she woke up, panting.

Rachel shook her head and looked over at Will. He'd fallen asleep, crammed up against the bulkhead, and Rachel was seized with a fear she'd had a couple times in the last few days, of what would happen if she died while he was asleep. Her fear had previously been just a vague anxiety, but now it shot all the way up to a gut-knotting terror when she considered that it might already have happened. How would she know? She didn't feel normal, after all, her body a wreck of pains and imbalances, her mind full of weird thoughts, memories, and feelings. When she put her hand out to touch him, was there still love in her longing, or had it turned into something more primal, savage, and evil?

Rachel pulled back her hand as she realized how hard her heart was pounding, and how fast and shallow she was breathing. She closed her eyes. "Thank you, God," she said in a whisper.

Chapter 3
Truman

Truman did not like the idea of piloting the ship. He loved helping Will with it, but for him and Lucy to try it on their own? That didn't sound good. Too much responsibility. And danger.

Before this day, all the wrecked ships he'd seen on the riverbanks hadn't frightened him. They were from long ago, barely recognizable as boats anymore, overgrown with kudzu, homes for birds and other animals. Truman would look at them and never think of the people who had died in them, and would even take hope from how thoroughly the living world had reclaimed the broken hulks. Not anymore.

Now when he looked at them he could think only of destruction, sinking down into the murky water, maybe getting caught on something so he couldn't get free; or he would think of the days of misery that would follow if they did escape the ship before it sank, days of trudging along the shore until they were found and killed by other dead people. Or live ones.

Will had explained to them, however, that since Rachel wasn't getting better, they'd have to get the ship moving again. He expressed hope that there'd be people downstream—a camp, a city, whatever they had set up, and they might have doctors and medicine. Any group that had survived this long must have something more than they had on the boat. It didn't seem like a very good plan to Truman, but he understood how Will couldn't bear to watch Rachel suffer and do nothing about it. Truman felt the same frustration, and it must have been much worse for Will.

"All right, Truman, just keep us out in the middle away from the banks," Will said, standing next to him as Truman gripped the wheel. It seemed easy enough, but what if something went wrong?

When he and Lucy had worked on the deck before, she had been able to raise and lower the sails, which she was doing now as Truman steered. "Good, Lucy," Will said as she raised the mainsail. "We're just going with the current, but raise the mainsail so long as the wind's good. You don't need the jib. And if the wind shifts, you can reef the sail. See, Truman—don't be so worried."

They sailed along for a few minutes, the only sounds the drone of insects, the occasional snap from the sail, and frequent bird calls from shore. Will clapped Truman on the back and smiled at him. "I'm going to go check on Rach. Just call me if anything changes. You'll be fine."

Truman nodded and watched Will slip down the stairs in the companionway. He turned his attention back to Lucy, who stood beside the mast with her back to him. As he often did, he wondered what she was thinking. They communicated more now, but he knew that didn't keep her from being nearly as much a mystery to him as she was to Will and Rachel. She liked working on the ship, he knew that—the sails, taking care of the water, even mopping the deck. She had the dexterity for fishing, more so than he, but she didn't have the patience for it; sometimes she'd get a worm on a hook and cast, and then hand the rod to Truman while she went to do something else. He liked that, when they'd cooperate on some task neither could accomplish alone, like when they dressed her late at night. He felt so close to her at times like that. But her impatience was a big part of her, too. She tried to keep down the hunger, thank goodness, but there was always something so angry about her—frustration at everything around them, and especially, Truman thought, at herself.

They were sailing along nicely when Truman noticed clouds off to the west. Typical summer day, with storms sometimes coming through, and these looked far enough away that he didn't worry.

Then the wind shifted suddenly, coming at them hard from the starboard. The wheel almost slipped out of his grasp, the force pushing against him was so strong, and he started really fighting the wheel to keep them in the middle of the river.

Lucy had immediately seen the problem as well, and she moved to reef the sail before they were driven too far to port. Truman looked with rising alarm as she struggled with the line. It must've fouled in the block, and the wind in the sail was putting so much tension on the line she couldn't free it. He'd seen this problem before, when they'd helped on deck, but with Will there, it hadn't posed much danger, as he could help and still leave someone on the wheel. But Truman couldn't leave the wheel unattended or they'd fly downwind, maybe even run aground. He was about to call for Will and hope he got up on deck quickly enough, when Lucy finally freed the line and lowered the sail. The force pushing against the wheel eased, and Truman felt safer.

Lucy turned toward him and dragged the back of her hand across her forehead. She even graced him with a little smile and a thumbs up. He shook his head at her but returned the gesture.

Even without adrenaline flowing, there was no question that excitement and danger still intoxicated them—it's just that such things made Truman feel weak and disoriented, while they seemed to make Lucy feel emboldened, invigorated, sometimes even a little playful, like the way she was acting now.

Truman watched Lucy secure the sail and settle down by the forward hatch. She often liked being a little distant from the others, even him. They had the whole night to sit together, after all.

She'd brought the portable CD player with her on deck, and now Truman heard some nice classical music in addition to the background noises of the river. It was a symphony, he could tell that much, but he didn't know music like Lucy did. He thought it might be Mahler, as she'd been listening to that a lot lately.

As she listened to the music, Lucy began working on a pile of long, thin leaves they'd collected days before. She'd gotten good at weaving them into baskets for various things.

Truman relaxed a bit after their excitement. The ship was back on course, and the wheel didn't feel so unnatural or dangerous to him anymore. He could do this, he thought—though he still doubted if it would do any good.

The storm coming in from the west would be a problem tonight, but by then Will would have anchored the ship and they'd be all right. Except for Rachel. Truman wished he had been a real doctor, and not just a professor of philosophy—a job which he wasn't sure had been particularly useful or enjoyable in his previous life, and which had definitely not benefited them in their present existence in any tangible way. The only difference he could observe was that it perhaps made him a bit calmer than Lucy. But even that wasn't entirely true. It just made him better able to articulate the anger that she felt as an inchoate, undifferentiated rage. He, on the other hand, could distinguish various ways in which the unfairness of Rachel's situation maddened him. But what did that accomplish? Lucy roared; Truman seethed. There wasn't much to recommend one over the other, and both were equally impotent, a fact that could only further infuriate them both.

As Truman reviewed all this, and tried to think if he could offer any better advice or propose a better plan than Will's, he became focused on some wisps of cloud to the port side far ahead. They almost looked more like trails of rising smoke rather than rain clouds. He resolved to point them out to Will when he came back up.

While Truman studied the smoke, letting himself get more hopeful that they might find help, Lucy turned off the CD player and started fiddling with the portable radio. She'd always done that, had always been curious about the possible existence of other live humans. Truman didn't know why, and if he had looked closely at her when she was turning the dials on the radio, he wouldn't have seen the kind of hope or curiosity Will or Rachel would display, but something more like concern and anxiety. It was a fear Lucy indulged in rather vigorously and enthusiastically, and one that Will had encouraged now that they were actively seeking other people.

Truman was so engrossed with the clouds ahead that he didn't notice the swirling, squelching static sounds of the radio at first. He didn't even notice when those sounds resolved themselves into music. Not the stirring orchestral sounds of a moment ago, but a driving beat and a male voice singing something insistent and urgent, followed by a chorus of nonsense syllables in a more cloying tone.

"Truman!" Lucy shouted after a moment. It always sounded more like "Tra—Man" when she said it; she couldn't really form her lips to make the long "O" sound.

Her cry yanked Truman out of his reverie and drew his attention to the radio she was holding up. Truman stared as a tinny song with a lot of snare drum and cymbal crashes leaped from the speakers. He was mesmerized by it. It took him immediately to a dark gym full of young people—happy people in brightly colored clothes, all of them laughing, moving their bodies to the music without talent or form, but with a vitality that demanded attention and longing. He no longer smelled the rankness of the river in summer, but instead the forgotten scents of perfume, cologne, flowers, a little bit of tobacco smoke, and that sweet smell of fake cherry flavoring laced with the sting of ginger and bubbles. The scene staggered him, both for its overwhelming, sensuous beauty, and for the guilty, bitter sadness he felt at having forgotten it for so long. It was one thing not to have thought of it since he died— most of his former life was swallowed up in that uncaring abyss of Lethe. But Truman knew as the music transported him that he had not thought of that darkened gym for years and years before his death, and that was his fault, his ingratitude and dishonesty.

"Will!" Truman shouted with equal amounts joy, fear, and hope. "People!"

Chapter 4
Will

Will bounded up the steps to the deck, his hand not far from the .357 Magnum on his hip. He saw no one besides Lucy and Truman, both of whom stared at him dumbly. The sail was down—that struck him as odd, but the ship was still safely in midstream, and the two dead people were just listening to music. It wasn't like Truman to get all excited over nothing.

"What? What is it?" Will asked.

"That's right, New Sparta!" a frenetic male voice answered Will from the radio. "That was Duran Duran—definitely one for you old-timers, really old school! When those guys tell you they're 'Hungry Like the Wolf'—they mean they really want to get with a lady!"

The man stopped talking and the sound of rapidly squeaking bedsprings came from the radio. Then the man laughed. "Someone says that today, they probably don't mean anything so nice!"

A moan rose from the radio, like dozens of dead people, followed by the sounds of shattering glass and screaming. The man laughed again. "You're listening to Crazy Man Kaufman! How about one more song before we send some news and announcements your way? Here's one not quite so old!"

Another song started, this time with a female singer. Will thought it sounded familiar, but wasn't sure.

Lucy turned the radio down some. Will could hardly believe it. Over the last couple days he'd nearly given up. He hadn't really slept, and he gnawed down his fingernails, thinking of what he might have to do if Rachel didn't make it, steeling himself for the event. Now all that fear suddenly evaporated at the words of this goofy radio announcer, calling out to listeners in—what was the name of the city? New Sparta? That sounded funny. Will knew it meant something else, but all he could remember was, way back in the old world, the only place you'd hear the word "Spartan" would be in the name of high school and college sports teams. But who cared now? They had named it whatever they wanted to.

"A radio station?" Will asked, beaming at Truman and Lucy. "There are people somewhere near here who have a radio station!" He gave Truman's shoulder a smack. "They've got to have medicine and doctors, then! You can't have a city that big and not have other stuff, like doctors. How will we find them, though? We can't have passed them upriver, I don't think, or we would've heard the broadcast before. But if they're not right on the river, we might sail past them and not know it." Will frowned.

Truman pointed down the river. Will considered the wisps of cloud there. "Yeah, you're right, Truman—that may be them. It doesn't look like just regular clouds."

Truman then pointed to the storm advancing from the west.

"Oh, yeah," Will said. "Is that why you reefed the sail?"

Truman and Lucy both nodded.

"Good job, guys. We'll have to deal with the storm tonight. Oh damn, the boat rocking makes Rach feel even sicker." He felt bad for her, but still confident the worst was over. They might even make it to this city before nightfall. Who knew? Anything good seemed possible, and nothing bad seemed real or threatening anymore, but more like just a nuisance.

The song ended and Crazy Man Kaufman started talking again. "Turn it up," Will told Lucy, taking a step toward her.

"Hey, everybody—the city council is glad to announce that work is almost done on the Victory Amphitheater on the riverfront!"

There was the sound of saws and hammers in the background.

"We'll announce the first concerts there real soon!"

Applause.

"The place was supposed to be done earlier, but, well, you probably remember it got pretty messed up. Really big cleanup before they could even start rebuilding. But until it's done, check out the Dead End—that's always open!"

There was the moaning of the dead again, but it ended with laughter this time instead of screams.

"Just outside the north wall you got all your favorite carnie games, shows, something for everyone! Come on by!"

More laughter and some kind of strange pipe music that Will didn't really recognize, he hadn't heard it in so long.

"Oh, sorry, time to pay the bills!" There was the ka-ching of a cash register, another sound Will barely remembered. "Be sure to stop by our sponsor, Freedom Food, in the south city market. Freedom Food has the only poultry and pork"—the sounds of clucking and squealing came from the radio—"that's been certified as meeting New Sparta city regulations, by city-council-appointed inspectors. You owe it to your family to buy Freedom Food."

Stirring martial music for a few seconds.

"And now, let's have some more tunes before the Crazy Man calls it a day!" The radio went back to playing pop music, and Lucy turned it down again.

"The guy said 'riverfront'!" Will exclaimed, smiling at Lucy. She didn't exactly smile back, but sort of nodded slightly and bared her top teeth. Always hard to tell what that meant, but Will didn't care too much at this point. "We just have to keep going and we'll find them and get help!"

"Same river?" Truman asked.

Will turned toward him. Boy that guy could be a downer. How pessimistic could one person be? But Will supposed he had to cut them both some slack. It didn't look easy, being dead. Both Truman and Lucy always appeared to be in some pain: when they moved or spoke, it seemed like physical discomfort, but even when they sat around, they looked anguished or worn out, like they couldn't be bothered with doing or feeling any more. Besides that, Will knew Truman worked hard to calm Lucy and get her to behave better. It was terrible to think, but without Truman to keep her in line, Will really didn't know whether they would've had to put her down. Again, it was hard to tell with her.

Will hadn't considered Truman's question, but he needed to feel optimistic right now and wasn't going to let Truman get in the way of that. "Well, I don't think they can transmit too far," Will ventured. "It's got to be this river. We'll sail until it gets dark, and I bet we'll have seen them by then! It'll be fine!"

Will made a move to take the wheel, then reconsidered. He'd run up here so fast, he hadn't locked the door to Rachel's cabin. "You keep steering another minute, Truman," he said. "I'll be right back. And you keep listening to the radio, Lucy."

Again, the nod and teeth from her.

Will dropped down the companionway and went to check on Rachel, who was still asleep, snarled up in the sheets. She looked awful, so much so that he paused a moment to make sure he'd seen her breathing, before leaning over her. He untangled her burning, slippery body and draped the sheet more neatly over her. She had to make it now. They were too close for this not to work.

"Just a little longer," Will whispered as he slipped out of the cabin and locked the hatch.

As he turned to go back up, Lucy was only a few feet away, staring at him. Shit, she could be fast and quiet sometimes. Will reflexively gasped and had the Magnum halfway out of its holster without thinking.

Lucy stopped, and her eye drifted down to the gun, then back up. No teeth this time. Just a stare. Eyebrow arched over that gorgeous blue circle, which looked listless, maybe a bit hurt.

Will was embarrassed and tried to hide the fact that he'd almost drawn a weapon on her, but what the hell did Lucy expect, sneaking around? It wasn't fair if she felt distrusted and ill-treated, if she wasn't going to behave, if she almost did her best to frighten everyone. He thought they should put a damn bell on her.

Lucy slid to the side and sat at the table in the middle of the main cabin. She had the radio with her, though it was turned off at the moment. "Send Truman down," she said slowly, then drew in another rasping breath so she could say more. "We'll stay inside. Strangers might not like seeing us."

Will was further embarrassed at how hard it was not to shiver when Lucy said too many "S" sounds in a row. He just couldn't help it. But then, neither could she, he thought, as he stepped toward the companionway. Lucy turned the radio back on, though she kept it low.

"Oh, okay," Will said. "I guess that's a good idea." He paused. "Um, sorry about that. It was my fault."

Lucy looked down at the floor. "Thank you," she said very quietly.

If it had been Truman he'd offended, Will might've patted him on the shoulder at this point. But Lucy—well, no.

Will ascended back to the deck and sent Truman down as Lucy had asked, then he stood at the wheel. The wind felt good for the first time in days, lifting his thoughts toward how soon Rachel would recover, how soon he'd hear her laugh again, see her incredible body swimming in the river, smell her, taste her. All that was finally a certainty again, and not a memory slipping away. The increasingly loud thunder didn't slow such thoughts, either.

Chapter 5
Lucy

Lucy watched as Truman shuffled over and sat across the table from her. The radio sat between them, playing music softly enough that they could just hear it. Truman looked confused, almost annoyed. Not that he ever looked really annoyed. He didn't have it in him, she thought. That was a nice way for him to be, most of the time, but tonight she feared it might be a problem later on. Being annoyed kept you on your guard, and Truman was seldom on his guard as much as he should be.

"You want me down here?" he said after a moment.

Lucy nodded. Talking still took too much concentration and effort.

"Why?" Truman persisted.

Lucy paused. How to put it to Truman? It was hard to explain things to him sometimes, things that seemed quite obvious to her. "If he finds people, I don't want them to see us."

Truman frowned. "No. We'll be all right. They'll understand."

Lucy leaned across the table and put her forefinger against Truman's forehead, then gave a little push. "Use your head. You know people. You know how they treat us." Still pointing at

Truman, she shaped her hand into a gun and snapped the thumb down like the hammer of a revolver. "Bang." The "G" sound at the end hung up at the back of her throat and sounded funny, like she was choking. Fuck, she hated when he made her explain ugly things to him.

"No. They're not all like that. Some are nice, like Will and Rachel. Please. Trust them."

Lucy's anger flared. She'd appreciated Will's apology, but when Truman said to trust them now, sounding like a beaten, defeated creature eager to placate someone you just couldn't please, it enraged her all over again. Didn't he know how hard she tried to trust them? But then they went and did something like Will had just done, nearly killing her just because she didn't moan like one of those brain-dead hulks out in the wild and let him know where she was all the time. How did it get to be her job to let him know what she was up to? She wasn't a child. How was that fair? How did that deserve her trust?

"He n—n—n..." She pulled her right hand back and clenched it tightly. God, it almost physically hurt to stammer like such a moron. She longed for the time before, when she'd just point and grunt. The frustration made her shake, and she inhaled slowly to try again, using a word she could pronounce. "He *almost* had his gun out. Just now."

"Oh." They paused. "It was a mistake. It happens."

"Yes. And when it happens—you and me will be dead, not them. That's what they do. They're good at it. You know it."

Truman looked down and fidgeted. "Maybe not."

Lucy shook her head. "Maybe..." She paused, because she couldn't think of the word. Damn it. She clenched her left fist this time. "Maybe something will fly out of my ass, Truman. Don't be stupid."

He looked up at her. From anyone else, the look of pity would've sent her flying into a murderous rage, and she'd be across the table and tearing his throat out. But with him it felt—okay for Lucy to let him show that for her. It meant he wanted her to feel good, to feel hope, so she didn't get so angry with him over it. But he needed to learn, too, or all his hopefulness would get him hurt. She unclenched her fist as she put her other hand on his.

"I'm sorry," she said. "Just stay here with me. It's better."

"Okay," Truman said. Then, after a second, "Monkeys."

"Huh?" Lucy said, wishing she had tried for "what?" instead, because it sounded less like a moan.

"You meant to say 'monkeys' before." He smiled that awful smile of his—crooked with lots of cracked and missing teeth.

Real laughter was beyond either of them, but Lucy had taken to making a huffing sound on the rare occasions when she felt like expressing amusement. "Oh," she said, and gave her sort of laugh. "You're funny. How do you remember so much?"

His smile was gone as he turned his hand over to grasp hers. "Not so much. Not enough."

Lucy squeezed his hand. So much more than she could remember, and still not enough? But he was right. That was just how it was with them. "I know," she said. "Me too."

She withdrew her hand and they sat. The voice on the radio, when it interrupted the music, came from a different man than before, and he didn't have any more useful information, as far as Lucy could tell. Just more talk about concerts and where there'd be construction and various stores having sales.

After a while, Truman took up a book from the table and started to read. He had many books, lying in all different places around the boat. Lucy couldn't read, and even when he'd tell her the titles, they were incomprehensible; truthfully, they seemed a bit worse than just indecipherable, sounding as though they contained something ugly or dangerous. She noticed neither of the living people bothered with Truman's literature, either, so it wasn't just her slowness and forgetfulness that made Lucy uninterested in the books, she decided. But they made Truman happy, and that was what mattered.

She tried to think of a better plan than just hiding below deck. She wanted to find a way out of the mess she thought Will was getting them into. Lucy felt bad that Rachel was in pain. As she sat there, several times she heard the girl moan and bang her knee or elbow on the bulkhead, and her heart went out to her. But Lucy wasn't totally convinced that trying to find a doctor or medicine was the best solution. It certainly wasn't the only one.

Why not let things go naturally? No one had considered that, and of course, no one had asked her. The pain would end on its own, as it did for everyone. It would start up again in her new existence, Lucy knew that well enough. But as she sat there thinking, she got more disturbed that this wasn't really about stopping Rachel's pain—it was about keeping her alive. And what was so important about that, really? Will was going to get Truman and her killed so Rachel could live? More of his terrible, heartless unfairness.

The sound of the radio receded as Lucy's mind raced over these ideas. So what made life so much better than death? It'd be different if she and Truman were going to sacrifice themselves so the other two wouldn't be killed completely. That'd still be unfair, since no one had consulted them, but at least it would be a balanced, even trade. But that wasn't the situation at all. She and Truman were going to be destroyed so that those two could get on with their precious lives, rather than one of them existing the way she and Truman had for years. Why did that chubby little girl have to keep on breathing? Why did people want that so badly, even people who seemed nice and unselfish much of the time?

"Her fault," Lucy whispered, without really thinking about it. Strangely, the words came out clearer than when she concentrated on them.

She was staring past Truman at the door of Rachel's cabin, thinking of how this would end so much better for everyone if the girl died before they found more wicked, violent people. It wasn't even that Lucy thought of killing Rachel, exactly. She knew how awful that would be, what a betrayal, and how disappointed and repulsed Truman would be if he knew she even thought such a thing. She was just trying to work it out in her mind, the true value of Rachel's warm breath, the heat of her blood, the wetness of all her flesh. How did it add up to more than her and Truman? What could Rachel do that they couldn't? How would she be so deficient if she were like them? Was it just the screwing? Lucy knew how the parts were supposed to fit together, though she had no specific memory of how it felt—only vague impressions that it was a very pleasant thing, but as brief as it was sweet. No, she didn't want to die so those two could screw some more.

Truman distracted her by standing up and slamming his book down on the table. Lucy looked up at him. He glared at her—or the closest his gentle features came to a glare. She hoped he knew her well enough to see she hadn't been thinking of hurting Rachel, but his look said he knew her thoughts had been heading down familiar tracks of frustration, rage, and blame. His look was quite unfamiliar, as though he would not tolerate such thoughts. Lucy rather liked seeing that in his face, as much as it startled her.

"Nothing's her fault," Truman said quietly but firmly.

Lucy considered him a moment. "Why do you get so, so…" Again she couldn't think of the word, so she made a gesture with her hand, lifting it palm up, then lowering it in front of Truman. "Like this? Over her? Why?"

Truman sat back down, still staring at her, though his look was softer. He took her hands in his. "Because she's our friend. She needs us," he said.

Lucy nodded. All right. It wasn't the girl's greater value, it was her greater need. That made some sense. And it was good to see Truman finally getting worked up. It'd give both of them a better chance, if ever there were trouble.

"I like her, too," Lucy said. "Both of them. I just don't always understand them. And I need you too, you know."

"I know."

"So if there are bad people out there, promise you'll do what I say. Promise. What I say, not what Will says. I promise to help her, however I can, but now you promise to listen to me."

He looked into her eye and didn't pause for too long. "I promise," he said.

Lucy got up and walked around the table, holding on to it as she did so, for the ship was rocking more and more. The storm must've arrived. She sat next to Truman, resting her head on his shoulder.

"Too much talk," she said. "I need rest."

Lucy closed her eyes. She was denied sleep, as always, so she just sat there, thinking, though the thoughts were calmer now. Truman was right not to blame Rachel. Everyone had to hold on to whatever amount of life they had left in them, and they had a right to expect their friends to help them do so. Lucy felt more at peace now that she'd stopped thinking how she and Truman might die, focusing instead on how they might get to kill some bad people who tried to hurt them.

She went over all the weapons in the main cabin—the knives and frying pans would be the easiest and quickest, if the attack were sudden. If she had a few moments to prepare, then there'd be the broom and mop handles that could be snapped and plunged into someone's chest, throat, or eye. That made a lot more blood than just smacking someone with a pan—so much of it, and so hot, sticky, and sweet. And of course—teeth were the best of all, when there was blood flying around. That would be as glorious as she remembered, and she snuggled up closer to Truman as she let such thoughts caress and soothe her.

Chapter 6
Rachel

She wasn't part of the equation anymore, Rachel figured. Funny to think of that, how they'd go on without her. Even when she'd been well, there was nothing she did around the ship they couldn't manage to do without her. They'd be fine, and that was not an insignificant comfort to her.

Oh, but it was getting hard to think. What was all that commotion before? It sounded like Truman had shouted something, then Will ran out, but now everything was quiet again. She must've dozed off and missed whatever it was about. It didn't matter. They'd do whatever they were going to do.

Rachel heard some shuffling, then Truman and Lucy talking. They sounded so funny when they did that. Long, drawn out syllables, pauses and wheezes. They couldn't really vary their tone or inflection, so it sounded like some sort of Medieval chanting by people who had colds. Weird. Must be hard for them. But they tried so hard to talk to each other. Not so much to her and Will—with them, the two dead people still mostly nodded or shook their heads. Of course, Will and Rachel encouraged that by phrasing most things as questions requiring "yes" or "no" answers. It was habit, and it made things easier.

Well, she guessed it didn't really matter much anymore. Will could talk to them however he wanted now. Maybe Lucy would warm up to him more than she had to Rachel, and not be so aloof and scary all the time. Or maybe she'd dislike him more and kill him one day. That thought frightened Rachel enough that she almost rallied out of her semi-conscious state, to call to Will and warn him, but she just didn't have the strength. When he came back down, she'd remind him to be careful around Lucy. Of course, she'd have to be careful Lucy didn't hear, but she'd try to remember to do that when she found an opportunity.

What was that other sound? It sounded like music, but not Lucy's classical stuff. It sounded like pop music. Lucy didn't have any CDs like that, and although she could be a little snoop—Rachel had caught her going through cabinets and things before—she'd never taken something that belonged to someone else, even assuming she suddenly got a taste for more recent tunes. What were those two up to?

Rachel almost thought she heard another voice besides theirs, too. She must be losing it, imagining things and drifting off, out of all this pain. As she considered it, she thought this would be a good time to go. She was alone, the hatch to her cabin locked. She could just go, and come back, and when Will opened the hatch, he'd see how she was, but she wouldn't be quick enough to hurt him. He'd have time to call Lucy and Truman and they could hold her while Will stopped the ship to drop her off somewhere. Rachel even thought how it might be nice to look at Lucy without fear, once she was dead. It looked as though the dead people still felt pain, but she'd never seen them show fear, especially not Lucy; that'd be really nice to be rid of that feeling. Perhaps Lucy would talk to her then, the way she was talking to Truman now. Rachel probably wouldn't be able to answer her—those two had taken weeks of practice to get good at it—but it'd still be pleasant, peaceful, like having a family. This would be the perfect time to go.

Rachel wondered if you could will yourself to stop living, and she tried concentrating on her heartbeat or breathing; she imagined them stopping, wanting them to stop with every bit of effort she could muster. But it wasn't like when she was little and tried holding her breath as long as she could—that felt good even as it hurt, and then it made her feel all dizzy and her friends would shriek with laughter. Now, in her present state, it was just too much effort and she couldn't be bothered with it. Besides, if you could actually will yourself to die, would that count as suicide? She was still afraid of that, so she stopped herself from thinking of it. It was bad enough, coming back as a zombie. No sense pissing God off worse with some last moment of bad behavior; he might make her a really bad, stupid zombie, one that deserves to be shot.

Maybe she was supposed to apologize for all the bad stuff she'd done. Rachel remembered that was how a lot of people used to talk about dying—you had to unburden yourself and feel all this guilt, and then God would make it easy on you, both when you died, and after. Milton and the other people in their city hadn't talked so much about that, but Rachel felt like trying to cover all her bases right now. She just didn't have the hang of the guilt thing. Embarrassment, a little shame, but not guilt.

She had felt ashamed around Will for how much she'd slept around before, back when they lived in the city, but she couldn't really think the sex was bad, in itself. It felt more like stupid and inconsiderate—immature, if anything, and not the kind of thing she'd need to dredge up now. In fact, thinking about it now was making her miss it more and wish she'd done it even more than she had, now that it was going to be gone forever. Worse than that, it even got her thinking about how Will might meet some girl when she was gone, how he'd want to live with her, have sex with her, even have babies with her.

Rachel had never been the jealous type, and knew in the abstract she had no right to be, considering her past, but it still made her seethe inside, to think of dying there in a wet, stinking mess of bodily fluids, then waking up as some zombie idiot just so Will could then bed down with a new girl—probably a taller, skinnier one, too. Guys always liked that, no matter how much they told you that you looked perfect. It made no sense to get worked up and jealous over it, but it convinced Rachel to stop trying to force herself to feel guilty, as it was only backfiring. No, better to think good thoughts, about being friends with Lucy, wanting Will to be safe, and wandering off to sit under a tree somewhere, all gentle and peaceful. Maybe God would like that. She didn't seem to have a lot else to offer him right now.

Okay, so much for the guilt. But Rachel still felt like you were supposed to say something to God at that final moment. She'd decided against asking for death, as that seemed too much like suicide. She had to be careful to ask for anything, in fact, like Will being kept safe, as it slid too easily into selfish thoughts of not wanting him to be with someone else. Telling God she loved him? She remembered that was another popular sentiment, way back when, but that was even harder for her to conceive of than guilt. No sense going out with a lie as your last thought. That couldn't lead to anything good. Hell, people often sniffed out lies and usually got really mad about them: Rachel figured God would certainly be able to uncover any final deceit, and would be even madder when he found out. Oh, this whole dying thing was too hard when it happened slowly. Too much time to think and worry.

All right. It was getting nearly impossible to concentrate. Just think of good stuff and thank God for it. How hard could that be, for just a minute? "Thanks," Rachel said, trying not to focus too much on the sex parts, though now that she wasn't making such an effort to feel bad about it, the sex seemed to fit much better into the pleasant jumble of memories. "It's been good. I'm ready now. Ready. Ready."

Rachel kept repeating the word as she drifted further from consciousness, finally finding herself in another dream, where she heard the refrain, "It's ready!"

Turning toward the voice, she saw it was her mother. In the dream, Rachel was fully grown, but her mother was still a young woman, like when she'd last seen her a dozen years ago. All of it, of course, made perfect sense in the context of the dream. They were in their old house—a comfortable ranch in a nice neighborhood. Rachel's mom was trying to hand her a small, plastic bowl of peas and carrots. "Dinner's ready, honey," she said again.

Rachel took the bowl and looked at the contents: especially tiny peas, mixed with perfect little cubes of carrots; the real kind, the kind you only got from a store. Again, it made perfect sense in the dream world, and Rachel's question also fit in: "These look good. They had them at the store?"

"Of course," her mother answered. "Canned this time instead of frozen."

Rachel nodded, somehow knowing that in the dream-world, the dead walked, but people could still shop at stores for some reason. She imagined her mother running through the supermarket parking lot, pushing a shopping cart as the slow, clumsy dead chased her; imagined her cheerfully loading her purchases into their van before climbing inside and backing over a couple walking corpses on the way out of the parking lot.

Rachel also knew that in the dreamscape she had a younger brother. This fact did register as somewhat confusing, because her only sibling had been an older brother. But she took the bowl of vegetables over to the toddler anyway. She probably had both a younger and an older brother - she just hadn't thought of them both before now. The younger one was a smiling, blonde-haired boy wearing overalls, and he sat in a booster seat at the table, fork in hand. She remembered he liked peas and carrots and was glad to see him enjoying them.

Rachel heard keys rattling and turned back toward her mother. "Honey, I have to go out again," her mother said. She was jangling her car keys in one hand as she handed another bowl of peas and carrots to Rachel.

"Oh," Rachel said as she took the bowl. "Can't you stay?"

"No, I have to go. Watch your brother while I'm gone. When you two are done, you can come join me."

"Okay, Mom."

Eating her food, Rachel stood with her back to her little brother, facing the door through which her mother had left. The vegetables tasted exceptionally buttery and sweet, the little cubes and spheres transitioning to a smooth, warm paste. There was no way of telling how long she stood there, just chewing, with no thought in her mind, only the simple, comforting sensations in her mouth.

Chapter 7
Truman

The ship wasn't moving forward, though it still rocked side to side. A while ago, Will had told them he could see lights and they should stay below, then he had closed the hatch. Now Truman could hear voices and footsteps from above. There really were people. Maybe Rachel would be taken care of. That much made Truman feel good.

Lucy was having a tougher time of it. She'd pulled him as far away from the hatch as possible and had pushed him to the floor. They'd huddled there since, Lucy clutching a cast-iron frying pan with one hand and Truman's arm with the other.

"They'll come," she whispered now as they sat waiting. "They'll hurt us. It's not fair."

"It'll be all right," was all Truman could think to say. Her suspicion was contagious and he increasingly didn't believe his own reassurances.

"You remember your promise. You do what I say."

"Yes."

"First thing. If they come in—we don't talk. Play dumb, Truman. They like that. Makes them feel good. Makes them feel smart and in charge. They like being in charge. Always. So don't talk. Pretend you don't know what they're saying. Grunt. Growl. You understand?"

It made sense. It was awful, but it made sense when she explained it. She was so smart in her own way.

"Yes. You're right," he agreed.

"Okay. That's all we can do, I guess." The "S" sound at the end trailed off for a second like steam from a broken valve. They'd have to practice that more, as it didn't sound nice. If they lived to have the chance to talk more.

The voices on deck continued, like they were discussing something back and forth. Their tone wasn't exactly angry, but they definitely seemed to have some disagreement. Truman only made out one voice other than Will's, but it sounded as though several people were moving around outside. He couldn't hear what they were saying, and some of the time the rain and thunder drowned out the conversation completely.

Lucy gripped his arm tighter and turned her head toward him. He looked into her one good eye.

"I love you," she said. "May not have another chance to say that."

She'd said it a few times before, but was still shy about it most of the time. It made her more desirable—a fact Truman thought she was quite well aware of. But now she came right out and said it, and that made Truman much more frightened, that she'd think these might be their last moments together. It was one thing if he were scared—lots of things scared him. But Lucy wasn't like that. Maybe the situation was worse than he thought.

"I love you too. Don't be scared."

"I'm only scared for you. I r—r—r—" Being unable to pronounce something didn't seem to make her angry this time. She relaxed her grip on his arm and took a deep breath. "I respect you. Not them. I like them, sometimes, but I don't respect them. They don't deserve it."

Truman shook his head slowly. "They can't help it. They're like animals or children. It's not their fault."

Lucy nodded and turned back to face the hatch. "Maybe."

The hatch opened. Lucy was up faster than Truman, pulling him to his feet. "Now," she whispered. "Remember."

Will came down the first two steps. He was soaked from the rain, and he shook his head to get his hair off his face. He looked around for a second before spotting them in the back. He turned to speak to the people on deck.

"Really, we need your help," Will said to them. "My girlfriend's really sick. I don't know how much longer she'll make it."

"I know that," came the reply. It was a male voice, calm but not gentle. "You told us a couple times already. But you're gonna have to show us everything on the boat. And if you got any of those things on board—we're gonna have to do something about that. Otherwise you can just untie from the dock right now and keep going. It's fine with us. Is that what you want?"

Will turned back toward Truman and Lucy. He stared at them a moment. "No," he said, and came down the remaining steps.

Will stood next to the hatch to Rachel's cabin as two other men followed him down the steps. One looked a few years older than Will; he had dark hair and an almost comically long mustache. The other man was younger than Will, with light brown hair and a clean-shaven, boyish face. Both men wore raincoats, though these were open in front, revealing holstered guns at their hips; each carried a shotgun as well. Their eyes immediately found Lucy and Truman huddled against the back wall. The young man leveled his shotgun at them; the older man just regarded them with a frown.

"See," Will said. "They're harmless. They don't attack. They're our friends. You can't just shoot them."

"Terry, put down the gun for a second," the older man said, pushing down the barrel of his companion's shotgun. "We're gonna discuss this. Nice and calm."

"Okay, CJ," Terry replied.

CJ's glance went from Terry to Truman, then to Will. "I already explained this to you. You can't just take your girlfriend to the hospital and leave these two things here. We know you're from somewhere way out in the wilderness and you're not used to civilization. Terry here's younger, so he doesn't know. But I've met wild people before. They come down out of the hills to trade. Not many left out there anymore, 'cause they act so crazy and stupid. But I've seen a few, and how some of 'em like having these things as pets. Or maybe it's their family. I dunno. But whatever it is, it doesn't matter—we got rules. Dead things don't go inside the city, and they can't be on a boat tied to a city dock. Either they're disposed of, or they're put in a work detail outside the walls, if they're good at something and they can be controlled."

Will's voice was plaintive. "They are controlled. Look at them. They're fine. They do whatever I tell them." He glanced at Lucy, then back to the man. "Whatever I ask them to. You don't have to do anything with them."

"Then you've got no reason to worry," CJ continued. "We'll just put 'em to work."

He had that tone of authority and condescension in his voice that Truman hated. From the corner of his eye, he could see that Lucy had raised the frying pan just a bit, but there was no way even she would try to cover the length of the cabin to attack. To Truman, her rage seemed nearly palpable as heat, though he noticed her expression was slack-jawed and uncomprehending. Women were so much better actors, he thought.

"They understand what you're saying?" Terry asked.

Truman wondered if the man had seen many dead people before. He didn't look scared, but more incredulous than anything, maybe even a little curious about them, as if he were seeing an exotic animal for the first time.

"Of course," Will said. "They're not like others. They can even..." Again he glanced at Lucy, and Truman felt her stiffen. "They help me around the ship all the time."

The older man nodded. "Yeah, you find some like that. Don't know why, but some aren't as messed up as others. That's why we keep 'em for work. So like I say—yours should be fine. They'll be useful. That's a good thing. But you got to decide. Oh, and we have to see this girlfriend of yours, too. If she's sick, you know what we're thinking. Maybe one of your 'friends' here bit her. And that means she isn't coming in, either."

"No, no, it's not like that." Will opened the door to Rachel's cabin. "Here, see. She's sick. She has a fever. I don't know what it is. But she wasn't bitten."

"Terry, cover those two," CJ said. "Especially the bitch."

The barrel of Terry's shotgun went back up. It was aimed right at Lucy's face.

"Don't call her that," Will said quietly, but Truman noticed he stood still and didn't intervene.

"Oh. Sorry." CJ pointed at Lucy. "But this is good practice for you, Terry. You got to learn which ones are more trouble. You can tell just by looking at her she's smarter than the rest. Even holding something as a weapon. And the way she's looking at us now, you know she wants it, even if she's behaved so far." He leered at her.

Truman hated him more, but he kept his mouth open and his eyes looking slightly up and over the man's shoulder.

CJ said, "Oh yeah, that's it honey, you know you hate us. You know you could take us if it weren't for the boomsticks, don't you? And that makes you just about as mad as you can get, doesn't it?"

Truman thought she might spring, she was getting so tense next to him.

Right as Truman felt certain Lucy would lose all control, and the two of them would be grey paste splattered all over the bulkhead, Will stepped forward, hand on his gun. "Stop it," he said. "Don't taunt her. You don't need to do that. Leave her alone. I said she was under control."

CJ chuckled a little and held his open hands up at shoulder level. "Okay, kid. We'll leave your friend alone. But keep an eye on her, Terry. Just everybody hold still for a second while I see what's going on."

He stepped past Will and looked in the little cabin. "Okay, kid, get in there and uncover the lady. All of her."

"You can see she's not bitten."

"I can see her pretty face, and her arms, and one leg. Plus, the place smells like rot and sick, just like when someone's bit and waiting to die. And she's not even moving. So let's see all of her. Come on. We've all seen tits and ass before."

Will grunted and pushed past him.

CJ put one foot in the doorway and leaned inside. "Okay. Pull her hair up over her head. Tilt her head. Lift up her arm. The other one too. I can't see her side. Now turn her over."

Pause. CJ emerged to stand next to Terry, while Will came out of the cabin.

CJ looked over Lucy and Truman again, before turning back to Will. "We'll take her to the hospital just as soon as you decide what to do with these two," CJ said. "It's up to you, kid. She sure looks worth saving from what I saw. Clean her up from all the stink, she'd be fine as hell."

Will's jaw tensed. He always did that. He was almost easier to read than Lucy, Truman thought; this could still end with all of them being shot in the face.

"Don't talk about her like that," Will said softly.

"Okay," CJ said. "I won't tease you about your woman. I know you hill people are touchy about seeing lady parts and stuff. Fuck, I'd forgotten how uptight some of you are. You'd think living out there you'd get more relaxed, swinging from trees naked and shit, but you get like damned Amish or something. But whatever—you got to decide now, or we'll leave and cut you loose and you can keep going downriver. And I'm no doctor, but I'd say you'll be throwing her overboard tomorrow or the next day if you do that. If she doesn't pop up and get you first."

Will paused and looked at Truman and Lucy, then back to CJ. "Go back up on the dock," he said. "Just give me a minute to decide."

"All right. We'll need a couple minutes to go get collars for those two anyway. But don't take too long."

"I won't."

Will closed the hatch behind them, and Truman could hear them stepping off the boat, and their muffled voices, along with some others, nearby. The rain seemed to be letting up, too.

Will looked more tired than Truman remembered. Truman hadn't realized how much the last few days had worn him.

"I don't know what to say," Will started. "You heard him. I can't force you to do anything. I don't even know what I'd be asking you to do, 'cause I don't know where they'd take you, what they'd do to you. I don't know what I'm supposed to do now. I just want her to be well again. I never should've brought any of you. It's my fault."

When someone—especially a big, strong man like Will—is about to cry, then you just stay silent a moment, because anything you say would only make him more anguished, or turn him to anger, embarrassment, or despair. For all his physical and mental limitations, Truman still knew that simple point of humaneness, and when he looked over at Lucy's one eye gazing at Will, he knew she remembered it, too. He loved her so much more than ever because of that, which only made him want to cry as well.

Chapter 8
Will

This really was his fault. They'd all be back home if it weren't for him. Well, not these two—they'd be out somewhere, doing whatever zombies who don't eat people do. Just milling around and being content, Will guessed. But now they would be rounded up by whoever these jackasses were—and what? Put to work? What could they do? Will wasn't sure, but he felt pretty certain it wouldn't be anything nice. He doubted they had zombies picking flowers or writing philosophy books.

Shit, why did people always arrange things in such fucked up ways? Worse—why did he always step right into it? He should've known better by now. He should've minded his own business back home, then he wouldn't have been sent into exile, dragging the other three along with him. He should've sailed right by these jokers, too.

What did that guy mean, calling him "wild"? He was normal. These people were the strange ones.

That hardly mattered, though. Blaming them wouldn't change anything. He had to sit down with two dead people and decide together. One look at Lucy and he knew no one was going to tell her what to do, even if Will wanted to—which he didn't. That'd just make whatever disaster followed even more his fault, if he made the decision on his own.

Will studied her now and she appeared alert again. She'd really looked out of it when the other men were around. And her emotional restraint when they were calling her a "bitch" and daring her to attack? Damn—Will knew from being around her how incredible that was. For a second there, he had been sure it would end with him either scraping her and Truman off the bulkhead, or with him hauling ass out of there after she tore the heads off those two jerks: he would've put even money on both outcomes, too. Lucy would know to use the furniture as cover, and that kid Terry looked too scared and nervous to get a good shot off before she brained him with the pan. But she'd played it better than that, and Will was grateful. That guy CJ was right about one thing—she was a smart one. She knew it was better if they thought she was a regular zombie. Good for her. It didn't remove the difficulty they were in now, however.

Will sat down at the small table. Lucy and Truman shuffled over to stand across from him. They needed to hurry up, so Will tried to start the conversation again. "I should just tell them we're leaving," he said. At least he wasn't getting choked up this time. Maybe they could continue and make their decision.

Truman seemed to appreciate the urgency of the situation and spoke up. "That would be selfish of us," he said. "We can't ask you to do that."

"You want me to tell them you'll go with them?" Will asked. "I can't. That'd be wrong. I'd be the one being selfish. We have no idea what they'll do to you."

"I know," Truman said. "I can't choose, either. Someone is selfish and someone is hurt no matter what we choose. I'm sorry. I'll do what you and Lucy decide."

Will had hoped Truman would come down in favor of staying in the city. He had to admit it to himself—it was what he wanted; he just couldn't bring himself to say it, that he'd sacrifice the two of them for Rach. If Truman had been in favor of it, that sure would've made it easier. Will didn't feel too good about having Lucy decide. But if she chose to leave this city and not submit to their rules—well, that was probably his fault, too, for nearly blowing her away earlier. More stupid choices and actions on his part. Shit just kept piling up, didn't it?

"Lucy?" Will asked quietly. "What do you want us to do?"

Lucy looked at Truman for a second. When her gaze returned to Will, it had that extra intensity she sometimes had. Usually you could tell there was some reservoir of rage boiling over behind that stare. This time, though, it was something else: concentration, like she wanted each syllable, and the thought behind each word, to make it to her lips without loss of focus or strength. She craned her neck forward before opening her mouth.

"Truman and I want to leave because we are afraid," she said very slowly, and Will's heart sank. He bowed his head, resigned to abide by her choice. He would take more punishment for his foolish errors, and accept more guilt for the harm they did to others, like Rach. It was a pattern he was getting used to.

"You want to stay because you love her," Lucy continued. "Fear is selfish. Love is never selfish. I want to stay."

Will looked at her in amazement. She didn't smile—she never did. Well, sometimes he thought she did, but it always looks more like a snarl. But right now, she just kept up that concentrated gaze, and Will had even less certainty about what the hell that meant. You never knew what was up with her. There was no way to know why today Lucy sounded like a Valentine's Day card, when most of the time she drifted around like a wraith who didn't quite remember what it meant to be alive, but knew she resented those who still were. What she said reminded Will of something else, too, but he couldn't quite recall where it was from, exactly. But whatever it was, whatever bright corner of her mostly-darkened mind she'd retrieved it from, there it was, laid before him with finality.

"Are you sure?" was all he could ask, though he knew from observation that once Lucy said something, that was that; she'd never discuss it or regret it. In this way, she was the opposite of him and Truman. That kind of certainty and simplicity must be a nice feeling, he thought, even as his heart filled with the strangest gratitude and wonder.

Lucy nodded and slipped her hand into Truman's. "I'm sorry, Truman. If you wanted to go, I would," she said, turning toward him.

Truman looked at her. "I know," he said. "You're better at choosing than I am."

Will normally gave them privacy for their displays of affection; it was just too weird—and a little gross, to be honest—to see them acting like that. But now he stared at them, trying to understand them better.

Understanding never came—just a slight tinge of joy added to his awe.

"When Rach is better, we'll come and get you and take you out of this place," Will said. He didn't really know if that would be possible, but he wanted it to be, at that moment. He wanted to give them hope. Most of all he didn't want to feel responsible for more harm to the people around him.

"I hope so," said Truman. His voice had an accusatory tone to it that Will had never heard before.

Will stood up and came closer to them. He still didn't know how to approach Lucy, but he knew he had to say something more, had to offer her something for the gift she'd given so freely and unexpectedly. Looking in her eye, Will wondered if she had even expected it herself, before she said it.

Perhaps she sensed his need, and his indecision, because she put her hand lightly at the back of his neck and leaned toward him till their foreheads touched—hers so shockingly warm and reassuring against his wet, clammy skin. Her perfect blue eye had some special depth to it, just inches from Will's: no warmth in its seemingly bottomless pit of blue—but its very dry, cold sharpness somehow let him know how much lay hidden behind it, and how much of that secret store was as beautiful as it was terrible, as lovely as it was awful. Her skin was so soft he could barely feel it, like down or cotton, though the pressure she put on his forehead and neck seemed more solid than any grip he'd felt, like nothing could shake it loose. For that one moment, everything about her was comforting.

"Thank you," Will whispered.

She pulled his head down farther, and he assumed she kissed his forehead, though it was hard to describe it as that, her lips pressing against him in another impossibly light yet forceful touch.

"You're welcome," she said as she released him and let him stand back up. She leaned against Truman. "Done talking. Too hard. Said everything. Tell them we're ready."

Will went back up on deck to tell the strange people their decision, as though it had been his. They'd understand even less than he did what had happened, so he would explain it to them in their terms and give in to their demands, even as he cursed himself for doing so.

Chapter 9
Lucy

Lucy hated people second-guessing her, especially if they were right. That dickhead CJ got way too much correct about her—how angry she was, how smart she was, how she *did* know that she could take him and his little friend and rip their throats out. Too close in here for their shotguns to help, either, and they'd never get to their automatics in time. She wouldn't have ripped their throats out though, as wet and exhilarating as that sounded—God, it'd almost be like being reborn. But no, using her teeth would've gotten her killed—getting in too close and giving them too much time. She'd probably have smashed the cute, younger guy in the side of his head—swinging the pan up from the side would take them by surprise—then she would've gutted both of them with the knife she'd hidden in her other hand. Yeah, at least CJ didn't know everything. But still—way too much for someone who'd just met her, and that infuriated her just as much as he thought it did.

All those plans of how to take them out were just a pleasant bit of hindsight, however. She'd left the frying pan and the knife on the counter before shambling up on deck. It was sometime in the middle of the night, and still raining lightly. Lucy stood with one foot on the gunwale, wondering how she was supposed to spring to the dock as the boat rocked back and forth. She eyed the four men there—the two who'd come on board, and two more whelps like that Terry kid. They just stared back at her, CJ standing firm and frowning, like when he first saw her, the other three shifting uneasily.

She thought the three young ones would piss themselves if she said, "Get over here and help me, assholes." Unfortunately, she was somewhat more certain CJ would shoot her in the face at that point. He was thinking it already, she knew as she watched him through the mist.

At least the cold drizzle felt good on her face, after the close, sick smell of the ship. And what was that other smell out here? There was the tar on the wooden planks of the dock, and a fishy, weedy smell from the river, but something smoky, too. Hell—the spoiled, lazy pricks had real cigarettes. Already this place was full of surprises, but Lucy very much doubted any of them would be good—at least not for her.

No, her days of being treated with some respect were over—her answer to Will had made sure of that. And the consequences were already becoming abundantly clear. She contemplated slipping and falling right into the river to be swept away, or maybe just down to the deck to sprain an ankle that would never heal. They'd no more lift a finger to help her than you'd try to do anything for a moth with a broken wing. As she paused, Will scrambled up next to her and took a surefooted jump to the dock. He turned back toward her.

"Come on," he said as he extended his hand down to her.

Lucy eyed him too. So different than the men on the dock, but still part of their kind—so needy and so confident all at the same time. She swayed with the rocking of the boat as she considered the moment they'd just shared. Will second-guessed her, too, but not very well: she knew he hadn't expected the answer she'd given. Good. People like him were so used to getting what they expected, so much in love with being right, so smug and self-satisfied about it, that half of her good feeling came from surprising him. The other half? An even split, she figured, between the pride of knowing she was better at suffering than they were; a grateful thrill that he finally trusted her—the kiss had seen to that, and had felt more delicious than any blood she'd ever tasted, so cool and moist, with just the tiniest hint of his sweat and fear and need; and a strange, compelling awe at knowing he and Rachel were better at living.

Yeah, she'd made the right choice. Will wasn't perfect, but was good enough that he deserved a chance to screw his girlfriend some more and raise a bunch of babies to be as imperfectly good as they were. It had to be this way, as much as she had an increasing taste and fear for how bad it was going to get.

Lucy clasped his forearm with her hand, as his fingers wrapped around her wrist. He was strong, for one of them. That made her feel good, too. With a nod he yanked her up and over, and she was on the dock next to him. She stumbled into him, and she could hear the others' surprise. "I never want to get that close to one of them.... Yeah, not without a collar or a muzzle.... Shit, she's right next to him! What the fuck's wrong with him?"

"Shut up, you knuckleheads," CJ growled. "I told you all to be quiet. Hill people's just different. So shush. You learn by watching, not talking. And you three got a lot to learn."

Lucy gave the three younger men a glare. She relished their fear. Maybe this place was full of soft, weak people and it wouldn't be so bad. A sideways glance at CJ and she thought no, she'd never get that lucky. There'd be plenty of bastards smart enough to make life wretched and degrading. There always were. Besides, weak people were a threat, too: they herded together, and thought even less of what they did and why. That made them the most dangerous of all, in some ways.

Lucy turned back toward the ship and helped Will pull Truman up onto the dock as well. He was all that had made her hesitate below. She didn't know if he could make it, being around harsh, brutal people. But on the other hand, he was smart in his own way, and he was so docile it might actually be easier on him. They'd heap more shit on him, sure, but they wouldn't be so skittish around him that they'd blow him away in a panic. Probably just make him push a broom around for fat, lazy people half as smart as he is. He'd be okay, and probably wouldn't get as angry over it as she'd already gotten. How'd that saying go? The weak shall rule the earth? Something like that. It seemed true in his case.

Lucy tensed at the sound of clanking chains. Two of the younger men were approaching with wooden poles about four feet long. A short chain attached a collar to the end of each one.

The one named Terry raised his shotgun.

"You collared 'em before, kid?" CJ asked.

Will took the collars in his hands, looking disgusted with their dirty leather and metal clasps. "No, we don't use these."

"You hill people are so crazy," CJ replied. "I don't know how you do it. But they haven't bitten you yet, so I figure you can get 'em collared easier than one of us trying it. They'll be spooked enough when we get 'em to their new place. So go ahead."

Will approached Lucy with the collar and put it around her neck. He leaned close to her left shoulder to lock the clasp. The leather was cold and slippery—not just from the rain, Lucy felt, but from all the blood and grease it had scraped from hundreds like her. She bared her teeth at the young man holding her pole. His eyes widened and he opened his mouth slightly.

Will moved in front of her so she couldn't see the coward on the other end of the pole. Will's eyes met hers again as he tightened the strap.

"Tighten that strap more, kid," CJ said. "I don't want her wriggling out, and we both know she's a limber gal—and quick. And you know damn well she don't breathe, so don't have any hard feelings about it. Get to it."

The strap constricted around Lucy's throat. It didn't hurt too much, though it still took every bit of her self-control to keep from telling these scared little shits to go fuck themselves.

"I'm so sorry," Will whispered. His eyes were wet. Lucy again thought she had chosen right.

Will moved over to put the other collar on Truman.

"Good," CJ said; he didn't seem as concerned with the security of his collar. "Cuffs next. Terry?"

Shotgun at his hip, the cute one approached, holding out some black iron manacles with his other hand. Will took them. Lucy remembered seeing handcuffs before—shiny metal rings with a chain between them. These ones were crude, and perhaps homemade—just curved metal bands that locked together with bolts.

Lucy held her hands out in front of herself, and Will sniffled a bit as he cuffed her. It took him awhile. Then he moved to cuff Truman.

When he finished, the men forced them around, the collars scraping and tearing at their necks. Truman nearly fell to his knees as they manhandled him. Lucy reached to help him up, but they yanked her away. She growled, but stopped herself. The men started to push them up the dock.

"All right, kid," Lucy heard CJ say behind her. "Ambulance will be here any minute. I hope your girlfriend makes it."

And that was that. The two of them were now under the control of these savage idiots, being pushed toward some lights up ahead. When they got to the illuminated area, Lucy saw a gate in a tall fence that stretched across the shore at the end of the dock. Another man with a gun was there.

"Whatcha got, CJ?" the new guy asked.

"Coupla dead fucks," CJ replied. "Two hill people back on the boat. There'll be an ambulance here for them soon. The girl's sick, but she's not bitten. I checked her."

"Okay," the guard said as he looked Lucy over. "These things good for anything, or is it time to pop 'em?"

"Oh, this one's a pistol." CJ laughed as he slapped the back of Lucy's head, then grabbed a handful of hair and yanked. It didn't really hurt, but it pulled the kerchief back. Lucy didn't like that at all.

She roared and whipped herself around so violently the man holding the pole couldn't keep her still. She batted at CJ's hand with her manacled arms and lunged for him. He stepped back, still laughing, and the man holding her tried to plant his feet and get enough leverage to wrestle her away from him.

The guard from the gate shoved a black rod with two metal prongs into her stomach and she felt something bad through her whole body. Her muscles didn't obey and she fell to her knees, twitching, her jaws clenched so tightly she thought her teeth would shatter. She spasmed for a few seconds before she could hear and understand what was going on around her again. All the men were howling with laughter, and it filled her with such fury she was able to force herself back to her feet. Lucy straightened the kerchief as she glared at CJ.

"See?" CJ said. "Gal's a piece of work! Look at that! Eight-thousand volts and she's right back on her damn feet! She's one for the patrols, for sure. Keep our city safe, this one will!" They laughed some more.

"The other one?" the guard from the gate asked.

"Don't know. Their owner said they were smart. He looks kinda scrawny." Pause. "What do you think?"

Lucy kept her eye on CJ, but at the edge of her vision she saw the guard move toward Truman. "I know a guy over at the Dead End," he said. "He's always asking me to send him some more smart ones, if we find any. You know how kids like that shit."

"Oh yeah, my kids love that—dead people doing tricks and shit. He pay you for that?"

"Sure, CJ. You'll get some. Don't worry. Just look for Doctor Jack."

"Good. Terry—you and Bart take him over there. We'll haul gorgeous here over to the City Patrol camp."

Lucy heard Truman wail. This time she could hear the zapping sound as the guard hit him with the same thing he'd used on her. Lucy tried to turn and lunge at him, but her limbs were stiff and unresponsive, and she immediately felt CJ kicking her legs out from under her. He followed up with a savage kick to her kidneys, as he and the man holding the pole shoved her face into the ground. CJ dropped his knee onto her spine.

The cold metal of the automatic jabbed into the back of her skull. CJ leaned down till he was panting in her ear. "You just don't know when to stop, do you, you fucking cunt?" he whispered. "Now darlin', I think you know what I'm saying. So I'm gonna do you a favor I've never done for a dead fucker before. I'm gonna explain things to you. City Patrol loves tough, smart things like you. Pays good money for 'em. So I'll have second thoughts before I put your brains all over the fucking ground here. But your boyfriend? You two seem kinda fond of each other, as sick as that sounds. So some carnies wanna pay something for him, and I got to split it with these other guys? That's not so much money. So Terry or Bart aren't gonna feel so bad if they have to shoot him. You think about that before you act up again."

She scraped her nose and cheek across the pavement as she turned her head to see Truman. They were hauling him back to his feet. He looked limp, but his gaze was on Lucy, his hands stretched toward her.

CJ sat up, the gun barrel still pressed against Lucy's head. "Terry, Bart—you two get moving. I'm gonna sit here with my new girlfriend while you two take him away. Then we'll try moving her. Gal's got almost too much spunk."

They chuckled and hauled Truman away. Then they got Lucy back on her feet. There was nothing more she could do at this point.

CJ holstered his pistol and brushed himself off. "See, that wasn't so bad." He started shoving her forward again.

It was bad enough, but besides the strange device that had incapacitated her, it hadn't been any worse than she had imagined. They were really pretty ordinary and predictable here, so they didn't bother Lucy that much. It only worried her a little, that Truman would be more troubled by their behavior. He still believed in silly, sentimental things, and expected all sorts of absurd impossibilities. She hoped he always did, but also worried that belief might make his ordeal too much for him to bear.

Chapter 10
Rachel

It had been years since Rachel had seen a room this clean. When she was little, her mother kept things really tidy in their home, but this was way beyond that. The walls and ceiling were almost impossibly white. The sheets on the bed were softer than she'd felt since childhood: now there, her mother would've been able to match the care and cleanliness; the woman must've done two loads of laundry a day, every day. And not just throw them in the washer, but the full deal—detergent (a special kind for delicate materials, too), fabric softener, bleach on the whites, dryer sheets; then everything folded and put away. Even when she lived in the city, Rachel barely bothered with such stuff, and certainly not since they'd been on the boat: there, she'd just rinse things out, hang them off the rigging, and call them clean enough. They always dried stiff and had an earthy, grassy smell to them, but what did that matter? Too many other things to worry about, and too many other things to enjoy.

As she slowly drifted up to consciousness, Rachel found herself wondering if her mother had been happy, doing all that work. And if her mother had been fulfilled by those things, what'd that make Rachel, with her lazy, sloppy, hedonistic ways?

Rachel's head throbbed and she felt a little woozy. Nothing like before, but still nowhere near right. Given how she'd felt the last time she'd been conscious enough to think, it was natural for her now to entertain the idea that this was wherever you went when you died. She toyed with that thought for a minute as her gaze drifted to the half-open window, where the sun was shining in. Rachel remembered something about rain and the ship rocking, remembered thunder and strange voices. So it made a sort of sense that this was some other world: the weather was different, it was so much cleaner than anything in the real world—quieter and calmer, too—and things didn't hurt anymore. Oh—and she was thinking of her mom so vividly, almost feeling her presence. That part made Rachel feel really glad to be here, and she half expected to see her mother when she turned to the other side.

No—just Will, asleep in a big chair. Rachel's mind shifted, first to chide herself for being so silly. If she'd died, she would've opened her eyes to find the regular old dirty world. She'd probably be seeing it through some cloudy gunk, too, since dead people's eyes were always so messed up, except Lucy's. And she'd almost certainly be wracked with the desire to kill everyone around her and tear into their warm flesh with her teeth. God, how could she be so stupid as to think she'd drifted straight to some heaven of clean sheets, bright sunshine, and her mother's love? That wasn't even a story you told kids anymore. It was just crazy.

Rachel sighed. It was nice to be alive, too. She'd fought so hard and rebelled against death for days when she was sick, it made her feel good and proud to know she'd won. But what was this place? She tried to roll toward Will, and she felt some resistance, something pulling on her left elbow. She looked down to see a tube running from her arm to a bottle hanging up above—more things she hadn't seen in years.

Keeping her left arm still, Rachel managed to nudge Will with her other hand. He woke with a start and looked at her. The smile spread across his face immediately. "Oh, Rach, you're awake," he said. "How do you feel?"

"Better," she replied. "Not great, but better. What happened? Where are we?"

"We found this city. They call it New Sparta. They brought you right to this hospital, got you hooked up to the medicine."

Rachel considered the tube and bottle again. "Medicine? How do they have medicine? It's all too old. It's been years since we had any."

Will took her hand. "They make it, I guess. They took one look at you and said you had malaria. They said it was common around here, with all the mosquitoes, but with drugs you should be better in no time. I was so afraid you wouldn't make it. I didn't know what to do."

Rachel smiled at him and noted how his countenance brightened. She so had him hooked. It was nice to be wanted so much, to have so much power, especially after nearly losing everything and being reduced to a wandering meat puppet with no control. How could she have been glad, even for a moment, to be rid of life and all of its perks—like having a gorgeous man who loves you and who'll do anything for you? She squeezed his hand— and if it were possible, he looked even more enthralled by her.

Rachel stopped smiling as she remembered something that bothered her. "Where are Truman and Lucy?"

Will lowered his gaze. "They took them away."

"You mean they—um, they killed them?" Rachel asked. She was grateful to be alive, but knowing those two were shot in the head would still make her feel like shit, especially for poor Truman. He wouldn't hurt anybody.

Will looked up. "No, not that."

"Oh, thank God."

"They said they would put them to work."

Rachel frowned. "Work? That's weird."

"Yeah. I don't know how exactly things are done around here. But they said some of the dead do work, if they're smart enough."

"And Lucy went along with that?" Rachel was sure Truman would've been okay with it—but Lucy? No way.

Will nodded. "She did. I asked her. I couldn't just force them to go with the people here. And she was—I don't know. Not exactly emotional, but like she was really determined to go through with it, if that's what it took for you to get better. Passionate— maybe that's the right word."

"Really? Wow." The idea of Lucy being passionate about saving her took some getting used to.

Will leaned closer and spoke more softly. "And then she kissed me. I think."

Okay, that was just too weird. Rachel cocked an eyebrow at him. "She—kissed you? Where?"

"On the forehead. I think. It was so lightly, I couldn't tell. I don't know why she did it."

"Kiss? Not bite? Come here." Will leaned forward and Rachel put her hand behind his neck to pull him closer, as she inspected his forehead.

"No. Really. She just barely pressed her lips against me. She was acting really strange, but she'd already said she wanted to stay here so you could get better, so I didn't argue. Don't worry, Rach, she wasn't being like a—well, like dead people usually are. She was being like a real person."

No, no marks, and Rachel ran her fingers all over his forehead a couple times. "That's really strange, Will. I don't think the two of them even kiss. I mean, not that I'd watch. It's too gross."

Will sat back up and took her hand again. He chuckled. "Yeah, I know what you mean. I told them we'd come get them when you got better. I don't think they'll like it here too much and we shouldn't leave them too long, wherever they took them. People can be mean. I don't want them to get hurt."

"Yeah, that's true." Well, Rachel would wait and see about that. They'd have to find out more about this city and what went on here before they went around demanding to have their zombies back. There might be rules about that. And Truman and Lucy might be okay, wherever they were. This place seemed too nice to leave without considering everything.

Rachel settled back down into the pillows. Damn, those were really soft, too. What the heck did they fill them with to make them feel that good, that luxurious?

She sighed. "I guess I better rest some more. Just that little bit of talking got me tired."

"Yeah, they said you'd need to rest a lot before you were all the way better."

Rachel closed her eyes and smiled. "I bet they have hot water here. I mean really hot water that doesn't run out."

"Yeah, I guess," she heard Will say as she drifted off. "Probably."

"Hmm, a hot bath is going to be so nice. I haven't had one in forever." Rachel thought of the water caressing her body, the warmth soothing her mind. Oh my God—maybe even bubbles. That'd almost be too much to hope for, but if they had rooms as clean as this, they might have any luxury she could think of. Yes, this place definitely needed more investigation before they went traipsing back into the malaria-infested wilderness.

Chapter 11
Truman

The two living men led Truman away. He couldn't see where Lucy had gone. He knew she could take care of herself—much better than he could, most likely—but it was just a man's instincts to protect the woman. The living took that away from him, and that made him ashamed—and angry at Will for getting them into this mess.

Lucy had been right about the other people. He'd told her everything would work out, but she'd been right to mistrust them. They didn't deserve trust, and they certainly didn't deserve all the comfort and safety of this place. They used a cattle prod on people—how much more barbaric could they get? Well, he'd probably find out soon enough.

And if they were going to treat him and Lucy like animals, maybe they'd get what they deserved: maybe some dead people would make them into food. Truman had never entertained or enjoyed that thought until he saw Lucy on the ground, writhing from their cruelty. Now he longed for it with every step he took.

The younger man, Terry, held the pole attached to his neck. The taller one, Bart, came up and walked beside Truman, who kept his gaze down.

Bart gave Truman a shove with the stock of the shotgun. "Hey," he said to Terry. "That crazy guy from the hills said he was smart. He don't look so smart."

Truman kept walking.

"Leave him alone, Bart," Terry said. The kid didn't seem quite so bad. "He's just dead. We'll all be like him someday."

"Not me," Bart said. "I'll eat a bullet first. Not gonna walk around like this bag of shit." He stuck the business end of the shotgun in Truman's face this time. "Right, Mister Smart Zombie? You're nothing but a bag of shit, aren't you? Shit for brains, is more like it. What the hell did that guy want with you, anyway? Were you his dad or something? Fuck—people got to shoot their own parents all the time. He should know better than to keep your sorry ass around."

"Stop it, Bart," Terry said more plaintively. "He can't help it. It's just how they are."

"Well, I can't help how I am, either. And I can't help he's a bag a shit. What're they gonna do with him at the Dead End, anyway?"

"I don't know. Put him in a tank full of sharks and have him fight them. I remember seeing that when I was younger. You remember that?"

Bart laughed. "Oh hell, yeah! That was fun. If the dead dude got a hold of one shark and bit into it so it'd bleed, the others would attack it and he'd be safe. If he figured that out in time. I don't know if this one's smart enough to do that." Bart smiled and looked back at Terry. "Did anybody ever tell you about the special shows there?"

"What?"

"You know—sex stuff. Naked lady zombies. You know, when you see some, they don't look so bad, and you think how you'd tap that, if she weren't all dead and shit. I heard they have some of them dancing around, doing stuff."

"That's just gross."

"No, really. I heard about that. I even heard they pull the teeth out of some of them, and you can put on a condom and--"

"Stop! That's sick. No one would do that."

"Yeah, I know I wouldn't. Sounds too risky. I'd still be afraid they might bite it off, even without teeth, or you'd get diseases and shit from them."

"No, I meant just doing it at all. Stop talking about it."

Bart shrugged. "Terry, you always act like such a girl about stuff like that." He smacked Truman in the back of the head. "Keep moving."

They'd marched around the outside of the city, within sight of the wall that surrounded it. It was uneven and crudely constructed, but Truman figured it was enough to keep dead people out. Shortly after the sun rose, they came to a collection of ramshackle structures—tents and various buildings made out of plywood and other materials. The settlement seemed to stretch out quite a ways from the city wall, sprawling irregularly.

They stopped and Truman looked around. A few people shuffled among the buildings, but none of them paid any attention to the three of them. One person even led a mangy horse, which Truman wondered at; he couldn't remember when he'd seen one before.

He heard some music in the distance, along with the occasional shout or bang of a hammer; an engine kicked on somewhere and backfired every few strokes before puttering off again. The air smelled of smoke and exhaust fumes, must and mold, damp animals and their droppings; cloying smells like popcorn and spun sugar wafted on top of the earthier undertones. Truman was surprised, but he didn't mind the place that much. It reminded him of the storage facility where he'd met Lucy—a place of leftover, forgotten, broken objects, but where one could find things other people didn't notice or appreciate. He hoped Lucy was in a place like this and that they hadn't taken her to a place of intimidation and violence, which the living always seemed to prefer.

"Where you figure this guy is?" Bart asked as they looked around.

"I don't know," Terry answered. "I've never brought anyone here. It's been months since I've been here at all."

"Me too. Looks like it's gotten bigger."

"Yeah. I heard on the radio they were adding stuff."

A little black girl emerged from one of the better kept buildings—a trailer with a proper door and windows. The windows had bars across them. The girl wore a short yellow dress, and red rubber boots with big black dots on them, so that they looked like ladybugs. Her hair was done up in two pigtails, one tied with a piece of blue yarn, the other with a piece of white ribbon. She was the first person to stop and stare at the newcomers. She seemed the most interested in Truman, studying his face from a distance.

"Hey," Bart said to her. "Hey, little girl. Do you know where we can find Doctor Jack? The person who runs the show? We want to sell him our friend here."

The girl stared another moment before answering. "Yes, Doctor Jack buys dead people. He's funny. I'll take you to him."

"Thank you." Bart gave Truman a shove as they started to follow the girl, who wended her way between the buildings and tents, her boots slopping in the mud.

She looked back at them. "Doctor Jack says he's not a real doctor, you know. But he's so smart. Teaches dead people to do all kinds of tricks. He says he's the only one in the world who can train them so good, and I believe him. What do you think?"

"I don't know," Terry said. "You might be right."

The girl turned forward to keep leading them.

"Smart—for a little jigaboo," Bart said in a lower tone, with a smirk.

"Shhh," Terry replied. "She'll hear you."

"It's okay," Bart laughed. "They're used to it. It's no big deal."

The girl stopped at a lopsided building decorated with red and green stripes. Glittery white paint decorated the roof with fake snow. "Santa's Workshop" was painted above the doorway, which had a canvas flap across it.

"I help Doctor Jack sometimes," the girl said. "You want to see the ones I helped train?"

"Sure," said Terry.

The girl pulled aside the canvas and Truman looked in. His eyes had to adjust to the dim red light before he could see.

The back part of the building was separated from the entrance by a barrier of chicken wire and metal bars. Behind it, a dozen dead children sat at a table. Three had been African American when they were alive; a couple of the others might've been Hispanic, but it was hard to tell in the odd light. They were all dressed in absurd green and red outfits—though, of course, they didn't seem to notice or mind. The children looked up and, if it were possible, showed some recognition of the girl, even some happiness to see her—and not as a prospective meal, Truman thought.

"See? They even look nicer now," the girl said. "Doctor Jack let me help with them and now they know me."

Truman strained to see what the dead children were up to; they seemed to be fumbling with small objects on the table. The girl noticed his gaze, and she took a step inside the building. She came back out holding a small, wooden box in her hand.

"Can I show him?" she asked, looking from Truman to Bart.

Bart stepped back. "Sure," he said. "Just don't get too close."

"I won't." She held the box closer. The pieces were dovetailed, with excess glue seeping out between the cracks; the children probably could fit them together like puzzle pieces, if they had enough time to work with them. "They make these! I know it's just a box, but it's so cute how they can do that now." She turned the box over. "One of them puts this sticker on when they're done."

Truman squinted to read the small black letters on the gold foil, even as he wondered why the girl would show it to him, as though she knew he could read. The label read, "MADE IN THE USA—BY ELVES!"

The girl turned and they started forward again. "Doctor Jack says everything used to be made in China. Do you know where that is?"

"Yeah," Bart said as he pushed Truman ahead. "I used to go there all the time."

The girl faced them, her eyes wide. "You did?"

Bart laughed. "No, I'm teasing you. Who'd want to go there anyway? Just a bunch of gooks and rice."

"Well, I don't know. But I think it's nice dead people make stuff here now."

"I guess. Are you sure you know where this guy is?"

"Yeah. He's sometimes here." The girl turned toward another odd building. This one was painted with lots of white and gold, and the tops of its plywood walls were notched, like the parapet of a castle or palace. Above the doorway here the sign read, "Las Vegas," while banners on the right and left said, "El Dorado" and "Taj Mahal."

The girl led them inside. It was much darker than the other building. A middle-aged man in a grey suit sat at a table there, separated by a wire barrier from a dead man in a black suit. The living man was pretty big—taller than Truman and much heavier. His head was bare about two-thirds of the way back; what hair remained was partly grey. He had a mustache and goatee, both trimmed neatly. Everything about him was clipped and well-groomed, though right now he appeared to be quite agitated and red-faced. He slapped the table with his open hand, then pointed to two cards lying there—an ace and a six.

"See?" he shouted. "Seventeen! But it's 'soft'! You can count the ace as one or eleven! So if you get something higher than a four, you can count the ace as one. Don't you get it, you stupid dumb ass?!"

The dead man's mouth hung open as he stared at the cards. He looked up at the angry man, then back down, then up, and shook his head.

The angry man ran his hand across his bald head and through the wisps of hair in back. "Oh, for fuck's sake! Never mind! We'll just have to keep the rule that the house stays on all seventeens! Can you do that? Stay on seventeen, all right?"

The dead man nodded and gathered up the cards. He shuffled them in his hands, concentrating on what he was doing. Finally the living man noticed the visitors.

"Dalia, I'm sorry. I didn't hear you come in," the man said as he turned and got up. Truman thought her name was about the prettiest he'd ever heard.

"Hi, Doctor Jack," the girl said. "These men wanted to see you."

"Well, thank you very much. I'll come fetch you later and we can work with the elves some more, clean some of the glue off them and make them look better for visitors. All right?" He smiled. His teeth were exceptionally white and straight.

"That'll be fun. Thanks!"

Dalia left them and the man looked over Bart briefly. "I'm Jack Madison," he said. "Folks around here call me Doctor, but that's just for show." He turned his attention to Truman. "You boys looking to sell this fellow?" he said as leaned to one side, inspecting Truman closely but still keeping a distance.

"Yeah," said Bart. "Some crazy hill people had him as a pet. Said he was really smart. He didn't look like much of one for fighting, though, so we brought him to you."

"Oh, good. They have so many big, nasty ones for the patrols. This one looks more promising for our little show. He understand people?"

"Yeah. He minds pretty good, too."

"That's the most important." The man looked in Truman's eyes. "You understand me, boy?"

Truman wondered what it was with all this "boy" shit. He wavered a moment, considering something violent. Nothing too much; maybe a lunge and snarl, just enough so they would treat him more like an animal and less like a child. Of course, it'd also bring on a vicious beating, or another zapping if they had one of those things around here. So he just nodded.

"You know your numbers? Adding? What's two plus two? This many?" The man held up all five fingers. Truman shook his head. "This many?" He held down his index finger with his thumb, so the last three fingers were still extended. Truman shook his head again. "This many?" His index finger came back up and Truman nodded.

"Not bad." The man reached into a pocket and produced some coins, keys, and two dice. He put one key, one die, and one coin on the table. "Okay. Let's see if you know which one's a square." Truman wanted to say it was a cube and not a square, but he went along with it, pointing to the die. "A circle?" Truman pointed to the coin.

The man smiled at him. "This one's got some potential." He got a wad of brightly colored paper out of his pocket and peeled off four bills.

Bart eyed the bills but didn't take them. "We got to divide it with some other guys back at the dock," he said after a moment.

Doctor Jack frowned, hesitated, then pulled off two more bills. "That's it, boys. Times are tough all over. You can take this, or you can take your friend here and go."

Bart took the money.

The Doctor said he wasn't sure where he wanted to put Truman, so they chained him to a telephone pole outside and left him there. It was too sunny there, too bright and exposed, and all Truman could do was turn away from the sun and lean against the pole, defeated and alone as people went by—some of them talking with one another, very few of them noticing Truman at all, and none of them remarking his existence in any way.

Chapter 12
Will

Will sat staring at Rachel after she fell back asleep. She was still a bit wan, but was looking better almost by the hour. She was so pretty to begin with—her body full, well-muscled, but with just enough softness to make her feminine and desirable. So strong and confident, too, and that just added to how good it felt to be around her. He couldn't believe how lucky he'd been, finding this city and saving her. This place was great. Maybe they could give him some more medicine and supplies, so they'd be safer when they went back out in the wild. He'd ask about that before they left.

There was a light tapping behind him, and Will turned to see a young woman in the doorway. Her black skirt ended just above her knees, and she had a black jacket over a button-up white blouse. Will couldn't help it, but, sitting in the chair, his eyes were right at chest level; for several moments he couldn't take them off her breasts. How the hell did they stay up like that? She looked really young, sure, but no woman's stayed up that high on her chest, especially not when they were as large as hers. Wait—did women here still wear bras? Everyone else he'd met had been a guy, except the nurses, and he'd been too distraught to notice their breasts. But that must be it—they wore bras as part of their regular clothes.

Will hadn't thought much about them when he was little, back before there were dead people walking around, and in his community since then, women just didn't wear them, except at special occasions like weddings. They were considered luxury items and were only brought out a couple times a year. He doubted Rachel even had one; he'd certainly never seen her wearing one. Well, maybe she'd get one now.

Still staring, Will thought of how Rachel's breasts would look in a bra, or what it would be like to take it off of her.

"Excuse me?" The woman's high voice finally made Will raise his eyes. Blonde curls framed her long face, flowing around glasses with black, rectangular frames. She tucked some stray curls behind one ear, that cute gesture all women seemed to have in common. In her other hand she held a clipboard. Besides bras, the women here wore makeup, too. Her mouth probably wasn't that striking when she got up that morning, but with bright red lipstick, and her pale skin and blonde hair, it was as captivating as her breasts had been.

Will finally managed to stop staring at her various parts and stood up to greet her. "Oh, hi, sorry," he stammered, stepping toward her as she took a step into the room. "I was just distracted. Haven't slept much lately."

She smiled. Looking and dressing like that, she had to be used to men staring. Hell, he must look like shit, Will thought, but there wasn't much to be done about that. As he came up closer to her, at least he had an excuse to look back down at her chest, as there was a nametag pinned there. It read "Peterson."

"Julia," she said, sticking out her hand, which Will awkwardly took. He wasn't used to that gesture, either, though they'd do it sometimes back in his old town. "I work for the City Council, Department of Citizen Accounts," she said.

What the hell was that? Sounded weird, and Julia looked a little less attractive when she said it. "Oh, okay," was all Will could manage.

Julia craned her long, shapely neck to look over his shoulder at Rachel, and for a moment the attraction came back full force. "How's she doing?"

"Much better, thanks. We're so lucky we found you."

"I know. We're so glad, too. Could we maybe step out into the hall for a minute, so we don't disturb—" Julia checked her clipboard, "Rachel? We need to discuss your payment options." That didn't sound quite as incomprehensible as "Citizen Accounts," but it sucked all the attractiveness from her, even though her smile was as broad as before, her eyes as sparkly, her breasts as perky. She suddenly seemed mysterious in a distinctly unsexual kind of way— now there was more of a threatening intractability about her.

"Okay, sure," Will said as he followed her into the hallway, out of the sunlight in Rachel's room.

The light in the hall was artificial, and it had that harsh glare Will remembered from childhood. He hadn't seen fluorescent lighting in years.

Julia went through the various sheets on her clipboard, clicking her tongue as she went. "Now, let's see," she said. "You should only be here in the hospital another couple days, and there's the dockage fee for your boat. Were you planning on leaving after that?"

"Um, yeah, that's kind of what we planned."

"All right, then here's the total." She got a business card out of her jacket pocket and put it on the clipboard to write some names and numbers on it. "This is my card. You can call me when you're ready to leave. I'm writing the names of some traders on the back. Call them first and they can meet you at your boat and you all can negotiate some prices for whatever you have to sell, so we can take care of your bill."

"Call?"

"Yes, on the telephone." She looked at him and smiled. There was some condescension in the expression this time.

"But I don't think we really have anything to sell."

"Oh." It had that note of deflating finality, like everything had been going according to plan, and there was no other way to do things, no other option, and now something very bad but completely undefined was going to happen.

"Well, let's see what we can do," Julia said after a pause. She gave it a hopeful, musical tone, like she could work some magical, impossible feat, if only Will had faith in her.

"Okay." Will had decided there was no amount of feminine beauty or physical comfort worth this hassle. But he didn't think he had much choice but to go along with her machinations.

Julia began to fill out a form, and she used a smaller scrap sheet to work out some figures. "Well, we'll need to put you up in a small house. We have lots of starter homes in town, all ready to move in. Utilities. Hookup fees. Food credits." More figures went onto the scrap sheet, more lines were filled out on the form, as though she were filling in some high-tech code or occult incantation. "You'll have to continue paying the dockage fees, unless you wanted to sell the boat?"

Will didn't hesitate to answer. "No. We need it."

"All right. You and Rachel will need to find jobs, so for now let's just fill that in at the average starting rate." Numbers were added and multiplied. "There. You should have your bills paid off in about a month."

"A month?" What was she talking about? What did it cost to have the ship tied up? And they'd just gotten a couple bottles of the medicine. How could it take a month for them to work it off?

"Maybe less." She smiled and blinked once. These people had that stuff ladies put on their eyelashes, too. Will had forgotten the name—masquerade or something. But her impossibly full lashes only distracted him for an instant from all the nonsensical stuff coming out of her mouth and all the seemingly unalterable, arcane symbols on her papers. "And of course, you never know—you might want to stay longer," she said.

"No, I don't think we will. And what about the two people who were with us? They took them."

"Other people?" Julia checked her paperwork. "You mean the two dead worker units?"

"Well, yes. How do we get them back?"

"Did you get a receipt for them?"

"A receipt? No. Nobody said anything about that."

Julia's brow wrinkled. "Those men at the docks are so sloppy and careless with paperwork. Well, it says here the female was taken to the City Patrol camp. She might still be viable after a month, but I wouldn't count on it. The male was taken to the Dead End entertainment center. He should be fine, unless he was a violent or disobedient one."

"No, not at all. He was very gentle."

"That's good. But without a receipt, you'll have to pay for them again. They're not worth much, so it shouldn't add too much time to how long you have to work."

"What? Okay. Whatever. But what do you mean that the lady *might* still be *viable?*"

Julia gave what looked like a very well-practiced expression of sympathy or concern. "Just that the City Patrol is very dangerous," she said. "They're not going on nearly as many patrols as they used to, but they still lose units all the time. I don't want you to get your hopes up."

No, there wasn't too much danger of Will getting his hopes up anymore—not after this beautiful woman had started talking about payment and filling out forms and acting like they were prisoners in this clean, efficient, orderly place. He'd much rather be around Lucy than this bitch. Definitely a lot more missing inside this one, even if she had all her parts and they were all so nicely shaped and decorated.

"Well, I guess a few weeks will be okay. We can rest and get ready to move out. Get supplies and stuff."

Julia beamed, an expression somewhat less insincere than her sympathetic one. "That's great! I'll write up all the paperwork and you don't need to worry about a thing!" She shook his hand again, much more vigorously this time. "I think you'll really like New Sparta! Have a great day!"

"Yeah, you too," Will said quietly to her retreating back, his gaze immediately drifting down to her swaying hips. As nice as the view was, Will no longer thought he'd like it here very much, and he had no doubts there'd be quite a few things to worry about in this strange, complicated place.

Chapter 13
Lucy

They'd trudged along up shore for some time, with a large wall to their right. The wall was a hodgepodge of different materials—brick, concrete, cinder blocks, wooden planks. In some places it was topped with spikes or barbed wire—or, as Lucy suspected from the glinting she saw at the top, broken glass. It was irregular in height: for the most part, it was as tall as two men, but lower in some spots, higher in others. The place stank, too, of humankind, so there must have been a lot of them behind the wall.

God, why did living people always smell so bad? How could they stand that toxic mix of shit and sweat they always had coming off them? The heady scent of rich blood and succulent meat underneath it all was intoxicating to Lucy, but hardly made up for the more piercing, stinging odors that wafted above it. Better just to smell nothing than their foul mixture, which made her feel hungry and sick at the same time, so Lucy refrained from inhaling, once she'd satisfied her curiosity.

The sun had come out and the day had grown warm as they followed the wall away from the river, into marshy fields with some twisted, thorny bushes in them, and a huge number of flies buzzing around. Only the dragonflies were of any interest to Lucy—big and purple with their wild, zigzagging flights; the rest were just nasty, ordinary flies—mostly black, a few of the bright green kind.

After a while the men started moving away from the wall, following a trail of cracked pavement into the fields, and eventually into a forest of scrubby pines barely taller than Lucy. She thought it was a pretty crappy-looking place overall—boring, stunted, and broken.

They emerged from the woods and Lucy saw a high chain-link fence ahead of them. A gate in the fence was flanked by two guard towers. From these, four rifle barrels were immediately trained on them. The collar pulled back on Lucy's neck and she stopped moving forward.

"Hold up, you stupid bitch," the man behind her said. Yeah—they went around pointing guns at each other, and they called *her* a stupid bitch. Dumb fucks. Some of them deserved to die more than others.

Lucy lowered her head, but let her eye wander about, taking in the scene more carefully. She now saw two larger guns on the towers; these were mounted on brackets and did not pivot toward them, but remained pointed into the enclosure beyond the fence. She also noticed the towers had no stairs or ladders.

Lucy breathed in through her nose. Ah—that wonderful, dry, dusty smell of dead people. This was a much better place, clearly.

She saw CJ out of the corner of her eye, raising his hands. "Hey, just me, guys," he called to the guards in the towers. "CJ. From the dock."

"Hey, CJ," came the reply. "Long time no see. Whatcha got?"

"Smart one," CJ answered. "Quick too. Thought you guys would be interested. Should be perfect for patrols. She can use tools, weapons. Some crazy hill person had her as a pet. Hardly needs any training at all."

"Really? Tiny little thing. Doesn't look like she'd be up to it."

"Oh, no, she's a firecracker. Lot of fight in this one."

"I don't know, CJ. She doesn't look it."

CJ laughed as he came around in front of Lucy. He pulled on two big leather gloves. "You guys," he said. "Always make me work for it. And it's just the city's money! You'd think you'd just hand it over and be glad to have another one for the patrols."

Lucy eyed him without lifting her head. "Come on, sweet thing," he said, leering at her. "Show the man what a crazy, fucking bitch you are."

Lucy gave a low growl. Fuck him. She wasn't going to put on a show so he could make some money. What the hell did he need money for, anyway? Everyone here looked pretty well-fed and spoiled, as far as she could tell. What the fuck more did they need?

CJ backhanded her across the face. Lucy lifted her head up part of the way and glared at him, but didn't make a move or another sound.

He squinted at her as the men in the towers laughed. "Not looking good for you, CJ," one called. "She's just somebody's pet. Leave her alone!"

CJ took a step toward her and slammed his left fist into her stomach. Didn't really feel like much—just a rough sort of pressing into her, not a real pain. But then he grabbed her chin and pushed her head back. She'd have a mouthful of gristly, crunchy thumb right now, if it weren't for those damned gloves.

"No more fucking around," CJ whispered to Lucy, his mouth next to her ear. "If you cost me money, or embarrass me, I'll snap your fucking neck, bitch. Fuck the money." He pulled back a little, so he could see her eye. "Blink, you cunt, if you understand me, or I'll do it right now."

A few more days of humiliation and pain? Or end it now? That is, if the little weasel had the balls and muscles to do it. Lucy half closed her eye. She knew it'd feel good, to have it over with. Real rest. That seemed like the nicest, most desirable thing imaginable. And not having to be pushed around by all the pricks in the world? That'd be incredible, too, better than anything she could imagine. But Lucy also knew she was just like Rachel—or probably like most everyone else who'd faced this kind of decision. She couldn't let go, even of this ugly, vicious semblance of life. It was just human nature not to. Nothing to be done about it but give in to the weakness.

She brought her eyelid down all the way and raised it back up.

"Good," CJ said, smirking. "You'll always be somebody's bitch." As he stepped back, he also pulled her kerchief off, just to make sure she'd put on a good show.

All Lucy's shame—at how she looked, at what she was, at how she couldn't even will herself to die—erupted into a howl of rage and pain. She swung her manacled hands—once to the left, then back to the right—catching CJ in the face both times, first with her fist, then with the metal band and her other fist. She would've lunged straight forward next, would have tackled him with the metal pressing into his throat, but the man holding her collar finally brought her around, pulling her off balance and keeping her from moving forward.

CJ stepped back, wiping his mouth with his sleeve. He wasn't smirking anymore, at least, but he smiled crookedly, showing his teeth all covered with blood. "Told you, guys," he said. "Bitch is twice as mean as a rattlesnake and almost as fast."

There was laughter again from the towers, but this time it sounded more appreciative than mocking. The one guard spoke again. "All right, all right," he said. "Maybe we were too quick to judge. You sure she can see, though, with her face all messed up like that? I've seen lots of 'em, but none with a face as jacked-up as that."

"She can see fine. Stop kidding around. She could see to clock me while you numb nuts sat up there and laughed. Now admit it. I was right."

"Okay, you were right, CJ. Girl's got potential. You fill out the form and turn it in at city hall and you'll get your money. Half now, half if she's still up and around after a month."

"Yeah, yeah, I know how it works. Always with the forms. Some shit never changes."

CJ approached Lucy, though he stayed out of her reach. The man behind her pulled back on the collar to keep her in place. "On your knees, honey," CJ said. "You did good and I appreciate it, but I'm not gonna take any chances, with you all riled up again."

The collar pressed on her shoulders and Lucy got down on her knees.

"Hands out in front," CJ said.

Lucy complied. He unlocked the manacles and stepped away as she got back up.

They walked her forward as the gate opened, then unlocked the collar. Lucy reached up to rub her raw neck. She turned to see CJ and the other guy backing away from her. She snarled at them, just to feel something good in her wretched state, but there wasn't much point in posturing now: they were safe and in charge and they knew it.

CJ gave a little wave—the mocking kind, with the hand held up, folding the four fingers down as one, then snapping them back up several times. "Bye, bye, darling," he said.

Prick.

"She know words?" the guard called from the tower. "Take commands?" They must not have heard when CJ whispered to her. Good. The less they knew, the better.

"Yeah. She won't always do what you say, but she knows."

"Get inside, bitch."

Lucy walked through the gate, which slid closed behind her. She sniffed the air again. Dead were around. Some were closer than when she smelled the air before. In the compound behind the fence sat various structures in advanced stages of decay—huts or sheds more than houses, though they might've started out as real dwellings once, a long time ago. No more commands came from the tower, which was fine with her, but after a few moments the silence made her anxious. Then Lucy heard some shuffling and scraping from one of the buildings.

A young dead woman emerged from one of the sheds—a girl, really, though she was nearly as tall as Lucy, and had a fuller, thicker body. Her brown hair was done up in two pigtails. Lucy didn't remember too much of fashion, but she was pretty sure only young girls wore their hair that way—or an older girl trying to look younger.

She had on a very short skirt, ruffled, with stripes, though the colors were so faded, you couldn't tell what shades they'd been originally; it was also spattered with mud and blood and God knows what other filth. Lucy remembered something about girls in really short skirts like that—they'd dance and jump around in front of crowds, though she couldn't remember what you called it or what the reason was.

The girl's top didn't match, but was made from some thick fabric, like denim or canvas; it had vertical black and white stripes on it and looked ridiculous on the poor girl, like something a person would wear to make people laugh, though this hardly seemed the place where people laughed very much. Well, except for those idiots in the tower, but they'd laugh at anything degrading or ugly. The girl held a bundle of the same fabric in her hands. Lucy noticed she walked with a limp as she approached.

"They're so funny, how they always send out a girl if it's a girl, and a guy if it's a guy," Lucy heard from the tower. "Like it fucking matters. They eat people, and they care who comes out to greet them? I can never get over how messed up they are."

The girl was now in front of Lucy, holding out the bundle. Her large, almond-shaped eyes were only a little cloudy, and set far apart on her round face. She must've been very pretty, with a voluptuous, young body, and a bright, innocent face. But now she just looked forlorn and stupid, gazing over Lucy's shoulder with her mouth slightly open, swaying there among the broken-down buildings. Lucy took the clothes from her and nodded slightly. She got no response before the girl turned to shuffle back the way she had come.

"The hot cheerleader's limping worse," Lucy heard one guard say. "We're gonna have to put her down."

"But she's so fucking hot," another one said. "I love watching her walk around. And it's not like with real girls: you can stare all day and no one cares, no one tells you to stop. You can just sit back and enjoy the show all day long."

Some chuckles and catcalls. "You're sick. How can you say shit like that?"

"Hey—what's wrong with looking? They're perfect for that. It's not like they mind. I don't see any problem."

"Yeah, you wouldn't. It's just gross. And besides, she hasn't been on patrol in weeks. We're gonna get written up if the inspectors come by. You know the rules."

"All right. Don't get all scared of the city council like a bunch of girls. I'll take care of it." Lucy heard a metallic click, and then someone shouted, "Hey!"

The girl stopped walking and turned back around. Her big brown eyes were looking right at Lucy, who shut her eye against the inevitable. She only flinched a little when the shot came a second later.

That was another thing about living people, besides their sickening smell: they were always so damned loud, with all their crashes and explosions, gunshots and screaming. Why couldn't they ever just shut up and be still?

Lucy opened her eye, and took a step forward. The body looked peaceful in the grass there, the eyes looking up at the sky; it had been as quick an end as one could hope for, so there was no logical reason for how much rage Lucy felt at that moment. But if anything, that only increased its intensity. She dug her fingers into the bundle she held and clenched her jaw till it hurt and her ears rang.

"Hey, new meat!" Lucy heard from the tower. She relaxed slightly as she turned toward them, readying herself for whatever new indignity or violence they intended.

"Put the uniform on," the guard said. "Rules."

Yeah, they always liked that word—"rules." Covered all sorts of ugliness that they loved so much. Lucy unfolded the stiff shirt and frowned at it. It smelled good, like dead people, but she still felt funny putting on such a weird piece of clothing. After a moment, she began to pull it on anyway.

"No," she heard when the shirt was over her head. "Take off what you got on first."

There were groans and laughter from the other men: "Not that again, you sick fuck! Oh, you can't be serious! You're one sick bastard!"

"Hey—you made me shoot my other piece of eye candy! This one's fine as hell too!" The one man pointed at Lucy. "Hey, honey! When you're done with that, put something over that mess on your face. I don't want to see that when you're sashaying around here. Ruins everything."

It was extremely difficult and slow, trying to get her dress off without Truman's help, but Lucy eventually got the buttons undone in the back. She stared at the girl's body as she worked, at the way the breeze now moved the grass around the corpse; it gave her something to focus on, something to distract from the shame.

Lucy let the dress drop to the ground. Though it had been warm earlier, the air now felt icy against her body.

Chapter 14
Rachel

Rachel kept her eye on Will as the tall blonde led them up the steps of the row house. This Julia character was definitely the kind you'd catch your man looking at the wrong way. Rachel was pretty self-confident in the looks department, and Will had always been more loyal than she, to be frank, but this gal had all those adornments she barely remembered from childhood—the clothes, the makeup, the girly-girl mannerisms. God, that thing she did with her hair, tucking it behind her ear—could she have practiced a gesture more affected and annoying if she tried? Rachel had even caught a whiff of Blondie as they walked around the city—somewhere between syrupy and flowery, but with something animal underneath it. What was that expression? She'd heard her older brother say it years ago, and they'd laughed hysterically at the naughty words. Oh yeah—she smelled like a French whore. That about summed up this skank.

Guys loved that shit, though, Rachel knew. And this gal had it going on every which way. With her height, she'd have great legs to begin with, and she was wearing high heels too. Who wore those anymore? You could barely walk in them, let alone run if you had to. Didn't seem ladies had to run too much here in New Sparta, if they played their cards right. Never mind the shaved legs and stockings. Rachel had forgotten how women's legs looked so different that way, it had been so long since she'd seen them. Kind of strange, actually—sort of lean and greasy looking. Rachel could be objective enough to analyze the oddity and unnaturalness of it, but she also knew objectivity was not the point. Attraction was all about difference, novelty. Rachel caught some of the city men checking her out like she was a new, exotic dish set on the table for them, even though she must look like some hairy nature-girl that swung down from a branch, next to this prissy bitch. Will couldn't help but have the same reaction to a Barbie doll like Julia.

Rachel half wanted to catch him checking out the slut's firm, slender ass. Make him feel guilty when she caught him, make him feel all eager and more forceful when they made up later. That'd be fun. But no, he was looking nervously at the house, the yard, the adjoining houses, anything but the bimbo's perfect body. Weird. On the one hand, Rachel didn't like not being able to figure him out, but on the other—well, it made him kind of cuter, too, that he was so shy and faithful. She leaned closer to him and rubbed his shoulder. He turned and gave her a smile, but it looked strained.

What the heck was he so nervous about, anyway? A guy had to be awfully bent about something to keep his mind off a piece like Julia. She'd taken them to three houses already this morning, and he'd been all mopey and shit. Over what? Rachel was enthralled by everything, even as she kept glancing at that tramp, kept track of her constant flirtations with Will, her subtle putdowns of Rachel. The bitch had to point out that one house had lots of sun—and she said it while looking Rachel up and down, as if implying she were too pale. At the next, she gushed over the large, elaborate kitchen, then asked Rachel if she liked to cook, noting how she, of course, loved to cook for her boyfriend. What the fuck did Miss Boobs-a-Lot think? She knew damn well they'd been living out in the wilderness and Rachel's cooking skills were more towards the gutting and cleaning end of things. And a supposedly sophisticated sperm bank like Julia knew how much a simple guy like Will would love to hear about her Marsala sauce and shallots and mint jelly.

Rachel had fumed over that, but those indignities paled next to the treasures Realtor Barbie dangled before them like candy or pearls. Rachel had been right about the hot water—my God, you could turn on the tap and have to pull your hand out from the stream of water, it was so hot. Ovens. Refrigerators. Microwaves. Washers. Dryers. Televisions. The city only had one channel, but they'd walked by a couple stores that rented DVDs. No having to ask for fuel to turn on a portable generator, either—the electricity flowed just like the hot water and gas. Even the phone lines were live. Hell—back home, she'd used the handset on her old phone to crack walnuts on the counter, but here you picked one up and it actually had a dial tone. The one house even had a garbage disposal and a dishwasher.

When they'd walked into the living room of another, the room had been stuffy, so the leggy bimbo had sashayed over to the window and turned on the air conditioner. Could you imagine—real air conditioning? Rachel could feel the air blasting half way across the room—nice and cold and damp. Yeah, all that stuff would be worth putting up with some stuck-up bitches like Julia. Besides, a few weeks here, and if Rachel got some nice clothes, underwear, some makeup—she wouldn't even have to feel self-conscious next to sluts like that.

At each house, Will didn't seem to see the attractions quite as vividly or desirously as she did. He kept asking about the cost, and since the city's currency had no real meaning to the two of them, he'd have to ask Julia to figure it, based on how long it would take them to work off the debt before they could leave. So each house was expressed as "five weeks" or "six weeks" or whatever. If the gal hadn't been such a bitch, Rachel almost would have felt sorry for her, having to crunch the numbers so many times, and for so little a purpose. Rachel didn't even pay attention to the calculations, she was so busy checking out the fun stuff. What difference did it make? What was the rush? This was going to be like a nice, much-deserved vacation.

Truman and Lucy didn't need stuff like this, they couldn't appreciate it one way or another. Set them in a corner, and they'd snuggle and stare off into space and be as happy as they were going to be. How different was it, really, than when she'd been little and they'd gone on a trip and left the dog at a kennel? It didn't know any better, even if she'd been worried back then that it'd be lonely. It was fine. Real people just needed more, and Rachel and Will had gone so long with so little. It wasn't their fault if they rested a bit here. Besides, it probably wasn't so bad, wherever those two were.

They entered the fourth house. A few hours ago, Rachel would've said it was the cleanest, most comfortable looking home she'd seen since she was a child. Now it looked pretty humble, after the other ones they'd been in. As Will dragged their slutty guide to the living room to run the numbers, Rachel drifted to the kitchen. Simple. Really small, made worse by having the washing machine in the kitchen itself. Rachel remembered that her grandmother's house had been set up that way. No dryer. She looked out the back window and saw the clothesline. Well, she never was one for laundry and chores, though seeing Julia's wardrobe, Rachel vowed to get nicer stuff and clean it up better.

The rest of the kitchen looked adequate, if cramped. Not much counter space, but she'd learn to make stuff. How hard could it be? Might be fun, playing house with Will for a change. My God—they probably had food here you didn't have to catch yourself, stuff in cans and jars and frozen from last summer. Yes, this could be nice.

Rachel had gone all the way around and emerged in the living room from the other side. The tramp was standing closer to Will than she needed to, showing him the numbers and a generous view of cleavage. He was still acting all chaste and nervous. He immediately noticed Rachel and stepped back from the temptress.

"Rach, this place is a little less than the others," he said. It seemed to be all he thought of, and this fact appeared to have made him happier than before. "We could be out in about a month."

Rachel hid her disappointment. "That's great," she said, flashing a smile at him and ignoring the bitch. "If this is the one you want, honey, it'll be great." He looked so relieved, so much more relaxed than before, that she couldn't help but respond to his happiness. If it made him feel better to stay less time, that was fine. She'd wheedle a few more days out of him, probably, and everyone would have what they wanted. You had to compromise.

"I'm glad you found something to fit your needs," Julia said with that annoying hair-tuck again. "Normally, you'd have to wait for the paperwork, but given your circumstances, I'm sure you can stay here tonight and I'll come by with all the paperwork tomorrow." Slut even dared a pat on Will's shoulder at that point. You had to give her points for being brazen. "You should carry her across the threshold. That'd be so cute."

Her? Who was that? The cat's mother? A normal woman who wanted to be friendly would've addressed it to Rachel, like, "Oh, Rachel, Will should carry you!" But of course, the bitch didn't.

Will didn't pick up on the slight, nor did he know to what she was referring. He looked around, confused.

"You know, it's a tradition," Julia said. "When a couple moves in—the man carries the woman in the front door. I know when I get married I'd love for my husband to do that. It's so romantic."

"Well, maybe later," Rachel said as she moved between them and steered the short-skirted annoyance toward the door. "Thank you so much for helping us find this place."

Julia took the implication. She was too sweet and cloying by half, but Rachel saw she could take a hint. Rachel also figured there wasn't much to be gained by hanging around, even if Will had the same jungle-boy appeal to her that Rachel had toward the men of the town. She let Rachel herd her out the door, smiling and promising to be back tomorrow.

"Whew!" Rachel said when they were alone. She walked over and pulled the curtains closed over the big living room window that faced toward the street. "Our own place! Isn't that weird?"

"Yeah," Will said, still looking around in something of a daze.

Rachel put her arms around his neck. God, his muscles were all knotted up. "But it's nice, too, don't you think? Comfy. We can relax a little. Things have been hard. We need a break."

Will finally seemed to ease a little, as he let his hands rest on her hips. "Yeah. That'll be nice. I'm so glad you're better. I love you."

"I love you too." Rachel pulled him down, touching the tip of her nose to his, rubbing it back and forth and giggling. When he laughed a little in return, she knew he was out of his funk enough for her to continue. She tilted her head to kiss his chin and the corner of his mouth. "We haven't done it in forever," she whispered. "And we finally have some privacy, not like on the boat. Come on, let's just have some fun."

His lips finally found hers for a full, deep kiss, as his hands went around to squeeze her butt and pull her close. God—one kiss and he was already so hard? Maybe his body had responded to that slut Julia, even if his mind were on other things. Or maybe Rachel just needed to do it to him extra good today, after such a long hiatus—hump any bothersome thoughts right out of his head, please his body the way she'd been wanting to have hers satisfied for so long. Her insides felt good for the first time in ages—warm and strong, their very neediness a source of so much overwhelming power. Rachel kissed him back more hungrily, her own arousal exploding at the idea that he needed to take her just as urgently as she longed to draw him in and possess him.

Chapter 15
Truman

Truman had been at the Dead End a few days now. Doctor Jack had been too busy with all his various undead amusements to bother much with him. At least he'd put Truman in a cage in one of the tents, so he didn't have to stand outside, exposed and alone. Truman's tent seemed to have some carnival or freak show theme. Next to his cage, the Great Lardo was chained—an enormous, fat dead man with wild grey hair and beard, dull eyes, and a mouth that always hung open. His nose and one cheek were torn off; his ears looked crooked, too. He was huge, not just in girth but height as well. They'd dressed him in overalls, with a giant belt around his waist; affixed to the buckle was a big metal medallion, the size of a serving platter. Truman thought he looked intimidating for about thirty seconds, before his sad demeanor made the poor man seem merely pathetic.

The Great Lardo was one of the two big attractions in the tent. Twice a night, with an extra show on weekend afternoons, three men would haul the unfortunate corpse to the middle of the tent and hold him there; two held the chains attached to his neck collar, while the third wielded a whip with great fanfare and noise. It was hardly necessary for controlling the dead man, who was completely docile. But the crowd loved it, and the Great Lardo knew to put on some show of hostility and aggression when the leather was cracked in front of his ruined face.

As they tormented him, Doctor Jack would wheel out a small cannon and train it on the growling pile of flesh. With a slack, irregular drumroll from another dead man—this one dressed in a marching band uniform—Doctor Jack would make a show of loading and aiming the weapon. A scantily-attired female assistant would quickly put aside her tray for selling peanuts and popcorn to the crowd, so she could come out and plead with him to fire the cannon and save the city from the monster.

"Oh no!" she'd squeal. "He's sure to break free from those chains and kill us all! He's so big he could probably eat everyone! Help!"

Doctor Jack would turn aside and smirk to the crowd, "I know one person in here I'd like to eat!" The men in the crowd would howl with laughter at that; some of the women would twitter more politely, while those who'd brought children might cast an embarrassed glance at them.

That was the penultimate signal for the act. The last was Doctor Jack shouting, "Step aside, woman! Those chains can't hold much longer!"

That was the sign for the assistants to drop the chains, as Doctor Jack lit the cannon's fuse. The crowd would gasp at the report, which was painfully loud in the enclosed space. The men had practiced their work enough that the projectile always hit its tormented target right on the metal disk at his waist; it gave a dull clunk as the impact sent the large man flying through the air. He'd land with a thud and the crowd would break out into wild laughter at his plight. Then the two assistants grabbed the chains, as the third man cracked the whip over and over to the crowd's applause. The people would shuffle out at that point, though photos were available with the Great Lardo for an extra fee. Truman almost imagined that the dead man looked happy at that point, with people paying him attention without trying to hurt him. Truman hated the smell of gunpowder after the show.

The tent's other big show was put on by Ravishing Ramona, Truman's neighbor on the opposite side of his cage. Her name said it all, so long as you made allowances for her being dead. She was tall and slender, with long, wavy hair that had remained remarkably dark, even after all these years. Truman didn't think she dyed it, as he'd watched her getting ready and had never seen her use anything on her hair but a brush. Against her pale skin the black mane was captivating, as was the red lipstick she put on. There wasn't a mark on her lean, sinuous body—not that Truman had ever seen, and most of her flesh was exposed for her act.

Ramona only had to do one late show each night, after the Great Lardo had been slammed into the ground for the second or third time of the evening. Her shows were only attended by men, the lights turned down low, and the whole spectacle accompanied by loud music with a driving, pulsing beat. Ramona would slink seductively out to the middle, her handler holding the chain slack and attaching it to the tent support there. As Ramona swayed to the music, the assistant brought out a bucket and laid it on the ground next to the woman. Ramona took her time peeling off two elbow-length gloves and a silver, micro miniskirt. She'd then roll down her gold, sequined top to expose her breasts, which were still perfectly shaped. The rose pink nipples provided the same mesmerizing contrast as her lips and hair. She always kept her midsection covered—Truman thought that was probably where the wounds that had killed her were hidden. When she revealed her buttocks and crotch, and then again when she uncovered her breasts, the crowd briefly erupted in shouts and applause, then settled back down to a rapt silence. That first night in the tent, even Truman couldn't take his gaze away from her, not knowing what she'd do next, and whether he'd find it to be hideous or erotic. He looked away for a moment when he thought it might be both - but only for a moment.

The dead woman reached into the bucket and brought out a gold-colored chain. It was covered in some oily liquid that dribbled off it on to her hand and arm. She kept pulling it out until she got to the end of it, where a metal orb a little bigger than a golf ball was attached. She lewdly mouthed it and rolled it around between her legs before the final segment began. Leaning her head back, she swallowed the ball, letting the chain trail down her throat after it. For a long time she kept feeding the chain into her mouth. Truman looked at the crowd. They couldn't make a movement or sound they were so entranced by the motions of her body. She paused, opening her mouth wider and reaching one hand down between her legs as she bent her knees. Finally, with a gasp she pulled the ball free of her vagina and showed it to the crowd, which roared its appreciation. She attached both ends of the ball and chain to the tent support, so she could rock back and forth on the chain, dragging it in and out of her body at both ends and loudly simulating masturbation for the crowd, which had again sunk into silence, to better and more fully revel in the woman's degradation.

Truman had finally been able to tear himself away from the scene at that point, though he couldn't block out the sounds she made. The chain in her throat made her choke and gag as she moaned, but that seemed to excite the crowd more. Ramona crescendoed from groans and sighs to finish with frenzied screams of feigned pleasure. Truman heard applause at that point, and looked up to see Ramona—the chain now gone, thank God— gathering up her clothes and blowing kisses to the retreating crowd. Like the Great Lardo when he had posed with children, Ramona looked almost happy, or even slightly patronizing, toward the living men.

That night, in the dark, after all the living people had left, Truman heard her moving around; the chain attached to her ankle rattled as she came closer to the wire and metal barrier that enclosed Truman. "What's your name?" she asked in a whisper. Her voice matched the rest of her—beautiful, thin, mysterious, though far less forceful and daunting than her body.

She'd spoken? Truman moved closer to where she was standing so he could see her better in the shadows of the tent. Some light seeped through the flaps, as did the sounds of living people—laughter, music, voices. After her act, she'd wrapped herself in a long, faded winter coat. It was made of some kind of fake, black fur, and although it was tattered and matted, it still gave her an exotic but much more demure look, with her long, black hair framing her thin face. With the color of her hair and the coat, Truman would barely have been able to see her in the semi- darkness, were it not for her pale skin. Her brown eyes were nearly as clear as Lucy's single blue one.

"You speak?" Truman said.

"Yes. So does Lou."

"Lou?"

She pointed over Truman's shoulder. "The other guy. The one they shoot at. He doesn't much, though. But when he wants to he can. We don't talk in front of the bosses."

"All right."

"So—what's your name?"

"Truman."

She repeated the name. It sounded nicer when she said it. She'd wiped off the lipstick and her mouth looked much more delicate now. "You can call me Ramona. It's a nice name they gave me. They gave poor Lou a stupid name, so I called him Lou instead and he liked it."

Truman nodded. "How can you do that?" he asked after a moment.

"Do what?"

"What they make you do. That show you put on for them."

"Oh. I think some stuff is missing inside, so the ball just goes through. I still have to work at it, but it's not too hard."

"No, I meant how can you do that at all? Don't you mind doing it?"

"Mind it?" She might've shrugged under the oversized coat, or she might've just been shifting her weight. "Sure. But they like it and it keeps them from shooting me. And it's comfortable enough here the rest of the time."

Truman didn't know what to say to that. They just stared at one another for a moment before she added, "I'm sorry if you don't like it."

"No, that's not the point. I just feel sorry for you."

"You don't have to. But thank you."

That had been a few days ago. They had spoken each night since, and Truman had spoken to Lou as well, who wasn't quite as taciturn as Ramona had indicated. Truman suspected he might've been shyer around her, just as Truman had felt intimidated by her at first. What normal man wouldn't be, after he saw her on display, and heard her matter-of-fact reaction to it? It wasn't natural; it wasn't right. But now Truman enjoyed talking to both of them. They didn't talk about the carnival and their present existence— there wasn't much to discuss in that, after all. Instead, they tried to remember different things, though their memories always tumbled out in a disconnected mess. But they helped each other remember snow and birds and all sorts of different people who'd made them happy in some way, though they usually didn't remember how, and they never remembered when, or what had happened to the other people.

As Ramona had said, it was pleasant enough in this place. Truman only wished he didn't have to listen to her entertain the living men. But turning his eyes away at least made it easier, and each night he looked forward to talking to her afterward, letting her soft voice push the evening's show from his mind. She'd always ask him about the books he'd read, what was in them, and Truman was glad and proud to tell her whatever he could remember.

The only time he'd felt really apprehensive and frightened was last night. When Doctor Jack was closing up after the show, he had looked at Truman and told him they'd have to get to work tomorrow on training him. Something in the way he'd said it sounded as if he might want to include Truman in the act with Ramona. So Truman spent the rest of the night trying to think of ways to kill himself, though nothing seemed feasible. It was another indignity of their existence: they couldn't even remove themselves from all the pain other people inflicted on them.

In the morning, when the tent flaps parted and were tied back, Doctor Jack strode in, the bright sunlight pouring in all around him. Truman could only feel the deepest despair and shame. Squinting at the larger man, however, one small but powerful revelation consoled him: a lunge and snarl and bite would most likely bring about the desired end of a bullet to his tortured brain. Truman bared his teeth slightly and prepared himself for that fate. The unfairness of it was far less appalling to him, the potential pain far less terrifying, than the powerlessness and humiliation he had felt throughout the night.

Chapter 16
Will

"Hi, Will," Ken called as Will walked down the path to the street.

"Hey, Ken," Will said, stopping to wait at the curb.

As Ken said goodbye to his wife, Shayna, Will watched a street sweeper churn up dirt and leaves down the street. There'd been a truck picking up trash the day before, too. They ran vehicles and machinery for everything in New Sparta. It was amazing, compared to how Will was used to living.

He turned his attention back to the couple in the doorway, his new next-door neighbors. Ken and Shayna were African-American, a few years older than Will and Rachel, with a baby girl named Aisha. Ken was a big guy and worked construction, which there seemed to be a lot of in the city. Shayna stayed with the baby for now, and they talked about trying to have another. They were both so polished, educated, well-dressed—sort of intimidating, really. Not uncomfortable, like the weird bureaucrat Julia, but Will felt as though he didn't fit in. Rachel seemed more at ease with their neighbors. They all had met the day before, as both couples returned to their houses with food and various other purchases.

People here bought an awful lot of stuff on what they called "credit." People didn't do that in Will's town, where you'd ask someone for something and then give them something in return at some point. This "credit" was something much more complex and long term, and it could only be expressed by lengthening the amount of time they had to stay here and work. Which is what Will had to take care of today—finding a job so they could start the process of cutting loose.

Will waved to Shayna as she stood in the doorway. Nice looking lady, with her hair straightened and some red tints in it. He hadn't seen that in years, and it looked good on her. She was about the same height and build as Rachel, and they seemed to hit it off yesterday.

Ken smiled at Will and started walking down the street with him. "Where you off to today?" he asked.

Will reached in his pocket and retrieved another of the business cards Julia had given him. "The lady from the city council said to go to the employment office as soon as possible. Is it this way? She said it was, but I didn't really follow her directions."

"Sure. It's on my way to the construction site. I'll show you."

"Thanks. Hey, do you know if they're hiring at your construction job?"

"I'd imagine. We're working on a couple big projects, now that the weather's nice. You'd probably like working there."

"Well, maybe, but I wasn't asking so much for me. That's what Rachel's always done for work—construction."

"Really? Wow."

Maybe he'd said something wrong or ignorant. Maybe women didn't do "men's" work around here. Julia sure was overly feminine. Shayna wasn't quite so much, but she'd worn a skirt both times Will had seen her. Maybe he'd just confirmed that he and Rachel were weird "hill people," the way the men had talked about them at the docks. Or maybe it was something more personal. Ken's tone didn't have anything judgmental or negative in it, really—he just sounded surprised—but Will felt himself getting defensive. Could the other man detect some suspicion in Will's tone, some hint of jealousy that Rachel was always around other guys? She'd been so wild when they first met, but he trusted her now. Well, sort of. He wanted to. He meant to.

"What?" Will asked.

Ken smiled again and put Will more at ease. The guy had that kind of personality. "Nothing. She just looks a little small and, you know, girly. That's all I meant."

"She's strong, and she's learned to work with the equipment. I mean, the equipment we have up in our town. I guess you guys probably have a lot more here. This place is so much more built up than we're used to, so much more developed."

"It's been good. We were lucky. But if Rachel wants to work at the site, send her over to the employment office. I'm sure they could use her."

"Great." Will tried his best to sound nonchalant. "I think Rachel should rest another day, but I need to go get a job right away."

"Yeah. Got to pay the bills. I know."

They walked in silence for a while. Will saw a man in a blue uniform putting papers into the mailboxes on the other side of the street; another man waved to them before pulling the starter cord on a lawnmower. Mailmen? Fuel being used to mow grass? This place was so different.

Will had enjoyed making love to Rachel on shag carpet that smelled of detergent and had probably just been vacuumed. Afterward, he'd laughed with her when they'd gone to the corner store to get popcorn, which they fixed on the gas stove and then devoured, before making love again, this time in the shower with that unbelievable supply of hot water. But overall, Will wasn't too sure about New Sparta and all its offerings. Things were simpler, safer on the boat. A little dirt never hurt anyone.

"Did you really live on a boat?" Ken asked. "Out there? With all those things? Now you just see them chained up and stuff, not running around loose and shit. I don't know how you did it."

Will took a second to process the question, which had come as such a strange coincidence with what he'd been thinking. "It wasn't so bad. It was kind of nice. Alone—the wind, the sun. Nothing to worry about." Best not to mention Truman and Lucy to the neighbors—that was definitely the kind of thing you kept to yourself when you moved in. That was what got him thrown out of his own town—it certainly wouldn't sit well with these people and their order and cleanliness.

Ken chuckled. It was deep and good-natured, but still made Will wonder if he'd said something wrong. "Nothing to worry about? Man, you are one crazy mother fucker, Will. I'm surprised you can walk, your balls must be so big. I haven't been outside in years. Well, sometimes the construction sites are right outside the walls, but then they have guards." He gestured to the pistol at his hip. It was a 9mm and looked so tiny on his large frame it was almost comical, like a man carrying a toy gun. "And I'm supposed to know how to use this, but come on. We have to pass a test on the pistol range once a year, but shit—paper targets just hanging there? I don't think that's the same as a bunch of those things around, trying to get you. I'd freak. And never mind if the girls were with me. They'd probably have to hustle me out of there themselves, and not the other way around."

"I guess we're just more used to dead people. They're not so bad. There aren't as many as before, and the ones that are out there move even slower than before. You just move away from them when you see them. Some don't even try to chase you. I think mostly they're tired and want to be left alone."

Ken slapped him on the back. "Crazy! You are so crazy! Now you're talking like they're people and shit." He pointed across the street. "Well, there's the employment office. They'll fix you up. Hey—why don't you and Rachel come over later? We'll put the baby to bed and we can talk, play cards or dominoes. You guys know how to play tonk?"

Tonk? Will guessed it was a card game, but he had no idea. "Um, no, but I guess we could learn."

"Sure. It's like rummy. We'll show you."

"That'd be fun. Thanks."

"No problem. I'll give you a holler when the baby's asleep. See you."

Will turned to face the building Ken had indicated. Carved above the door were the words "City Library," but a different sign had been hung under that, designating the building as the "City Employment Office." Will imagined a building full of people like Julia—clipped, pert, sparkling women and men. They would be shuffling mountains of papers, scribbling lines of figures, all of it to enforce myriads of stated and implied rules, most of which could not exactly be explained or rationalized, but none of which could be questioned or altered in any way. The thought so terrified Will that he nearly ran back down the street. But after a moment, he had steeled himself enough to duck his head and bound up the steps to the entrance, two at a time.

Chapter 17
Lucy

The first few days in the compound had not been as bad for Lucy as those first few minutes. Not knowing where to go, and with no further demands from the guards, she had entered the building from which the girl had emerged. It was the ruins of what had once been a small home. All the windows were broken, and the front door was a pile of shattered wood and glass next to the doorway. Lucy stepped through the entrance and let her eye adjust to the darker interior before proceeding.

Lucy heard a grunt and scrape to her left. She turned and saw a tall, dead woman. She wore the same stupid striped shirt as Lucy now did; under that her pants looked like black jeans, covered with mud and grime. Lucy had been forced to pull on similarly filthy pants, though they were a lighter color. The woman stood in the middle of the room next to a chair, the cushions of which had split open, letting the stuffing spill out in grey strands.

The window was partly covered by tattered cloths that flapped in the light breeze, but the woman must've seen what had happened outside. She had a long, black metal rod in her right hand, which hung down at her side. It was one of those pointy metal poles people used to stab at the fire in a fireplace. What were those called? Not stabbers, not pointers. What was it? Pokers—that was it. The scraping sound had been made by the tip of it sliding along the wooden floor as the woman turned toward Lucy.

They faced each other for some time. The woman did not appear as uncomprehending as the girl had. The gaze that came from under her short black hair had more reason and purpose behind it, though her eyes were much cloudier and uglier than the girl's had been. And her movements were stiffer and less graceful than the girl's; she nodded to Lucy, then turned to walk toward the other doorway that led to a room farther back in the house.

Lucy followed her, their shoes crunching on the bits of plaster and glass everywhere on the floor. Most of the ceiling and walls had disintegrated, leaving the beams exposed in many places, though here and there pieces of wood, cloth, and cardboard formed makeshift patches.

They entered the other room, which was darker, so Lucy paused again to adjust. After a moment she could see two more dead women sitting in the room—one on a sofa, one on a large stuffed chair. The furniture here was in better shape than the chair in the first room, and the ceiling and walls here were also more intact. The back of the room, however, was a jumble of broken furniture, as though someone had barricaded this room off from the back of the house. The furniture blocking the back windows was what made it darker in here. Only a little light seeped in from the front room, and from a small window on the side, which was covered more thoroughly with cloths than the window in the other room. This back room seemed safer, more private.

As the tall woman sat down in an empty chair, Lucy surveyed the other women. The one on the sofa looked like she had a larger frame than the rest of them, though it was hard to tell under the striped shirt—they were all cut so large and loose-fitting. She had shoulder-length brown hair that had become a nondescript, sandy color; it might've been much darker before—there was no way to tell. Her face was torn on the right side—not as badly as Lucy's, but she'd lost a lot of hair on that side of her head as well, so it looked ugly in its own way. She was probably the oldest of the group, while the other woman who sat in the chair looked like the youngest. Her red hair had faded to an odd rust color, the sort of shade that human hair wasn't supposed to be. Lucy thought she looked a little like Rachel—similar hair color, allowing for the age and decay; same eyes, too, though now they were clouded; same plump face; same build—busty, with a short, thick body. Though she didn't look nearly as miserable as Rachel had when Lucy last saw her, Lucy knew this woman would never have the joy of the living girl. None of them would, though this was probably the calmest and most content she'd seen dead people—other than Truman, of course.

"Angie's g-g-gone," the tall woman said softly after a while.

Lucy couldn't help letting her jaw drop at that. She and Truman had struggled so hard to relearn speech, and this woman could talk too. She had the same problems they did—the pauses to take a breath or to think of the next word, the little catches and stammers, the vowel sounds coming out wrong—but she could speak. If the living people in this place were not particularly surprising or interesting, the dead people certainly were.

"I should've gone," the short red-haired girl said, looking down.

"No, they were gonna get her anyway," said the brown-haired woman on the couch. "They liked her better. Fed her more. Always looked at her ass. Then she got hurt. They got tired of her. That's how they are."

The other two nodded in silent agreement.

"You talk?" Lucy finally asked.

"Yes," the tall woman said as they all stared at Lucy. "So do you. Good. Sit. We'll talk."

"Thank you." Lucy sat on the sofa next to the brown-haired woman.

"Most of us talk," the tall woman continued. "But not in front of food men. Never. You remember that."

"Food men?" Lucy asked.

"The living," the tall woman answered, tapping the tip of the fire poker on the floor. "They bring us food sometimes, so we call them food men."

"Yes, and some day maybe they are the food again," the woman next to Lucy said. The three women gave the same awkward, huffing kind of laugh that Lucy did.

"I'm Carole," said the tall woman.

"Becca," said the redhead.

"Christine," said the brown-haired woman.

"I'm Lucy. You remember your names from before?" Jealousy overwhelmed her at that moment, to think that they might.

"No," said Christine. "They're just names other people picked. When I got here, women called me Christine. Said I looked like a Christine. They're all gone now. All dead."

Lucy nodded, looking again at each woman, getting more used to them and their ways. They seemed so gentle, and sort of resigned, like Truman.

"Did you remember your name?" Becca asked.

"No, it was like with you. Someone called me that."

"Not a food person, I bet," said Christine. "They always call us something stupid—like Lucky or Skinny or Cutie. Dumb fucks."

"No, it was a—one of us."

"Your man?" asked Christine.

"Well," Lucy hesitated. It was so weird, trying to explain it to them, and she didn't know how they did things here. "Yes. I guess that's what he is."

"What happened to him? Dead?" asked Christine.

Lucy turned to study her more closely. She was so damned matter-of-fact. But it didn't seem to Lucy as though the other woman didn't care. She looked genuinely concerned and kind—as kind as dead people ever looked.

"They took him. They said something about the Dead End. I don't know what that is."

"Another place for us," said Carole. "We hear about it. Food people like to go there, make fun of dead people. Not so bad. No food for dead people, but it's safe. Mostly. He should be okay."

"You want to have a man here?" asked Christine.

"What? What do you mean?"

"Some girls like it," Christine said as she shrugged. "They stay in houses with men. The girl picks one and lets him touch her, lick her, hold her down sometimes, in front of others. It's not like they can do anything, really, but the men like that. Makes them feel strong, in charge. If you want that, we can tell you which men are looking."

"And which are nice," said Becca.

Lucy looked from one woman to another. Becca appeared slightly embarrassed by the conversation, but Christine and Carole were completely unmoved and impassive—again, not uncaring, but just not upset, even though what they suggested seemed bizarre and sickening to Lucy.

"No, I don't think I need a man. Can I stay here?" Lucy asked.

"Of course," Carole said. "That's why we sent Angie, so you'd come to us. It's nice to have friends."

"Yes, it is," said Lucy. "I'll stay here if you want."

"Good," said Christine. "You want something over that?" She pointed to the left side of Lucy's face. "I don't mind it with me, but some girls like to cover theirs."

"Oh. Yes. Please."

"Turn around."

Lucy turned so her back was to Christine, who wrapped a coarse piece of cloth around her head and tied it in back.

"Thank you," Lucy said.

"You're welcome."

That had been a few days ago. Since then Lucy had met more of the dead people in the compound. The population was mostly men, but there were quite a few women and even some children in the group. Most of the time all of them milled around aimlessly, or got in various kinds of trouble. Many weren't as smart as the women Lucy first met, and most weren't nearly as nice. Sometimes the dead men would wrestle and fight each other, but not to do any real damage. They had even made some clubs with padding on them for practice.

There were lots of places out of sight and earshot of the guards and people would gather and talk, or play simple games with dice or cards they had made. It was boring, but not nearly as bad as what Lucy had expected. She had also learned the real purpose for the camp: to send them out on patrols to kill other dead people that might threaten the city. Lucy was not sure how bad that would be, but the other women in her house spoke of patrols as very unpleasant and dangerous: an injury like Angie's could be fatal, even if one made it back to the camp.

It was a bright, sunny day, and Lucy walked around to the side of their house, away from the guard towers. She had a small, old metal pot with her, and she placed it under one of the drain spouts from the gutters. The gutters were bent and broken all over the place, but she wanted to see if she could catch some rain water.

She remembered when Will had shown her and Truman how to drink water. It had been one of those pleasant, innocent, generous gestures of his, and Lucy thought it might be nice to share it with the other women sometime. It was funny how they'd forgotten how to do that on their own, but also funny how it was still so enjoyable. They'd forgotten so much, but to forget how to have joy? That was a truly bizarre curse.

Once she'd done this errand, Lucy came back around the house to the yard in front of the guard towers. She always looked down when she walked in that part of the camp—better not to draw their attention and more abuse or mockery. The guy who liked how she looked was a special nuisance and would demand some display of her body or he'd make it unpleasant for her and her friends all day.

As she walked, an older dead man passed near her and grabbed her arm. Lucy looked up, and although his face was dull and slack, there was no mistaking that look of lust—even without sex, the need to dominate and use another person was still driving him on, perhaps more strongly than it had in life. Lucy, being new to the camp and physically small, had probably brought this urge out in him.

He had a hold of her left forearm, and Lucy spun and twisted his arm around as she smashed him in the side of the face with her right fist. With a shriek, she wrenched her arm free and punched him again, kicking him in the knee as well. Then she stepped back and growled at him. Dumb, sick bastard. It was bad enough, having to put up with the living. Her own people ought to know better.

Catcalls came from the tower. "Oh! Old guy wants some! You gonna give him some, sugar?" They laughed.

The dead man charged, getting his arms around Lucy's chest and slamming her against the wall of one of the buildings. She was afraid the whole thing would collapse, it creaked so loudly and gave way so much as he pressed her against it. Then he started humping against her and grunting; with his size and leverage, Lucy couldn't push him off herself. Fucker didn't even know why he was doing it, probably, but just had that urge, like a fucking dog. The catcalls from the tower increased, along with hysterical laughter, and they were joined now by moans and grunts from a gathering crowd of dead.

Lucy roared with rage and disgust, as she grabbed the man's ears and pulled. The one in her right hand came off and she flung it aside, but that only seemed to make his thrusting against her redouble. She dug her thumbs into his eyes as she brought her mouth down on the back of his skull and tore off a piece of scalp with her teeth. Not like real flesh—it was brittle and bitter and she spit it out as she finally pushed him back. He landed on his ass, clutching at his face and whimpering. Fucker wasn't just stupid and sick—he was weak, too. How could he even think, in his rotted-out brain, to touch her? Lucy leaned her head back, her fists at her sides, and howled, trying to release all her revulsion and fury.

The laughter continued from the guard tower. Then one of them called, "Finish him off, darlin'."

Lucy looked up at the tower, then at the crowd. One dead man tossed a length of pipe that landed at her feet. Lucy looked back to the tower. Fuck them. Like she was going to do their dirty work? Give them more to laugh at? All she'd wanted to do was get the sick bastard off herself, and she'd done that. She considered raising her middle finger, as she remembered that was the right gesture under the circumstances, but worried that might be pushing it. She kicked the pipe and turned to walk away.

As she entered their home, Lucy could hear the thuds of the other dead men beating the one who had attacked her. There was a wail, which was joined by many more until it was a roar of agony and triumph, while the thumps were accompanied by tearing, ripping sounds. Then there was just moaning that gradually trailed off until it was indistinguishable from the light wind.

Lucy found Carole standing where she had been when they first met. Lucy didn't look out the window where Carole was staring, but just walked past her, and into the back room. She sat down next to Christine on the sofa. It had become their usual seating arrangement, and Lucy had come to accept and even long for the other woman's stoic responses and attitude. Lucy leaned against the larger woman, drawing on her solid strength.

"Somebody get killed?" Christine asked.

"Yeah."

"Anybody we know?"

"No. Just some guy."

"Good. You okay?"

"I guess. Not really."

"Yeah, me neither."

They sat there and were joined eventually by Carole and Becca. The four sat as the faint light in the room faded into a darkness far more embracing and hopeful than the piercing, harsh light ever could be.

Chapter 18
Rachel

"Will, you seen my shoulder holster?" Rachel called. He was still in the shower, and she was rummaging around in a pile of clothes next to the bed. She wished she had a better place to put her stuff, but Will had refused to buy much furniture at that store with the funny sounding name.

"What? I think I saw it downstairs, hanging on one of the door handles."

"Okay." Rachel twisted her arms back to hook her bra. The things were a bitch to get used to, either in terms of putting them on, or how they chafed and squeezed in all the wrong places. She stepped into the steamy bathroom and wiped off the mirror to admire how well the garment did its job. She put her hands behind her back, pulled back her shoulders, then brought her arms up over her head. Yeah, it sure was a different look, as were the shaved pits.

She felt a little funny, putting the girls on display like that. You'd laugh at a guy if he stuffed a sock in his pants, but this was different—it was just helping out what you already had. Besides, if that's how things were done around here, you had to go with it. Same for the little bit of lipstick she put on now. She wouldn't get all dolled up like that tramp Julia, but you had to look nice, if that's how everyone else dressed and kept themselves.

"Okay, hon," Rachel said as she pulled on a t-shirt and tucked it into her jeans, ruffling her hair and admiring her bust just a bit more. "I got to go meet Ken and walk to the construction site. Don't want to be late."

Will pulled back the shower curtain and she leaned in to give him a little peck. "Blech," he laughed when he tasted the lipstick. "I don't like that stuff."

She smiled at him. "Love you. I'll see you later. We can tell each other how work went."

"Love you." Was there that hurt, suspicious tone? Rachel liked to hear a little bit of that, but she didn't want him getting all weird on her. Her wild days were past, and she just wanted to have the normal level of jealousy from her man—the amount that kept him attentive and interested, but not stalking you or getting abusive or looking around on his own. As predictable as guys were, they still took some fine-tuning to get them right where you wanted them. She'd be extra nice when she got home tonight and he'd be fine.

Rachel got the .38 short barrel off the floor next to the bed—again, no extra furniture like a nightstand, as per Will's instructions. Walking down the stairs, she swung the cylinder out, even though she knew there was a round in each chamber. Rachel snapped the cylinder back in place, the steel cold and reassuring on her palm. It took her a second to find the shoulder holster, but it was hanging on the handle of the hall closet, just as Will had guessed. Carrying a gun that way just felt more comfortable than at her hip, especially if she were sitting and operating a vehicle. She strapped the holster on and stowed her weapon, checking herself one more time in the hall mirror.

Ken was waiting for her at the curb. "Hi, Ken."

"Hey, Rachel." He and Shayna were so darned good-looking—thick and muscled, both of them, except he was so tall, and she was as short as Rachel. He had such a deep, sexy voice, too, and so polite. That card game they'd taught them had been fun. Nice to do something with other people for a change. They even had some beer, and peanuts. Rachel had never had the former, and she hadn't tasted the latter in years. The cold, bitter liquid and the salty, slightly greasy nuts had made her feel satisfied, full, and warm. That had been a good evening, the best in a long time.

They started walking down the street. "We had fun the other night," Rachel said to make small talk.

"Yeah, us too." It was easy talking to him. He'd look you over, but not in a nasty, predatory way—just appreciative. It felt good. "Sorry the baby woke up and we had to call it a night early."

"No, that's fine. She's so cute!" You had to say that to parents, of course, but in this case it was true. The kid was gorgeous, alert, always laughing.

"Thanks. I think she liked both of you. You and Will trying to have kids?"

"Yes, but—" Rachel hadn't reckoned with this. She'd never talked about it, really. She thought of skipping it, but Ken seemed kind and sympathetic enough maybe she could. "We—I had a baby and lost it."

"I'm so sorry." Like the kid comment, you kind of had to say that, but he made it sound better than that. The brief touch to her shoulder as they walked was sincere and compassionate too, and didn't seem awkward or aggressive, like it might with other guys. "That happened to us, too. Really hard. Maybe you can talk about it with Shayna, if you feel like it."

"Yeah, maybe. Thanks."

"Was yours far enough along that you had to put it down after? That was the really hard part for us. I mean, they let us do it ourselves, or they would've done it for us at the hospital, but I think it's hard either way for parents."

"I know." As much as Ken put her at ease, this was dicey. Here in New Sparta they clearly didn't keep people penned up after they died, so telling them her baby was locked up with other dead people back where they came from—that was going to be a hard concept to introduce this morning. It also made her look at Ken differently, at his big hands and his biceps stretching the fabric of his t-shirt. What had he done? Smashed it with a mallet? Driven a spike into its head? Set it on fire? He seemed so gentle, how could he do such a thing to his own child?

"We didn't have to do that, thank God," she finally said. Things were just done different here, and she had to accept that. She also had to try not to stick out as some freakish hillbilly.

"Good. You were lucky. I know things were hard for us for a long time after that. I wasn't sure we were going to stay together. Don't tell her I told you about that part, if you talk to her about it."

"I won't. I understand." That voice and soothing demeanor had pushed the image of him killing his child out of her mind, thankfully, and she could again enjoy his company.

"We couldn't stop worrying and fighting when she was pregnant again, but then Aisha was born and things got back on track. I know the same will happen with you and Will. You're both good people. It'll work out."

"Thanks. You're so sweet to say that." It was hard not to be flirtatious with him, and it was all so natural and harmless anyway.

"No, I mean it. You'll see. First we got to get you to work, so you can afford a family." He laughed and they walked a bit faster.

They went by the employment office Rachel had gone to yesterday, and Will the day before. Rachel smiled to think of Will's description of it, like it was some office of zombies or robots out to steal his soul. God, why did he get so worked up over people and authority? They were easy enough to work around. Sure, the place was too clean and cold and impersonal, but you just had to watch yourself, and size up the person you were talking to. Hell, she'd gotten along well enough with Julia to make things work—she figured she could handle some people who filled out forms and filed them. They were harmless enough, and if it meant the electricity and gas and television and phone all ran the way they were supposed to, then it was worth a few minutes of her time, putting on a mask and answering some dumb questions.

They kept walking, Ken pointing out some of the other buildings—theater, restaurants, shops. When Ken noted Shayna's favorite hair salon—Rachel hadn't even heard that phrase since she was a kid—he let his gaze wander over Rachel's big mane of red curls. If it were Julia pointing out the store, the glance would've implied some negative evaluation of Rachel. If it had been another guy, it probably would've looked too lecherous. But this seemed like neither, and Rachel could smile back and think that some styling sounded like a good idea.

They got to the end of one street where there were lots of construction vehicles. Rachel saw the city wall now, though at this point there was a big, ragged gap in it that men and machines passed in and out of. Besides the loaders and trucks and cement mixers, there was a military-looking vehicle, a Humvee with a man standing in the back at a machine gun. Another man with a rifle stood next to the vehicle.

Ken introduced Rachel to the foreman of the construction site, a middle-aged white guy named Joe. Rachel had to produce some papers she'd been given at the employment office, which Joe examined between glances at her chest. His checking her out wasn't quite as discreet as Ken's, but it wasn't too bad by guy standards, either. He was up to ogling, not quite all the way to leering, and she could stand that easily enough. He went in a trailer and emerged with some keys, using them to point at a Bobcat track loader.

"You drive one of those, darlin'?" Again, not too bad—not "babe" at least.

"Of course." Those things were a blast to drive, in fact. Rachel could remember when she'd been little and seen two of them at the state fair, digging a huge hole and filling it back up, over and over, for the two weeks the fair went on. She'd never been a tomboy, except in that one respect, and she'd stand there in a dress and ponytails, watching those two Bobcats tearing around, rather than go look at ducks and bunnies and other things at the fair.

"Good. Drive it on down there, past that telephone pole. Ronnie's down there—he'll tell you where to start. We're still working on leveling the ground there." Rachel doubted he worked on much of anything, but guessed that's how bosses talked here. Again, you had to adapt.

Joe tossed her the keys. Rachel waved to Ken as he walked off to another part of the construction site and she got into the vehicle. As the engine roared to life and the whole machine shook underneath and around her, she thought this wasn't going to be bad at all—hauling around in this all day, then relaxing with Will each night, eating good food, talking and playing games with Ken and Shayna. This was definitely a great place.

Chapter 19
Truman

Truman's fingers clenched the wire and bars of his cage as he tensed for the attack he felt sure was coming. But as Dalia stepped around the tent flap, Truman relaxed. Not even these people here could be so perverse as to bring a child along, if they planned to do the things Truman had feared. No, his anxiety must've been unfounded, at least for now.

Doctor Jack and Dalia paused in the doorway to let their eyes adjust to the dimness inside the tent. He was wearing his grey suit again, while the girl wore another simple dress—this one white. She had on the same boots, and she'd found another white ribbon so her two pigtails matched this time. She pulled a red metal wagon behind her. Truman couldn't quite see what was inside it.

Doctor Jack looked around and breathed deeply through his nose. "Ah," he said. "That's about the only nice thing about dead folks—they don't smell much after a while. That, or you get used to it. I'm not sure. But it wasn't that way, back when we had more animals in the carnival—always shoveling their shit and things always stinking so badly, especially in the summer. Oh, that was awful."

Doctor Jack took a few steps closer, glancing over at Lou and Ramona. The large dead man had gotten up when the two live people entered, but Ramona remained sitting on a lopsided wicker chair, its high, rounded back rising above her head like a crown or those things above saints in religious paintings; Truman couldn't remember the name of those. Ramona just stared over the visitors' heads, thinking of something pleasant or horrible from years or decades ago—her face was too impassive for Truman to guess.

"Now, don't get me wrong, Dalia," Doctor Jack continued, turning his attention to Truman. "I still hate 'em, deep down. No sir, I can't abide zombies. They ruin everything. There used to be so many different kinds of people: young ones, old ones, black, white—all wanting different stuff." He pointed an accusatory finger at Truman. "Then they just turned into *this*. Can't buy stuff. Can't do anything. Heck—teach 'em a few tricks is the best I can do, to bring in some folks and their money." He brought down his finger, then raised his hand to run it across his bald head and through his thinning hair. He sighed so long and deep that Truman could almost feel sorry for him, if he hadn't just tried to heap all his shortcomings and disappointments on Truman. "Some days it doesn't hardly seem worth it. Just should go try a new line of work."

Dalia peered around her companion, smiling first at Truman, then up at Doctor Jack. "Oh, stop, Doctor Jack," she said. "I think they're nice, most of the time, just like real people."

She dropped the wagon's handle and came closer. "Hi, mister!" she said to Lou. He raised his head and gave a wheeze. Truman couldn't say the man's face lit up—that really didn't look possible anymore—but he was clearly happy to see the little girl.

"Hi, Miss Ramona!" Dalia said, turning to the other side. The thin dead woman brought her gaze down and nodded just a bit, then returned to staring at some spot on the tent's ceiling that only she found interesting.

Doctor Jack put his hand on Dalia's shoulder. "You're too trusting, dear," he said. "You people, of all folks, ought to know better. You got to be hard. You try too much to see the good in folks, and it's just not right. You got to just size 'em up—figure out what you can get from 'em, how to get over on 'em. That's how a person survives. Your momma knows that: works hard in the fields when it's time, comes back here to work at night, to make some money for you and her. Does real good, too, 'cause she knows how people are, knows what men want. She's smart. But we got to get you up to speed, darling, or you're gonna turn into some holy roller or something." He chuckled. "Not that there's anything wrong with religion, mind you: you just got to know when to use that, too, and not let it get all out of hand." He patted her head, the affection of the gesture only partly tarnished by the ugliness and cynicism of his words.

Up came the finger again—not accusatory this time, but pointing Truman out in a demeaning way, making him want to cringe or hide. "You listen up, Dalia. You look at this one. Skinny, not much left on his old bones. Cage will hold him fine. But you see over there? Two locks on the door. He'd watch me dial up the combination on the one, if I weren't careful. He might even figure out how to pick the other one with a piece of wire or something. So two locks for this one."

The living man stepped closer to Truman, drawing aside the jacket of his suit to show a small revolver in a holster at his hip. "He knows what this is, too, and he knows why I'm showing it to him. Now, mister, do we understand each other? Are you gonna mind this fine young lady and try to learn what she's showing you?"

Truman looked over at Dalia, who smiled at him again. He nodded.

Doctor Jack let his jacket fall back in place. "Good. Now, Dalia, you keep an eye on this one. I think he'll make a good show, but I don't know. I kinda have a bad feeling about him, like he's up to something. I paid good money for him, but if he does anything funny, you come running and tell me." He looked over at Lou, and then Ramona. "That goes for you two as well, though I figure you both know to behave by now."

Dalia picked the handle of the wagon back up and patted the man's arm. "Don't worry, Doctor Jack," she said. "I think he'll be fine and we'll have a good time."

"All right. We'll see."

When Doctor Jack had left, Dalia came closer to Truman's cage, hauling her wagon with her. Truman could now see it was full of large, paperback books. She leaned closer to Truman, squinting at him. "What're we gonna call you?" she asked.

As charming as Truman found the little girl, he heeded Ramona's warning not to talk around the living, so he just stared back at her.

Dalia reached into the wagon and held out one of the books to him. "Can you read any?" she asked.

Truman considered how to answer that, then nodded as he took the book.

The girl beamed. "I just knew you could, as soon as I saw you. Those men who brought you in—they didn't see you the way I do. Some people just look, but I see things. Not even Doctor Jack sees everything the way I do." She lowered her voice. "But he does see a lot. He sees something in you and he doesn't like it." She raised her voice again and laughed. "But I do!"

Truman looked at the book in his hands. It was some kind of book for helping people study for a test. Page after page was full of multiple choice questions.

He jumped a bit when Dalia's hand shot between the bars and grabbed the book. "Don't look in the back!" she said. "The answers are in the back!"

Truman put his hand on hers, caressing the back of her hand. She didn't flinch or pull back. Perhaps Doctor Jack was right and she was too trusting, though Truman was grateful he could relish the touch of her. In the last few nights, sometimes he and Ramona would both lean their backs against his cage, and he could feel her pressed against him. But with living people it was always different—something so fragile yet powerful about them, something so warm and terrifying. With Dalia the overweening, frightening part of life was almost imperceptible and there was only a sweet, delicious presence. The whole time he felt her hand, she only smiled up at him.

"You look sad. Do you feel sad, 'cause you think you scare me?" she asked as she pulled her hand back finally. She was as perceptive as she claimed. "You don't. Doctor Jack's wrong about that: I know which people to be afraid of. Some dead people, some regular people. I know.

"I'll call you Professor, okay?" she said after a brief pause. If anyone were frightened, it was Truman, at how much she could tell. But he just nodded.

She pointed at the book in his hands. "Doctor Jack and I were trying to think what you could do. We were going through all kinds of junk he's got, trying to get ideas. He thought of wrapping you up in cloths and setting them on fire, so you could climb up a ladder and jump off into a little tub of water. I said that was dumb, for a smart person like you. You needed something better."

Truman was already in her debt, clearly.

"Then I saw this pile of books," she said. "He's got lots more, too. Nobody wants them. They just use them to start fires when it's cold. But I saw what they were, and I bet him you could answer questions and surprise people. They'd pay money to ask you a question from here, you'd point at the answer, and I'd check the answer in the back. So try some. Go ahead." She handed him a stub of a pencil.

The book she'd given him was full of analogies, like "book is to shelf as plate is to cupboard," where one of the items was missing and you had to pick it from four choices. The test must've been for younger people, as the vocabulary was basic and the relationships uncomplicated. Truman felt like he knew most all of them as he went through a page and handed the book to Dalia. She turned back and forth, checking his answers against those in the back.

"I knew you could do it!" she said after a moment. "You only missed one!"

Truman was glad she was pleased and would win her bet, but he frowned at having missed one. He reached out for the book, to see the page again.

"Oh, you want to know which one you missed?" Dalia asked. "You are a good student!" She opened back to the test page and looked at the questions, then held it up to Truman. Truman peered at it. He'd had to guess on that one, as he didn't remember what a "nave" was, so he'd circled the answer "pulpit" even though it didn't fit the analogy.

"It's okay. I don't know that word either. Some of the questions are harder than others. I don't know why. I'll go tell Doctor Jack the good news, Professor!"

As Dalia skipped from the tent, singing nonsense syllables as she went, Truman sat down on the ground.

"Nice kid," Ramona said from her chair.

Truman nodded. "Yeah. She deserves better."

Ramona gave a remarkably lifelike giggle—light and chiming. It was much nicer than Lucy's horsy, snorting sort of laugh, though it mostly made Truman miss that familiar sound. "Truman, we all deserve better," she said. "Why do you say it about her and get yourself all upset and down?"

"I don't know," Truman said. "It actually makes me feel better, thinking there are still people like her."

"You're so funny, Truman. You crack me up."

If he stretched and wedged his shoulder between the bars, Truman could just reach the wagon and take some more books. He wanted to see if there were more words he'd forgotten.

Chapter 20
Will

Will bounced up, then his butt smacked back down on the metal bench, as the wagon trundled over the remains of an ancient road. The vehicle had obviously been built from cannibalized parts of trucks, so it had some shock absorbers, but there was only so much they could do. There really wasn't anything left of the pavement.

"Should've told you to bring a pillow like everybody else," chuckled Garrett, the older guy who sat across from Will. His short hair was grey, while his mustache and scraggly beard were still mostly dark. "You're gonna be black and blue after this."

"Yeah, I'll remember tomorrow," Will said.

Chris, sitting next to Will, offered him a cigarette. The kid was young, blond, still had some acne. Will took the cigarette and dragged it under his nose. It wasn't corn silk, like he was used to. The last time he'd smelled real tobacco, he'd been a kid and didn't even smoke. Back then he'd thought it was gross. That last year in school they'd even told him all the "Just Say No" stuff.

"Real? Wow. Thanks," Will said.

Mike, sitting next to Garrett, handed Will a lighter. "They don't have that where you come from?" Mike asked.

Will lit up and couldn't help but cough on the first puff, and everyone else in the back of the wagon laughed. The driver, Jake, on a bench in front and slightly above the others, turned and joined in too.

"No," Will wheezed after a pause, handing the lighter back and laughing with the others. "Somebody showed me how to roll and smoke corn silk cigarettes, but this is the first real one I've ever had."

"Ah, you had it rough where you lived," Mike said. "You'll like it here—cigarettes, booze, movies, women."

Will smiled and played along. "Oh, yeah, it's great. I got a girl though." They all laughed at him again, and he determined to keep quiet about more stuff.

Mike held up his left hand, showing his wedding ring. "Yeah, I know what you mean. Jake's married, too. I don't know about these two fags." He shoved Garrett playfully, who punched his shoulder. "But it sure is nice to look. Or even touch. We'll take you to one of the titty bars one day after work."

Will smiled but didn't answer. He leaned back some, looking along the side of the wagon at all the different containers strapped and bolted to the sides, there for them to fill on this foraging mission into territory outside the city. He brought his gaze forward to the two big horses pulling them. The second drag from the cigarette didn't hurt, and sent a nice rush through him.

"They're quieter," Garrett said.

"What?" Will said, returning his attention back to the inside of the wagon.

"The horses. That's why we use them. Run an engine out here and there'd be zombies from all over headed our way. You know how they love noises, especially engines, machines, that kind of thing. There aren't many left, wandering free, but we still don't want to get any more attention than we have to."

"Makes sense."

"Saves fuel for the city too. Speaking of which, that's what we'll be working on mostly in the town. We'd been going to the truck stop up north, but last week there were just too many zombies around. The city patrol will take care of them and we'll go back there, but for now we got to check out other places."

"City Patrol?" Will asked. Shit—that weird, gorgeous gal Julia had said that's where they'd taken Lucy. "What's that?"

Garrett eyed him a bit before answering. "Some zombies they got kinda tamed. Not really, but they feed them and shit. Makes them want to hang around and do stuff, so they send them out to kill other zombies when the foraging groups find a spot that's too hot for us. They haven't been going out so much, since things quieted down, but we need that truck stop. Lots of fuel there. Besides, don't want them to get lazy. Lazy zombies on the dole— that's a hoot. That fat guy on the radio would have a helluva time making fun of that."

The men chuckled again. Will couldn't join them, knowing Lucy was out there, fighting, maybe getting hurt. He had to get her out. He'd do whatever it took, but for now he didn't see anything he could do, other than working to earn the money so he could then go looking for her.

"Anyway," Garrett continued. "We'll pull up near the one gas station and fill up the Jerry cans. There shouldn't be any of them around, but keep an eye out. Your application said you had extensive weapons training. With what?"

Will shrugged. "Anything."

"Anything?"

"Not cannons or grenades or something like that. But yeah— any handgun or rifle or shotgun." Will shifted uneasily and left out any mention of how he'd been taught not to shoot dead people unless he had to. That definitely didn't seem like something that would go over well.

"Yeah? You think you're good, kid?" Garrett's tone wasn't exactly hostile—he was even smiling—but it had that familiar, masculine air of mockery and challenge.

"Well, sure. I mean, everyone in my town learns to shoot. You get good at it with enough practice."

Garrett reached under the bench and slid out a long, plastic case. "Hey, Jake," he said. "Hold up a minute."

The wagon stopped as Garrett opened the case. Will recognized the rifle inside as an M4. Great gun. He didn't usually see it with a scope and silencer like this one, though.

Garrett offered him the weapon. "I don't usually waste ammo, but I like to know what the other guys in my group can do," he said. "You know what I mean?"

Will took the rifle. "Sure."

Garrett's hazel eyes narrowed as he tilted his head back. "Up on that hill behind you. I think it's a gal."

Will turned. The figure was just barely identifiable, swaying side-to-side. It seemed to be approaching them with a slow, uneven gait. Will raised the rifle, settling the eyepiece of the scope to his eye. Garrett was right. It was a woman—naked, emaciated, her hair nearly the same sick grey as her skin, her jaw slack. She couldn't seem to move her left arm, and all her motions had a jerky, involuntary quality to them.

"Shit, I can barely see her," Chris said in a low voice. "You can't hit that."

"Yeah," Garrett said. "But for a guy with a lot of practice, it'd be easy. So—that shot too hard for you, kid?"

Will tightened his grip and started to sweat. He needed this job. "The shot's easy," he whispered.

"Good. I could use a good shooter in my group. These three are useless most of the time. A guy who could really shoot could make some extra money. So do it and let's get going."

The woman's eyes were the only part of her that looked dark, and oddly, though they resembled blank, empty holes, they seemed the only part of her that was vital and real. It was crazy to think she might be able to see him, but Will had one of those moments when you're convinced of something, regardless of its senselessness. Whether that deep, steady gaze he imagined were accusatory or imploring, however, remained completely uncertain. Even when he could force himself to see it as making some urgent request of him, he still could not decide if it were asking him to pull the trigger.

Through a huge effort that made his head hurt, Will forced all such thoughts down, pressing them into a hard, sharp lump at the base of his skull. That woman didn't see anything. She wasn't even a woman anymore—not even a "she," more like just an "it." She wasn't a real person. He needed this job. He needed the money. He exhaled as he pulled the trigger.

"Damn," Chris whispered as the body crumpled to the ground.

"Shit," said Garrett as he took back the gun. "I thought for a second you were bullshitting, but you're for real, kid. Might have to call you Deadeye from now on."

"Yeah, you might," Will said, looking down at his boots.

So what if he'd shot her in the knee? So she could lie there for God knows how long, looking up at the sky? What kind of mercy was that? What kind of respect for humanity did that show? Maybe it was worse than shooting her in the forehead. Would he have been able to put the gun down, if it'd been Lucy up on that hill? She was part of the reason he needed this job, and now he had to kill or maim others like her. What sense did that make? What was he doing to himself? Such doubts made Will's head continue to ache. This was going to be a long, shitty month.

Chapter 21
Lucy

The room was still mostly dark when Lucy heard the blast of a car or truck horn outside. The four women got up, while the sound repeated several times.

"Food men want something," Carole said to Lucy. "Patrol, probably. We haven't been out for a while. Get a weapon."

Carole went to the pile of weapons stashed under the furniture in the back of the room. She picked up the fire poker she usually carried around, while Becca took an aluminum baseball bat. Christine stooped down and got a crowbar. She lifted her shirt to stick it through a belt loop in her baggy pants, and Lucy saw that her stomach was ripped open. Her ribs poked out from flaps of dried skin around an opening that extended from her waist to the middle of her chest. She was hollowed in the middle. Her breasts were missing, too—just some shreds around scabbed flesh. Lucy couldn't help but stare at the mysterious cavity, dark and dusty, with so much of the poor woman missing. Christine pulled her shirt back down.

"What?" she said to Lucy. "It doesn't hurt. We all have stuff like that."

Lucy looked in her eyes. "No, it's just—it made me wonder. What we were like before. What you were like."

Christine shrugged as she picked up a broken table leg; it was dark wood with a big, round knob at one end. "I don't remember. Fat, probably. Me—not you. You were skinny. And pretty."

Lucy took a golf club and put it back. Those could break. She chose a shiny pipe about two feet long. It flared slightly at one end, and tapered at the other, like the pipe for one of those machines you pushed around the house to suck up dirt. She couldn't remember the name of the thing, but this part seemed like a good weapon—light and strong.

"Thank you," Lucy said. "You're not fat. But it made me think of babies, if we had any. Do you think you did?"

Christine patted Lucy's shoulder. "Maybe. I'm sure if I did, they're all dead now. It's just what happened. You think of yourself now."

Lucy followed the others through the front room. She wanted to think of herself, to simplify things in that way. But her head always got so filled with other things—the hunger, of course, but also anger and disgust at other people, and those feelings seemed to grow stronger rather than weaker. She couldn't ignore them. But they grew equally as fast and powerful as other thoughts: worries about an ever-growing list of other people—at first just Truman, but then she'd added Will and Rachel, and now the three women here were just as important to her. Then at times like this morning, Lucy would worry about the craziest things—like whether she'd had children, and what had happened to them and whether they might, just possibly, be all right. Think of herself? She didn't really remember what that would be like, and it seemed like a long time since she had. Sometimes it seemed like she was the last thing she thought of.

The sun was low, not even over the tops of the trees. It was still cool, too, with mist off in the forest and hanging in some of the lower places in the fields. Everyone assembled in front of the gate, the black and white stripes of their uniforms swaying in a mass. Outside the fence Lucy saw a large vehicle. She didn't know anything about cars and trucks, but it was one of those big, squat things the Army started using, after they got rid of Jeeps. It was done up with greys and greens in an attempt at that pattern hunters or army men would wear, with the letters "NSP" stenciled on the hood and door. A man dressed in a uniform stood at a machine gun mounted in the open back of the vehicle. He raised a bullhorn to his mouth.

"All right, you pus fucks!" the amplified, crackly voice from the bullhorn announced. "You've got work to do. If you understand what the hell I'm saying, make sure those other dumb fucks around you follow orders. If you do what we say, then there'll be lots to eat when you get back. I'm talking the real stuff."

The crowd murmured and seethed around Lucy. Even Carole and Christine looked excited by this offer, though Becca appeared more noncommittal.

"Yeah, yeah," the man spoke from the army truck again. "You understand that part, don't you? Follow the road northeast. We marked it along the way with yellow paint. Just follow the yellow signs. There's a big truck stop. You'll see the sign—really tall. You can't miss it. More of you dead fuckers must have moved in there, because our foraging parties were attacked. We need it cleared. Then keep going till you find a town. That must be where they're coming from."

Two other men came from behind the truck with big duffel bags, which they set on the ground. "When you get to the town, use these," the man with the bullhorn said. "I know some of you old timers know how they work. But do *not* use them at the truck stop. If any of you do, I'll shoot every one of you myself. Do you understand?"

Enough of the gathered dead nodded to satisfy the man, apparently. "Good. So let's review." He held his hand up and extended a finger for each instruction. "Follow road. Attack truck stop. Follow road some more. Open bags. Attack town. If you do all that right, then it's feeding time when you get back."

The truck started up and drove a little ways off, then the gate slid to the side. The group marched slowly through the opening. Lucy watched the men in the towers and on the truck. They didn't look too concerned at having so many dead people now loose. They'd gotten used to it, and the dead around Lucy looked pretty unlikely to go against orders. Everything went according to plan. Everyone here was too used to rules, too used to how things were "supposed" to be. Lucy didn't really know how things should be, and if she tried to think about it she got distracted and confused by all kinds of thoughts, but she knew somehow that shuffling along in a crowd like they were now was guaranteed to fuck things up worse, turn them around and make them uglier than they were to begin with.

As they got farther from the compound, the mob could spread out more and they weren't jostling one another so much. Lucy looked off into the fields and woods and considered just wandering away. But then she'd definitely never find Truman again. And what about Will and Rachel? She doubted they'd ever really come back for her. People made all kinds of crazy promises. Maybe they even meant to keep them at the time they made them, but life got in the way of that. Life had its own demands and schedules and it seldom matched up with anybody's plans.

She didn't really blame them. But she did want to get back to Truman. She didn't think there were many dead people like him. He'd need her help to survive, and she needed him to make survival more bearable. The women here were nice, but most everyone else was a sick savage, and God knows anyone she'd find out in the wilderness on her own would probably be worse. No, better stick with the group for now and see what happened. Not everyone had someone to come back to, however, so why were the others marching along so obediently, once they were away from the living people and their guns?

"Why don't people wander off?" Lucy asked.

"Better to stay in a group," Carole said. "Safer. Easier."

"Food," Christine said. "No more food anywhere out here. Nothing good out here. Just wild people and broken things."

Lucy didn't know what to think of that. Killing was one thing—that was a thrill she missed even more than life itself, because she didn't remember what life had been like, while she contemplated and longed for the perfection and purity of a good kill every day. And to eat after such an act? That was glorious and fulfilling in every way. But to kill dead people, whom you couldn't eat? That didn't make much sense. And then just to be given food? Handed it like a pet? That didn't sound right either, but all Lucy could do was go along with it for now.

They marched all day at their slow pace. As the man had said, various abandoned vehicles and other things like overpasses and telephone poles were marked with yellow paint to remind them of the route. Then the sign he'd spoken of loomed ahead of them. It was shattered and bent, but it was definitely the one. Under it the large, low building of the truck stop spread out, surrounded by islands of fuel pumps. Most of these still had roofs over them, though some had collapsed. Burnt-out vehicles were everywhere.

The horde stopped at a distance from their target. There was some shuffling around as some of the dead men went through the group, growling orders. Lucy noticed one tall black man in particular. His name was Ben, and she had seen him in the camp before, usually with a couple men following him, as if he were special or in charge. Ben and his current group of men took the children and some of the women to one side and told them to stay there, along with the two big bags and whatever they contained. The men then separated the remaining people into two groups, which would attack the building from different sides. Lucy stayed close to her friends so the four of them would be in the same group.

At the end of these preparations, one dead man jumped on top of a wrecked car, holding a pipe above his head as he shouted, "New Sparta!" The crowd gave a low rumble of approval. "Fresh meat!" he shouted louder, and the response was much more vigorous. In the distance, Lucy could hear an inarticulate moaning in response. She thought how much more comforting that sound seemed when you were a part of the group making it, compared to how chilling it seemed now.

The man jumped off the car and the two groups surged forward. "Kill! Kill! Kill!" they chanted. Now the group identity and hysteria were much more infectious and intoxicating, and Lucy felt herself chanting with them—at first just in response, but quickly building in intensity as the feeling took hold of her.

Plants had reclaimed the parking lot entirely, with grass up to Lucy's waist. Suddenly she heard screams up ahead, and she stumbled into the people in front of her, who had stopped running. The chanting stopped, too. When the group started moving again, sifting off to the right and left, Lucy saw what had stopped them: a large pit, into which three of their men had fallen. The pit must've been covered and they hadn't seen it. They were writhing and moaning, impaled on dozens of pointed sticks, the tips of which were now stained black from their insides. These dead people they were fighting were smart enough to lay traps? Lucy didn't know if her group had expected such behavior, but they didn't show any fear or concern at this development. The pit was too deep to reach the wounded men, and the sides too steep to climb in and help them. Lucy seemed to be the only one concerned with them anyway, and she doubted the three men could still move even if they were pulled out.

"If I get like that, finish it," Christine said next to her. "No sense sitting around, waiting for someone else to do it. It looks like it hurts."

Lucy nodded, then turned her attention forward as the crowd again picked up momentum. Off to their left, the other group seemed to have encountered some similar traps, because they'd fallen behind. Lucy and those around her came around the building, milling around the fuel pumps. There was no more chanting or moaning, just the shuffling of their feet and some sniffing as they tried to locate their enemies. The wind must not have been right, because Lucy couldn't pick up any new scents.

Inside the building was dark and she couldn't see any motion through the windows. Shit—they were probably going to have to charge in there? Lucy tightened her grip on the pipe.

None of this felt right. It was—what would you call it? Not just foolish and dangerous—it was definitely those things, but that wasn't what was bothering her. It was wasteful, senseless, even— dishonorable? She didn't really know what made her think of that, but the word stuck with Lucy as she looked around. Then her gaze went up to the canopy above the fuel pumps. An enormous log hung there, maybe eight feet long and two feet thick. It looked like it had lots of short branches sticking out from it, like one of those prickly plants people used to have in pots on their desks. What the hell was that doing up there?

Lucy only walked away from the truck stop that day because it suddenly clicked in her mind that the log was another trap. With a shriek, she lunged to the left, slamming into Christine and sending both of them down behind a fuel pump. They knocked over a couple other people, just as Lucy heard the whoosh of the log swinging by, and more screams. She also heard what sounded like the metallic ring of an aluminum bat clanking on the pavement.

At almost the same moment Lucy and Christine landed on the concrete, there was a shout, and people came streaming from the building. Lucy stood, hauling Christine up next to her, just as their attackers came within reach. Filthy, nasty things they were. Half naked, they looked like they had lain in the dirt every night since the world ended. Worse than living people, if that were possible. At least they didn't smell bad, like the living, but their bestial, ruined faces and bodies more than offset that slight grace and made them the most repulsive things Lucy had ever seen.

As she raised the pipe over her left shoulder for a backhanded swing, she knew she'd been correct a moment before: this was sickening and stupid and—most of all—pathetic. But looking at these open-mouthed wrecks was so revolting, it made swinging the pipe seem the only reasonable response. Then when she felt the shock of the weapon impacting a skull, that made it seem not just right, but good. Really good.

As the first hideous thing fell to the side, Lucy remembered that, try as you might to dress it up before or after, and call it honor or rightness or necessity, killing finally came down to that glorious moment of power, when you took away someone's last bit of energy—their last hold on this world—and let it flood into you, as though it would fill you with everything you ever needed or wanted, in one rapturous burst. Then Lucy didn't need to think, didn't want to. It all just came naturally and beautifully, her arm coiling and uncoiling with an agility she had previously only felt when playing the violin. The whole experience was quite close to that, in fact—furious, passionate, and beautiful.

Christine moved beside her, swinging both her weapons, as well as slamming her shoulder, butting her head, or kicking her feet into everything that got in her way. The larger woman was slower and more methodical than Lucy, but no less graceful. As she fought, Lucy realized the usefulness of their absurd uniforms: in the chaotic jumble of flailing, grappling bodies, there were several times she would've smashed some of the people in her group, if they had not been wearing the distinctive striped shirts.

The whole fight lasted no more than three minutes, certainly less than five, though it seemed as if they had been hacking their way through the stiff, ugly bodies for hours, turning such unclean matter into a perfect, sublime spirit of destruction and cleansing.

They both turned as soon as the last one fell, and climbed back over the bodies to where the log trap hung from the canopy above them. Lucy now saw that wooden and metal spikes covered its surface. Becca's baseball bat was on the ground there, and Lucy bent down to pick it up, then looked to see what had happened to the girl. She lay about twenty feet away, on her back. Her arms moved up above her, like she was trying to clutch at something, or swat something away.

Lucy and Christine went to her, kneeling down next to her. She smiled up at them. "I'm sorry," Becca said. "I didn't see it. I should've—I should've warned you."

Lucy brushed the girl's hair from her face. The exhilaration of the battle had drained from her as soon as she saw the poor woman on the ground. Now Lucy felt numb, even a little dizzy. Becca obviously couldn't get up. Her back was probably broken and she was going to die here in this shitty little dump, so some loud, stupid assholes could get fuel to drive their noisy, useless cars and trucks. It shouldn't be this way. This didn't make any sense, but this is what happened when you did what you were supposed to, what you were told to do. Lucy seethed inwardly—not just at Becca's injury, but at the fact that they were all denied the tiny relief of being able to shed tears. Why was that so much to ask?

"No, no," Lucy said. "I should've seen it sooner. It's my fault."

Christine stood up as Carole came over to them. "What do you want us to do?" Christine asked.

"I don't know," Becca said, turning her head to look at the grass next to her. She reached over to pull one of the stalks down, rubbing it between her thumb and forefinger.

"When food men come, they'll just run over you," Carole said. "Or more wild men will show up when we leave. They'll tear you up, throw pieces of you all over."

Lucy turned and glared at the two other women for a moment. They took to studying the grass and didn't say more. Lucy pressed her hand against the girl's cheek.

"You decide," she said softly. "We'll do whatever you want."

"So many times I thought of dying, of how it must be nicer than this, and now I don't want to. It's so stupid, but I don't. I can't."

Lucy nodded. "It's just how people are. Don't feel bad."

"It doesn't hurt. I don't feel anything."

"That's good. I'm glad."

"Can you just leave me somewhere? Maybe up against a tree? Would that be all right?"

"Of course."

"I know it'll probably be worse when they come, but I can't help it."

"I know. It's just how it is."

Though the girl was stout, she was quite short and easy enough for them to carry over to the trees not far from the battleground. As they carried her, a male voice called from behind them, "Hey! Where you going? Come back!" This time Lucy did extend her middle finger.

They leaned Becca against a thick tree. There were acorns all around its base; Lucy couldn't remember the name of the tree that made those. She thought it was *oak* or *maple*, but wasn't sure. Lucy laid the bat across the girl's lap. She wouldn't be able to do much to defend herself, but it'd make her feel better to have something cold and solid to hold on to. Lucy had made sure they'd gone a few steps into the forest before setting her down. Maybe the living people or other dead people wouldn't spot the girl there and she'd have a better time of it than Lucy and the others. Lucy doubted it, but who knew? It was all too fucked up even to worry about. You just had to do what the weakest and most hurt in the group needed done, and then hope. Or else just try to forget.

"Thanks," Becca said.

Lucy bent down and pressed her lips against Becca's forehead. She didn't taste as good as Will—dead people never did—but Lucy held her lips there longer, to prolong the moment that would have to sustain the girl until she was either snatched out of this hideous, broken existence, or until the world itself passed away, finally unable to withstand all the pain and injustice that filled it.

Chapter 22
Rachel

"How are you liking work?" Ken asked as they walked to the construction site.

"It's great," Rachel replied. "I love driving those little track loaders. It's like playing in a sandbox all day. I'd do it for free. Well, I guess I sorta did, back home."

"What do you mean?"

"Well, not exactly. I mean, we didn't have money. We just worked, and traded with people. I don't know how it all evened out, exactly, but you did whatever you did for the city, and you picked up food and stuff from other people when you needed it, and you gave them stuff when they needed it."

"No money? But how'd you know you'd worked enough, to get the stuff you wanted? Why would people work, if other people just gave them things? I don't understand."

"I guess it's hard to explain, if you haven't lived there. It's not like here. There weren't nearly as many different things. Just simple stuff. So I guess we didn't have to keep track of it as much. And we didn't work nearly as much, either. I'd work a little in the summer, and most of the rest of the year I'd just putter around and help other people out. I guess we were kinda lazy and spoiled."

Ken laughed. "No, you're fine. Will, too. You both work hard and you're so honest and open."

Rachel blushed to think of all the stuff she'd deliberately left out of their conversations.

"We're glad you moved in."

"Us too. It's nice to have regular people around or I don't know what we'd do in this city. We'd never be able to find our way around."

"Oh, you'd manage. How's Will?"

Oh God, another time when Rachel had to decide how much to tell the neighbors, no matter how nice they were. "He's been kinda down the last couple days. I think he's stressed about his job." That'd probably be about enough to say, and true as far as it went.

"I don't blame him," Ken answered in his soothing, compassionate voice. "I'd be scared and nervous all day, out there with those things. I don't know how he does it."

Rachel felt bad she couldn't really explain why her boyfriend was all depressed about the other guys in his group shooting dead people. She didn't really understand it herself. It was different if you'd known the person, or even if the dead person were nice, like Truman. But to just see one of them, wandering around in a field, looking hungry and stupid—what was the big deal with putting one of them down?

"Well, he should be used to dead people. I wish he'd just snap out of it." Rachel let a little more anger slip into her tone than she'd intended. She glanced at Ken. She didn't want him to think she was a bitch. If she told him everything about Will's attitudes, Ken would definitely see her point of view and not blame her for being pissed. But she kept it to herself. Letting people know your boyfriend was a little kooky always ended up backfiring, anyway, and made them think you might be weird, too.

"I'm sure he will. He'll be fine. It's a big adjustment for you two, living here. He'll come around." Ken was always so supportive and encouraging.

"You're probably right." Rachel certainly hoped so. Will hadn't even had to do the actual shooting, after that first day when he'd proved himself, so why was he so distraught he barely ate? And never mind the sex. Four days without it—that was like a record for them, and she'd even been trying to coax him, so she knew he must really be in a funk. Funny how guys always thought girls were the moody ones, and they were ten times worse. Well, maybe tonight she'd get him to do it. Rachel sighed as they walked on without talking for a while.

"Hey—look at that," Ken said, drawing her attention to a crowd near the entrance to the construction site. It was especially noticeable, as they weren't the usual construction workers, but mostly young women.

"What're they doing?" Rachel asked.

"Oh, I heard the guys talking about it yesterday. Since we're almost done with the new amphitheater, they said one of the musicians might come by and give out tickets to the first concert. I bet I know who it is. Come on. We should get you some." Ken hurried her along.

Rachel laughed. "Why me? Don't you want them too?"

"Nah, we have to stay home with the baby. But let's get two tickets and you can take Will." Damn—could he be any more considerate? The guy was a dream.

The crowd seethed around a man on a low stage that had been set up in the street. Several larger men kept the people moving along as they approached the stage and then moved away from it. The man who was drawing all this attention walked around the stage, giving people tickets, squeezing their hands, smiling. Sometimes he'd even bend low enough to accept a quick kiss on the cheek from a girl, before moving on to the next person. He was exceptionally good looking, in a way Rachel hadn't seen in a long time. With the tousled hair, long but neatly-trimmed sideburns, button-down shirt under a rumpled jacket—he gave off an air of deliberately casual confidence and perfectly rehearsed spontaneity that was like a precious but fragile relic from the pre-zombie world. Observing him more closely, Rachel could see he was older than he appeared at first, but he still looked familiar, like an older version of someone she'd seen years ago.

"Oh my God!" she exclaimed, nearly as loud and screechy as the other women in the crowd into which she and Ken now jostled their way ahead. "I know him!"

"Yeah!" Ken laughed as he pushed her forward. "He and his brothers were in town back at the beginning. The other two didn't make it. He dedicates each concert to them." Rachel couldn't help thinking how sweet that was.

As Rachel and Ken made their way to the front of the crowd, she kept her gaze on the singer. She'd had a picture of him on her wall when she was a kid, and now she was going to meet him. Not the young, famous him, but still. She'd never met anyone like that before. It was funny how she'd forgotten about such people, as though none had survived. But practically the cutest one of them all was still alive, and just a few feet away. God, she hoped she looked okay. No time to do much about it, so she just tried to stand up straighter and stick her boobs out a little more, and gave her red curls a little fluff with her hand.

Ken said, "Thanks," as he grabbed a ticket from the man, then quickly shoved Rachel to the front so someone else wouldn't take the spot. She looked right into the guy's eyes as she reached up for a ticket, and his gaze overwhelmed her—not just with how gorgeous he was, but how easy and calm, the way he smiled at her, shook his head a little to throw his hair back out of his face. Regular people didn't look or move like that—they either looked worn out and ordinary, or if they were a little better than average, then they were intolerably stuck up, like that bitch Julia. Not him. She wondered how long you'd have to be around someone that perfect for the rush and the fascination to wear off. Maybe never—maybe they just floated along, above all the shit that made people distracted and tired, constantly emanating their energy and good fortune on those blessed enough to be near them.

From the time she reached up, until the crowd pushed her aside, must've only been a second or two, though the moment seemed unbelievably long and vivid to her. Ken pulled her from the crowd and put his ticket in her hand, laughing at how dazed and disoriented she was. Rachel couldn't believe her good luck. She'd just have to convince Will not to be such a downer, and life here would be great.

Chapter 23
Truman

As Dalia had predicted with her unusually astute business sense, Truman's trick brought in lots of customers on the following nights. Doctor Jack was very pleased, as it brought people in before the Great Lardo's performance, and kept them around after, spending their money to ask Truman where the Pyrenees were, or what was the chemical formula for salt, or the measurement of the hypotenuse of a right triangle. During the day Truman would try to learn new words and facts from the books.

All in all, it wasn't too bad, and he also noticed that Doctor Jack was pretty good about dividing the evening's take with Dalia. Truman didn't know if it was good or bad, that people so unevenly distributed their cruelty and compassion to other people. Most of the time he thought it was an inconvenient, annoying glitch in the universe, as it made it slightly harder for him to hate the living man for how he treated all the dead people. But Truman knew he only had a few hours to wait before he'd hear Lou groan and fall to the ground once more, and then just a little while longer before he'd have to cover his ears, trying to keep out Ramona's moans and screams. Then he'd remember quite well how to regard the living man in his tidy suit and well-groomed beard. If Dalia's goodness elicited some small response in the callous, rapacious man, then that was to her credit, not his, Truman decided.

Dalia had coached Truman ahead of time, to throw some of the questions if he got too many right in succession. He didn't have to do that too often, since he didn't know the science questions very well, and the customer would usually pick up on that and keep asking him those. Whenever Truman gave an erroneous answer, the person would get back his or her money, plus some silly prize. As Dalia had said, Doctor Jack kept all sorts of things lying around, and now next to Truman's cage there was a big box of such detritus to give out as rewards: dolls, inflatable hammers, snow globes, mirrors painted with supposedly funny sayings, and all sorts of rolled-up posters—mostly of rock stars who were long dead, or wandering around out there somewhere, no longer interested in their music or their fame. In addition to these, there were dozens of copies of one picture that had a poem written next to some footprints on a beach. Truman much preferred the dead rock stars; they at least looked happy, or amusing, or even intimidating.

When Truman got a question wrong, he'd also have to wear a dunce cap for the next few questions, until he earned back the right to wear his regular costume—a crudely made mortar board, or a large purple turban with a plastic jewel and a feather in the front. He'd look at the props during the day and burn with anger at the mockery heaped on him, but each time he'd remind himself of poor Lou and Ramona, and such self-pity would disappear, even as his rage redoubled at their tormentors.

Tonight Truman felt tired. It'd been a long day, with Lou's afternoon show, and Truman having to keep people entertained and paying until his evening performances. Inside the tent was hot, and the people reeked of sweat and some kind of alcohol. Not the strong, bitter smell of liquor, but that sick, sour smell of beer. Something a little rancid about it, too, like it had gone bad, but they kept swilling it. Some smoked cigarettes as well, adding to the general stench.

Truman eyed the living and thought how awful they were— greasy, lazy, ugly, and stupid. So many things to do, and instead they came here to laugh and add to the misery of some people who were more wretched than they were. Degrading outfit or not, he was glad he could answer their simple questions and maybe remind them how hideously, colossally moronic they were. In between customers, he looked down at Dalia and gave her a little smile. If it got her some money, too, then that was a bonus.

Lou had gotten up from his third gut-smashing of the day. As he posed with some children for a picture, men and women sauntered back to Truman's cage. He answered some questions as Dalia collected their money and hawked the novelty to the crowd. With her usual yellow dress, she now wore a little black bowler and carried a bamboo stick, to complete the look of the impresario or hawker. Truman also noticed she'd gotten new, shiny, black leather boots, and that filled him with pride that he'd helped procure them.

"Come on, folks," she shouted. "The Professor will answer all your questions. You pick from all these books, all these hard questions, and we check the Professor's answer. No fooling around! You'll be amazed! The smartest zombie on earth!" Truman forgave her the derogatory label. The people expected it, and besides—it didn't even sound so bad when she said it.

After a while, the women and children left, as new men filtered into the tent for Ramona's show. They were more drunk and smelly than the previous crowd. Most didn't even pay to ask Truman questions, but just taunted him. One man did finally step up and give Dalia the required fee. He was a little shorter than Truman, but broad, well-fed and muscled, with taut skin and angular features. Truman immediately hated him a bit more than the others. He wasn't even as loud and abusive as some, necessarily, but something about him had that special confidence and arrogance the living— especially men, and especially younger men—so often had. It was that empty, reflexive vanity that came from no more remarkable accomplishment than being alive, that monumental self-assuredness that would never consider or blink at its own obvious fallibility and ignorance. That was the sort of man who faced Truman, and even if he were here primarily to see Ramona put herself through much worse degradations, and even if Truman's act could make Dalia some money, Truman still took the man's easy, affable grin as the most personal affront imaginable.

"Okay, mister," Dalia said to him. "You can pick any of these books. We have lots. Pick a question, any question."

The arrogant man looked to his friends, laughing and joking with them as he picked a question. When Truman looked at his choice, however, he remembered the side-angle-side postulate, and

Dalia got to keep the man's money. He laughed and shook his head as his friends egged him on. Truman could tell he was trying to play the big sport. Truman didn't doubt for a minute he'd give Dalia more money. Good for her. As Truman looked at the next question, he thought he might have to put the dunce cap on, but was mightily glad that he guessed correctly on the question about mitosis. He risked a little combination of a snarl and a smile at the expense of the man, who seemed much less easygoing this time as he shoved more money into Dalia's hands and grabbed up another book.

The man finished off a brown bottle of the foul smelling beer as he looked over the potential questions. He dropped the bottle on the ground, taking more time than before to find the question he wanted to ask.

"There!" he said, an extra note of triumph added on top of his normal tone of presumption and entitlement. "Ha! I know that one. Most people don't!"

He handed the book to Dalia, who held it up to Truman. He looked at the question she was pointing at. Truman was surprised, as the other two had been much harder and required some thought. This one seemed pretty simple, and he wondered if the man were trying to trick him somehow. But all he could do was point at the answer he knew was correct this time.

The man looked over the top of the book to see his answer. "Ha!" he said. "See! He's not so smart!"

Dalia brought the book down and turned to the answers in the back. "No, mister," she said. "The Professor's right!"

"What? Give me that!" He looked at the contradictory evidence on the page, his face going crimson. "Trenton's not the capital of New Jersey! I was born in New Jersey! It's Newark!"

"Sorry, mister," Dalia said, casting a sideways smile at Truman. "It's been a long time. You must've forgot." The man's friends loved that, punching his shoulder and teasing him.

"I didn't fucking forget, kid. That isn't right."

"The answer's in the book. We have to play by the rules. We follow the answer in the book. If you want to pay for another question, you can ask one."

"I don't want to ask this stupid fucker another question!" the man said as he threw the book down on the ground and kicked at it. He got up closer to the bars of Truman's cage. "How do you do it?

It's a trick. He doesn't know anything. None of them do. They can't. They're all messed up."

Truman stared back at him. He didn't snarl or even glare this time, but let the man's friends work him to a further fury with their jeers, as they slapped him on the back and said he was dumber than a zombie, that maybe when he died he could be smart like one of them, or maybe he'd just get even stupider. Truman relished the moment.

The man pointed at Truman. "If you were out here, you sorry piece of shit, I'd snap your stupid faggot neck."

Of course he would. He was big enough and strong enough to do so, and drunk and barbaric enough to want to. But Truman wasn't out there now, was he? And the man was way too drunk to be making dumb-ass threats. And way too alive. He should realize in this world that being alive was not something to brag about, but a fragile liability that only a very few could hold on to, and then, only with the kind of enormous expense and sacrifice that a buffoon like this would never appreciate or understand. Truman tensed and thought how someone should remind him, in fact, of all those inconvenient truths.

"Don't talk that way to the Professor, mister," Dalia said with an unusual sharpness. "And keep away from his cage. I don't think he likes that."

As Truman lunged, he still wasn't sure anything would come of it, since the man was so powerfully built. But he didn't really care about the outcome. About all Truman could accomplish in his pathetic existence now was to surprise people like this with something their dim, selfish minds couldn't comprehend or expect. That was his only meager satisfaction, but the shock and horror on the man's face as Truman grabbed him with both hands made such satisfaction seem not at all paltry. Truman got a hold of the man's thick, hairy arm, twisting and yanking it back into his cage. Truman had enough advantage from the leverage and surprise of the attack that the man fell forward and slammed his face into the bars as Truman pulled him off balance.

They started to struggle, and the man nearly wriggled out of Truman's grasp, but with a roar, Truman threw himself into it, pushing the man's elbow back the wrong way. This drove him to his knees, howling in pain. Truman held his open mouth right next to his forearm. It stank. The other men banged on the cage, trying to help their companion, but what could they do? None of them dared stick their arms inside, lest they be grabbed and bitten instead. The man's whimpering and blubbering made Truman hate him more, made him long to release all his frustration and humiliation, to burn it into this idiot's mind, to rend his healthy, vibrant flesh and tear it away from such an undeserving soul. But Truman wavered, as he imagined the prospect of defiling himself with the blood of such a disgusting simpleton.

Then he felt the tiny hand on his shoulder, its grip so firm and resolute. So accusatory, too, in its smallness and fearlessness.

"Don't, Professor," he heard Dalia say beside him. "You be nice and let this man go. You do that or I won't be your friend anymore."

Truman only hesitated a moment after that, before shoving the arm back out between the bars. He nodded to Dalia as Doctor Jack and some other assistants pushed their way through the crowd.

The man Truman had attacked rubbed his arm and pointed at him. "That fucker attacked me!" he shouted. "I want him put down!"

"Now, now," Doctor Jack said. "I'm sure there's been some misunderstanding. Dalia—what happened?"

She scowled and pointed at the man. "That man said we cheated. He called the Professor bad names. He got up in his face, and I told him not to. Then the Professor grabbed him, but I told him to let go and he did. The Professor listens to me—not like you, you big, mean dummy! You're just jealous 'cause he's smarter and nicer than you are!"

"Now, see, a misunderstanding," Doctor Jack said, coming between Dalia and the men. "You boys failed to follow the instructions of a show employee, and that got you in some trouble. But now everything's fine."

The man rubbed his elbow. "Hey—I was in school to be a lawyer. You can't get away with this. That thing's dangerous."

Doctor Jack laughed. "Oh my God—a lawyer! What the fuck does that matter, you dumb ass? Besides saying you were a politician or you liked little boys, is there anyone you could've thought of that people would feel less sorry for, anybody they'd rather see eaten by a zombie? Lawyer! You boys get along. You're outside city walls and I've got a business to run and we don't want any more of your commotion. Now get!"

The men went off—grumbling, shouting intermittently, but they went. Doctor Jack turned back to Dalia. "You did really good, dear. I'm very proud of you," he said in as tender a tone as Truman had heard from him. Then he turned to Truman. "And you, sir, are in for a long night tomorrow. We're gonna set things up special, and show people we know how to teach our zombies right. Now, Dalia, you gather up your stuff and run along. We can't have you around when Miss Ramona does her thing."

As Doctor Jack and the others walked away, Dalia slipped her hand into Truman's. "You shouldn't have done that, Professor," she said, her face very serious. "They're gonna hurt you so bad tomorrow, and I can't do anything about that. Please don't be mad at me. I wish you hadn't done that."

Truman leaned close to the bars. "S'okay," he said in a sighing whisper that could almost be mistaken for an exhalation of breath, by someone not as wise and discerning as this child. But as Dalia's eyes widened, he knew she understood—understood there was much more than even she'd seen, and understood that he trusted her with his secret. Truman understood something then, too—that surprising these living people could sometimes be as beautiful as it was exhilarating. Dalia slipped her hand from his and backed slowly away, a look of the purest, most sublime awe shining from her face.

Chapter 24
Will

"Isn't that some shit?" Garrett said as the four of them looked into the pit. Three zombies were down there, impaled on sticks. They obviously couldn't move, but their moaning had caused Garrett to stop the wagon to investigate. All of them had on weird striped shirts. Will remembered cartoons when he was little, where men in jail wore shirts like that, as they ran around with big black balls chained to their ankles. It was all funny back then. "What the hell happened to these fuckers?"

"Somebody didn't like the City Patrol taking back the truck stop yesterday," Mike said.

"Yeah, but a pit trap? Now we'll have to fill out a report when we get back. That's something serious." Garrett got a can off the side of the wagon. It was a small, rectangular can with a nozzle at the top, so if you tipped it up and squeezed it, the liquid inside would shoot out. Garrett started squirting the contents all over the dead men. The stinging scent of lighter fluid filled Will's nose. The smell made him wince nearly as much as the dead men did, as the liquid hit them in their eyes and mouths. They spit and gurgled and tried to thrash free, but remained stuck. The best they could do was swat at the stream of liquid. Their pathetic gestures made the other men chuckle. Will looked away.

Garrett put the can back. "Well, on behalf of the city of New Sparta, we'd like to thank you boys for your service," he said. Will heard the strike of a match. "Now, we'd love to give you all a Christian burial, but today it's looking more like it's gonna be a barbecue." More chuckles, then there was the whoosh of the flames and Will could feel the heat on his neck and the side of his face. The moans increased in pitch and volume, then subsided.

Garrett led the others around the side of the wagon. "All right, Jake," he said. "You drive alongside us. We'll walk in there, real careful. Don't want the horses falling into anything like this. Keep your eyes open, boys."

They proceeded toward the ruined truck stop, the four men walking alongside the horses as they pulled the wagon. Will didn't feel too frightened of what the dead might do. He just didn't know how many more scenes like the one he'd just witnessed he could stand.

"Damn, boy, what a mess," Garrett said as they stopped. Jake climbed from the cab and they all inspected the carnage from a distance. There were bodies all over the place by the fuel pumps, most of them naked and emaciated, a few wearing the striped shirts. Some still clutched filthy weapons. The building's windows were smashed out, and the only sound was the scraping of some blinds against the window frames.

"Don't get close to the building or the pumps," Garrett said. "No sense risking it. Too many places for them to hide. The caps to the tanks are out here somewhere. Look for them." He turned to Will. "You—F.N.G.—get the rifle out of the back and keep an eye on the trees and the building. We'll get the fuel."

"Ha—now you're the 'fucking new guy,'" Chris laughed. "It's been me for weeks."

"Yeah, and before that it was some other dumb ass who couldn't keep quiet," Garrett said as he started kicking and poking in the grass. "So shush."

Will got the M4 out and stood near the wagon. Everything looked deserted. Maybe the rest of this trip would go smoothly and uneventfully.

"Here," said Garrett, as he pulled the weeds aside to uncover the metal caps to the fuel tanks underneath. "Get the hoses and jerry cans."

Will kept looking around as the others worked. There was definitely some movement in the trees, but it wasn't coming closer so Will said nothing. He wasn't afraid of whatever dead people they'd find there, but of what he'd have to do to them if they were found.

"Hey," said Chris. "What's that? Something moving?"

Shit, now he'd spotted the movement. Kid was kind of a pest, even if he weren't as cold and brutal as the others. Yeah, that about summed up the guys—cruel or clueless, and only the former seemed to last very long.

Will raised the rifle so he could look through the scope. "Something," he said. "Can't tell what." He wasn't lying, either. He could just see an occasional motion at the base of one tree, but it was too much in the shade for him to make out what it was.

Garrett stepped up next to him, observing the trees, then looking around closer to where they were standing. "Chris—take the F.N.G. and check it out," Garrett said. "We're out in the open here, none of them can sneak up on us while you're out there. But snap it up. And do *not* go further back in those trees to where we can't see you. Just walk up and shoot whatever the fuck it is. Be sure you use a silencer, even though I bet they know we're here already. We need to hurry up. This place is still too hot."

Will and Chris started off toward the trees, Will dividing his attention between the tree line and the ground just in front of them, wary for any more traps. When they were right next to the spot where he'd seen motion, Will could finally make out a human form, sitting under the one tree. It was a dead girl, wearing one of those striped shirts and holding an aluminum bat across her lap. She looked enough like Rachel that it made him shiver—same build, same hair, even if it had faded to an unnatural hue. Just sitting there. Didn't even snarl. Just stared at him with clouded eyes, her mouth open a little.

"What's it doing?" Chris said. "Why doesn't it attack?"

"Probably injured, can't move."

"Well, shoot it and let's go."

"Why? She's just a girl. She's not doing anything."

Will turned to see Chris's shocked expression. "What?" Chris said. "It's not a girl. It's just a dead thing. It's not good for anything anymore. Just kill it. It's grossing me out."

"How can you say that? People don't have to be useful for something."

The kid's look hardened a bit, like he'd been coached in a certain way of looking at things, certain phrases that had to be said to brush aside doubts. "Yeah, they do, actually. But that's not even a person. It's not even alive. So kill it."

Now the girl did snarl as she raised the bat. She'd looked resigned before—now she looked defiant. "See—it's dangerous," Chris said. "Put it down."

"She's just doing that because you're standing right next to her, talking about shooting her in the head. So shut the fuck up."

Now Chris looked amused as well as shocked, and still with that hardness of someone who could deny the reality right in front of himself with complete certainty. "No—you shut the fuck up. You gone crazy? They don't understand anything. She just wants to eat us. She would if she could."

"Maybe, but she can't. And look at her—she knows what we're saying. You can see she does."

Chris looked at the girl, then back to Will. "All I know is it needs to be killed." He reached for his own weapon and Will grabbed his wrist. That was a big step, and Will didn't know where it would lead, but it happened before he could really think about it.

"Hey!" Chris said. He looked like he also knew they'd gone too far now, that it had escalated past posturing, past the point where you could laugh it off.

"Don't," Will said. He knew he could probably smack the kid around pretty easily, but an altercation with another team member was going to complicate life considerably. He'd probably be working at the corner store after today, making half as much money. The girl wheezed and Will knew he'd made the only choice he could.

Chris glared at him and Will didn't know how to end or defuse the situation. Then there was a shout from the direction of the truck stop. After a second it was followed by a long scream and a series of gunshots—not one weapon, but several, firing maybe as many as ten shots in a couple seconds.

Will pulled Chris away from the girl and shoved him toward the sounds. "Come on," he shouted. "They need us. Go."

Chapter 25
Lucy

After setting Becca in the woods, Lucy and her two remaining friends shuffled back to rejoin the main group of dead. Lucy looked around the crowd. She hadn't done a head count before the attack, but the battle had clearly taken its toll. She guessed twenty or so hadn't made it back, and the mob was now maybe a little over a hundred—not counting the smaller children, whom she couldn't see among the others.

Lucy still wondered why such young people had come on this outing—or why they were even in the camp in the first place. She'd asked the other women about the children before, in camp, but they'd shrugged and said they were there to fight, like everyone else. That really didn't make much sense, though when they'd left that morning, some of the men had made a point of shoving the children along with the crowd leaving the gate.

Walking to the truck stop and battling the other dead had taken all day and it would be dark soon. They couldn't risk tripping and hurting themselves, so they sat down beneath a nearby overpass. Some of the men went among the abandoned cars there, sniffing. Lucy thought at first they were checking for hidden enemies, but she couldn't quite make out what they were doing, it had gotten so dark. From their sounds, they were dragging stuff around and breaking things, but these were not the screams and howls of battle. Then Lucy caught the scent of gasoline. Another hideous stench the living people loved so much, and it made her recoil and shake her head.

"What the hell are they doing?" Lucy asked, looking from Christine to Carole, who both sat near her.

"Fire," Carole said. "Keeps wild men away."

"Yeah," Christine grunted. "Scares regular people like us enough. Wild men really hate it. Makes them run far away." There was a pause. "They'll probably ask you. They never can do it themselves. Men—clumsy and scared." She gave a coughing kind of chuckle.

"I know," Carole said as she got up, joining her friend in laughter as she brushed herself off and ran her fingers through her hair.

Lucy was about to ask what they meant, when Ben approached them. Lucy studied him more closely than before. Most of the dead looked much paler than when they were alive, including black people, but his skin had remained a very dark shade. He'd kept a lot of his bulk and muscle tone as well. Lucy remembered how Becca had said he was one of the nicer men in the camp—not just because he was in better shape than most of them and more pleasant to look at, but because he was respectful, didn't try to intimidate others or demand things. But he was still a man, so Lucy eyed him and rose to her feet as he got closer.

Ben looked at Lucy and gave her a little nod. "What's your name?" he asked. He had a nice voice, too.

"Lucy."

"That's a pretty name—pretty like you. Who gave it to you?"

"My man."

He smirked. "Ah. So you don't want to be my woman, either? Why do all you pretty ladies treat me so badly?"

Carole laughed at this as Ben turned toward her, holding out a small object. Lucy couldn't see what it was in the darkness.

"You light it, lady?"

"Yes, Ben," Carole answered. Her voice sounded different than normal, higher and more nervous.

He smiled, showing rows of teeth better than most living people had. "You sure you don't wanna be my woman all the time?" he said to Carole. "I keep lighter. You light fires. People would respect us. I'd protect you. It'd be nice."

Carole gave her huffing laugh as she took the lighter. "Oh, Ben, you ask that all the time," she said. Then she surprised Lucy by slipping her arm around Ben's waist. "I like things the way they are. You can hold me as we walk over, so your friends will see. Then I'll come back and sit with my friends. Okay?"

Ben put a big arm around her. "Yeah. That's okay. Nice to hold you sometimes."

"I know. I like it too," Carole said as they walked away.

"She likes to flirt," Christine said when they'd gone. "It's good for her. You should try, too. It's normal. Makes things easier."

Lucy sat down next to the older woman. "Yeah, maybe someday," she said. "I don't trust people too much."

Christine nodded. "Yeah. That's normal, too."

There was a crackling, whooshing sound as a large flame leaped up nearby. The assembly of dead people sent up a collective gasp, then settled into an agitated murmur for a few moments as they struggled to overcome their fear. When they nearly had, another flame erupted from the other side of the overpass, so they were flanked by fires. Their murmuring resumed, then finally died down as Carole returned to Christine and Lucy.

They sat there through the night, then resumed their march as soon as the sun was up. Walking by the blackened circle of debris that had been the fire the night before, Lucy thought it didn't smell so bad now.

They continued through the morning, until they reached the outskirts of a town. Stopping at the top of a hill, they looked down on the remains of the settlement—just a collection of low buildings around a central cluster of multi-story structures. Most everything was so overgrown you could barely tell they'd been human constructions at one time, though the top floors of the taller buildings were still visible.

Lucy squinted. She thought she saw movement among the buildings, but couldn't be sure.

The crowd was jostled around again, as they had been at the truck stop, though this time the men came through and rounded up the children, taking them to the front.

"What are they doing?" Lucy asked.

Carole shook her head. "It's not nice. Don't ask. Just wait till we have to fight. Isn't that bad enough?"

Lucy tried to see over the other people, but she wasn't tall enough. She had the most driving curiosity about this, as well as a sense of dread. Just ignoring it wasn't going to work.

"No, I want to know," Lucy said as she started to make her way through the crowd.

"I'll go with her," she heard Christine say from behind.

Lucy got to the front of the crowd, with Christine emerging a moment later to stand next to her. Eight small children—they looked like they'd been about five or so when they died—were in front of the main group. Ben was off to the side, looking down on the town through those things that make everything look closer. Not a telescope—that was one long tube, whereas these were two short ones that you held up to both eyes. A microscope? No, that was something else.

It almost seemed as though Ben were supervising or directing, while the other men took bundles from the duffle bags and attached them to the children's backs. Lucy looked more carefully at the children who were facing her direction. They appeared as ambivalent as the dead usually were about anything other than fire and live humans. They didn't show fear or nervousness or even much interest in what was being done to them, their heads lolling around as they were jostled about. One boy who caught Lucy's attention looked rather nasty and belligerent, baring his teeth as she stared at him. But he might have been squinting at the sun, or grimacing at the strap being pulled too tight. You never knew.

When the children were prepared with their backpacks, the men turned them all toward the town below. Ben stepped forward to address them.

"Men down there are *not* our friends," he shouted. His voice was soothing and commanding at the same time. "They are bad men. They hurt our friends yesterday. You understand?" The children grunted and nodded. "You go down there." He pulled two aside. "You two—go inside their big buildings." He came down the line to the next two and separated them. "You two—there's a pile of cars and trucks in the middle of town—climb up on it. The rest of you—make noise. Get bad men to chase you. Then run away from them—but do *not* come back here. Stay down there and find as many bad men as you can. Then let them get close to you. Pull the strings in your hands. Then you go." Ben held his hands over his head. "You go—up to where Santa and bunnies and fairies live forever. They'll be nice to you. They'll give you so much love. You'll be happy. You'll never be hungry or scared again. You be proud now. You are heroes. Now—go!"

The children lurched down the hill as best they could, in an uneven, tottering sort of jog. Lucy watched their small heads bobbing in the grass, which was almost as tall as they were.

She turned on Christine. "They send them in there? With—things?" She hated it when she couldn't remember a word, especially if she was trying to say it to someone else, but now her anger was increased by this monstrous scene, and by her own complicity in it. "With b-b-bombs?" She was so worked up she was stuttering now too, which further added to her shame, frustration, and rage.

Christine looked completely unperturbed—though there might have been the tiniest spark of sympathy for Lucy, a shred of pity, almost, for someone who could still feel the obvious wrongness of all this. She put her hand on Lucy's shoulder. "It's better this way," she said. "A few die, so others won't."

Lucy pushed her hand away. "I don't care. This isn't better. This isn't right."

"It doesn't matter. This is the way it is. You don't like it, then go away. Or maybe they can strap a bomb on you, if you hate it so much." The two women glared at each other for a moment.

"We can, but we won't." It was Ben's low, steady voice.

Lucy turned on him. She hadn't noticed him coming over, but now he stood quite close to them. To think she'd been told how nice he was. To think she'd looked at him and thought how attractive he was. It was all maddening and disgusting now.

"How can you?" she growled at him.

He shook his head. "You don't like this?"

"No."

He nodded. "Good. Then you're smart. I don't like this, either." He pointed to Christine. "She doesn't like this." He shrugged. "We do it to survive. Maybe someday we'll stop doing it and find another way to survive. Maybe you don't judge us until then. Okay—smart, pretty, dead lady?" Although his smile now wasn't as perfect as before, tinged with something cold and sharp, it was still reassuring and captivating.

Lucy waited a moment. "I'll think about it," she finally said.

His smile seemed to brighten and broaden. "Good. They hate it when we think. Maybe your thinking will help us. Maybe it'll do some hurt to the people who really are bad."

He turned back toward the town, raising the magnifying things to his eyes again. Binoculars—that's what they were called. Funny word.

Lucy followed his gaze. In a few minutes she heard the first explosion, like a dull thump. It was followed immediately by another, then a much louder one. This larger blast was simultaneous with a small fireball in the middle of the town. Lucy thought she saw a car flipping backwards through the air as well. There was a pause before she heard another explosion, though this one sounded muffled. There was a rumble immediately after it, as one of the taller buildings collapsed, falling over and crushing several of the smaller buildings near it.

Lucy turned from the destruction and extended her hand to Christine. The other woman took a step toward her. "I'm sorry," Lucy said. "It's not your fault."

Christine nodded as she took her friend's hand. "I'm sorry too. We do bad things. You're right to r-r-remind us how we're supposed to be."

Carole came up alongside them and together they watched a huge cloud of dust slowly rising up from the ruins of the town, flames leaping up here and there amidst the obscurity. The scene was punctuated by more explosions and occasional screams, while underneath it all, a rising chorus of moans accused and threatened them.

Chapter 26
Rachel

Will had shown polite interest in the concert tickets, but Rachel could tell he wasn't interested. Maybe he really was scared about the job, though she couldn't understand why, after he'd spent years out there among the dead, often alone. He'd said last night that they were going back to some truck stop that was supposed to be especially dangerous, and that made her wonder if he'd lost his nerve. She almost wished that was it, because at least she could sympathize with that, and try to reassure him or express her concern. And she was concerned—but only for him and not the zombies: that was the difference that was coming between them now.

After dinner, she'd swung her leg over his lap and had straddled him, resting her butt on his thighs. She'd laced her fingers behind his neck and had told him how much she loved him and worried about him. It felt good to think maybe she knew now what was bothering him, at least in part. But she couldn't very well tell him he was going to go out in the wilderness and not see zombies getting shot. That was just part of the deal and he should get used to it.

She'd punctuated her consoling him with enough snuggling and kissing that he couldn't help but get it up, and they'd done it on the floor—nice and hard and rough. Rachel congratulated herself on breaking the dry spell—God knows, it never would've ended if she'd left it up to Will. But as he slept next to her, she reflected that it had been pretty perfunctory—she'd only come because she hadn't in so long—and he still wasn't into it. Well, pity sex was still sex, and she'd work on him some more tonight.

Rachel stayed up a while thinking of how to go about it. She'd had trouble sleeping the last couple nights, even though she'd been feeling tired during the day.

After a fitful, uncomfortable night's sleep, Rachel got up. Will had already left for work. It was her day off and she looked at herself naked in the bathroom mirror. She ran her hands down her thighs, and then back up. Those felt nice and firm, but as she dragged her hands over her hips and then her belly, she felt fat. Maybe that was another part of why Will wasn't interested in sex. That thought made Rachel feel so worthless and gross she nearly started crying, though she managed to pull herself together before the tears actually flowed. She'd just have to lay off the Chinese takeout.

It'd been okay to binge a little at first with all the new stuff in the city, but now she'd let herself go too much. She'd take it easy on the late night snacks, even though she'd been having such a craving for spicy food. A little restraint there, together with the long walk to work, and she'd get back in shape in no time. That and some nice stuff from today's outing with Shayna, and things would be fun again.

Rachel wrapped a denim skirt around her waist and again considered her body. The piece of clothing looked pretty dumpy—it made her hips look bigger and her legs shorter, too—but she never got to wear a skirt at work, and they were so much more comfortable anyway. She lifted her foot and pointed her toe. Yeah, her legs still looked pretty nice. Rachel considered going braless—the things had been fun at first, but now they seemed to chafe and pinch more than before—but there was no way she could in public anymore. The catcalls and stares would quickly escalate past flattering all the way to humiliating and threatening. Well, again, you just had to put up with some things in a new place with new people and rules. She wouldn't be a big crybaby like Will.

Rachel strapped on the bra that hurt the least and pulled on a tee shirt. Nice, tight, low V-neck, lots of cleavage on display. She didn't feel so bad anymore.

Rachel checked her .38. That was another problem with the skirt—she'd have to wear her shoulder holster, which was feeling as uncomfortable as her bras lately. She slipped it on, though, and holstered her gun as she went out the front door.

Rachel could hear Shayna fussing around with the baby as she knocked on their door. The door opened and Shayna greeted her, then turned to fumble with her purse and diaper bag.

"Hi," Rachel said as she again admired Shayna's tall figure and the red highlights in her hair.

Aisha was already in her stroller, and Rachel helped with the door and with hassling the contraption down the couple steps to the sidewalk. She cooed and smiled at the little girl, who was done up all in white and who returned her attention with equal enthusiasm.

"How you doin', girl?" Shayna asked as they started down the street.

"Great," Rachel said. It felt more natural to keep things from her, for some reason. With Ken, Rachel always felt a little guilty about her half-truths. But she told them equally to both of them, she knew, so it didn't seem to make too much difference. One just took more effort than the other.

"That's good. We're gonna have a nice time, just us three girls."

They chatted as they walked—just the usual small talk about the baby, Rachel's work, the prices or scarcity of different food and other products. They stopped at several stores for practical purchases. They both opted for canned peaches at the food store, while Rachel also needed detergent, and Shayna more diapers. At the drug store Shayna wanted some sunscreen for the baby, and Rachel bought some as well: she hadn't used any since she was a kid, but she wondered if it'd be a good idea to try it. With red hair and pale skin, her freckles got pretty bad in the summer and maybe that'd help.

As they came out, Rachel saw one shop she hadn't been in yet. It was a small storefront, with its name stenciled on the window in fancy, script lettering—"Fulci Leather." She gravitated toward it without consulting Shayna, who followed along, pushing the stroller.

"Oh, you like that?" Shayna said, pulling up alongside Rachel in front of the window, which was full of coats, boots, shoes, and bags. "The man does make nice stuff. Ken got me some shoes for Christmas. You should go in. Aisha's good for a little while longer. Come on—let's go in and look."

"Well, okay."

Rachel gravitated toward the display of boots along the one wall as a small, older man approached them from the back. What was left of his hair was still black, and slicked back on his mostly bald head. A yellow measuring tape hung around his neck.

"Ladies, welcome," he said, smiling as he took off his glasses and slipped them into the pocket of his shirt. The accent might've been fake, and Rachel wasn't sure where it was supposed to be from, regardless.

"Thank you," Rachel and Shayna both said. Rachel smiled back at him before returning her attention to the goods, though she could see from the corner of her eye that he continued examining her.

"You're new here," he continued after a moment.

"Yes," Rachel said. "We—well, I'm not from New Sparta."

"How nice. I'm so glad you stopped in. You're interested in boots? Those are very nice." Rachel was holding a knee-high, black leather one with about a three-and-a-half-inch heel. She was sure a pair of them would look awesome on her, but even without asking the price, she sighed and put it back, knowing it wouldn't help get Will passionate about sex again. Didn't matter how good she looked or how hard she tried—if he were all depressed about money and staying too long in the city, he'd be totally uninterested, even angry.

"Hey, girl," Shayna said from the other side of the store. "Here's what you need." She held up a large, black handbag.

Rachel walked over and touched the leather. It was softer than any she could remember feeling. The maker had riveted triangular pieces of silver metal at the corners; these were like mirrors, they were so shiny. The handle was rigid leather, connected to the bag with round metal hoops, which also had leather fringe hanging from them. Around the handle there was another shiny metal band. This one had "Fulci" engraved on it.

She didn't want to seem like an ignorant hick by burying her face in the bag, but she risked leaning closer to inhale the pungent leather smell. It was an elegant, graceful piece, no question, but Rachel couldn't really quite imagine what it was for. She'd never had a purse as an adult—just play handbags when she was a girl—so the item fascinated her; it just didn't have the raw, sensual appeal of the boots.

"I do?" she said with a smile.

"Ah, you have excellent taste, miss," the man said to Shayna. "I make everything myself, but the handbags are my favorite—so functional and beautiful. So much attention to detail, but so rugged and practical. Every lady needs a bag like this."

"He's right," Shayna said, still holding the bag before Rachel. "I didn't want to say anything, but you really can't go around packing like you do, with your gun all out in the open. You don't see other gals doing that. I mean, maybe at work, since you're out there on the site—but around town? You need to put it in a bag like regular folks."

"She's right," the man said, nodding and gesturing to her .38. "Such a lovely lady—you can't have this ugly piece of metal strapped to your beautiful body. I saw your pretty face when you walked in, then I saw this gun, and for a moment I was scared and thought you were a robber." He chuckled. "This bag would be perfect for you."

"I don't know." If Rachel had had doubts about the boots improving her sex life, she was virtually certain this thing wouldn't, and it probably cost nearly as much as the boots. On the other hand, if it were something practical, something she needed to have, then Will could hardly object. He couldn't ask her to go around town being ridiculed all the time, could he? That would be so unfair.

"Yes, please, I want you to have this bag. I can make you an excellent deal on it. It'll be my gift to you, as a newcomer to our city. Barely more than the cost of materials. Just for you."

The ridiculousness of a "gift" for which the recipient has to pay was not lost on Rachel. It made her smirk and almost push the bag away. But the man had that fawning and insistent quality of all good salesmen, that way of making you feel guilty if you don't buy. And now he and Shayna really had made her self-conscious about carrying her sidearm in the open, so much so that the handle of the

.38 rubbing against her left boob was almost unendurably irritating and embarrassing.

"How much?" Shayna asked, pulling the bag slightly away from Rachel. They exchanged a glance, and Rachel could tell that her friend would be a bit better at bargaining, and she should go along with it.

The man named a price much less than Rachel would've guessed for the boots, but still a lot under their present circumstances. Shayna balked at it, and Rachel played along by acting surprised and disappointed, even taking a step back, as though she were going to abandon negotiations. Aisha cooperated by starting to fuss right then, and Shayna was lifting the bag to hang it back on its hook. The price came down, and with a slight indication from Shayna, Rachel took the deal.

They were barely out the door when Rachel wriggled out of her holster and put it and her gun in her new bag. She shouldered it, trying different ways of settling it between her elbow and her body. Although it didn't really rub against her boob that differently or less annoyingly than the holster had, and though she was terrified now that she would put it down somewhere and forget, or that it'd be stolen, she was sure she'd get used to the feeling of it against her. And it still smelled really good.

Chapter 27
Truman

After the living closed up the tent, Truman and Ramona leaned against each other, her thin shoulder just touching his between the bars. Her presence wasn't nearly as comforting as the beatific look on Dalia's innocent face, but it was more solid and longer lasting.

"You got that asshole good, Truman," she said after a while. "Showed him he's not all that."

"He was stupid," said Lou, though Truman couldn't see him in the darkness. "They call Lou stupid, but plenty of them are dumber. Talk too much. Talk all big, when they don't know anything. Another minute and maybe Lou would've pulled his chain out of the ground. Go over and help Truman break the little lawyer-man. Tear his stupid arm off. Lou would give it to Truman to gnaw on for days and days, just like old times before."

Ramona chuckled. "Don't make me hungry, Lou," she said. "Most days I don't think about it. But yeah, he was yummy looking. Juicy. Him being such a dick would make it tastier, too." She turned to Truman. "But your little friend was right—it's gonna be bad tomorrow for you."

"It's all right," Truman said. "I knew I shouldn't do it. I knew they'd do something to me. I'll be okay."

She tilted her head down a little, and even reached between the bars to touch his cheek. She hadn't done that before. "I hope so, Truman. We need to send you back to your woman before they hurt you too bad here."

Women had the oddest ideas about intimacy and trust and when to bring up certain topics, Truman decided, not for the first time.

"What are they going to do?" he asked. "It can't be that bad."

"Electricity," she said. "It hurts."

"The cattle prod?" That had been bad, but nothing unendurable, and it didn't last long.

"No," she replied. "Big thing, like a bed. They'll strap you to it. Keep zapping you over and over. They like to watch. You'll have a big crowd."

That definitely sounded like something the living would do and enjoy. It still seemed like something he could survive, though Truman couldn't remember feeling electricity before that time with the cattle prod, so he didn't know exactly what the effect would be.

"Yes, that'll hurt, but I'll make it."

Ramona nodded, still stroking Truman's cheek and chin. "You might," she said. "I never felt it. Neither has Lou—right, Lou?"

"No," came the reply from the darkness. "They never did that to Lou. Lou only pretends to be mean. They like that. But he never hurt someone here. Truman did, 'cause he's braver than Lou. Truman needs to be extra brave and strong tomorrow, though."

Ramona smiled at Truman and lowered her voice so the other dead man couldn't hear. "He looks up to you, I think," she whispered. Then she raised her voice to a normal volume. "He's right," she said. "One guy they used it on didn't make it. I mean, he did, at first, but he was all messed up after. Couldn't talk or move right. That was the end of him. Remember him, Lou?"

"Martin," said Lou. "They called him Rat Boy. Tall, skinny, pale kid. Bad people saved up all the rats they'd catch around here. Starved them till they were crazy, mean, mad. Then they'd drop Martin in a big, metal tub with them. They'd put a metal grate across the top, so poor Martin couldn't get out, but the people could see him and the rats. It was loud, him and the rats rolling around, biting and screaming. He'd have to fight them so long, before he'd get them all. Bite their heads off. Tear them in two with his hands. So many of them. So much blood all over him. Martin hated it. I told him it's not so bad, it takes them a long time to save up so many rats, and he just sits around the rest of the time. But he hated it too much. He tried to get away. They zapped him. He was slower after that. His hands and face twitched. Next time with the rats, he couldn't fight them so good. They got him. Nothing left. Just rats. Then the bad people got them, too: poured gas in the tub and set it on fire. More screaming from the rats. Smelled bad too."

Ramona turned and again leaned her shoulder against Truman. She lowered her head as she snaked her hand between the bars to lace her fingers with his. "You'll survive tomorrow, Truman," she whispered. "Then we'll work on getting you out of here."

"You too," he said. "And Lou. You shouldn't stay here either. We all should go."

She tightened her grip on his hand as she nodded. "I think we've been lazy. I don't know what we'd do out there."

"You're just scared. You'll go somewhere. It doesn't matter where."

"You have someone to go to, Truman. That's different. Lou and I don't. But maybe you're right. Sometimes it's pretty bad here. We get afraid of what's outside, though."

"There's so much space out there, so many places with just dead people, or sometimes even with no one at all. It's not perfect, but it's better than here. You have to try."

"We'll see, Truman." They were silent for a while.

"Did you like to drive cars?" Ramona asked finally.

Truman had to think for a minute. He had no specific memory of the devices, though when he'd seen wrecks of them lying around, he often thought how large and graceful they looked.

"I don't know," he answered. "I'm not sure I did. But it might be nice to try again."

"Yeah. I don't see how we could."

"You never know. We do a lot more than we used to."

"That's true. I think I liked to drive. I wonder what kind of car I had."

"When you get out, you'll find a car and learn how to drive it."

"I might. Where will you and your woman go?"

That thought had been bothering Truman lately. "I don't know. I hope we can find Will and Rachel—those are the living people we were with. We were happy, the four of us. But I don't know where they are, or if they like it here, and I don't know if we'll be able to find them. I don't know how to find Lucy, either. But I have to. And you have to get out too."

They sat quietly after that, and Truman considered how much time they—and all the billions of people like them—had spent, making plans that never happened. More importantly, he wondered whether those fruitless plans were what made all the inevitable suffering endurable, or whether they added to its agony and wretchedness. He supposed he only had until the following evening to find out, though perhaps even then it'd remain a mystery, a tantalization forever beyond his grasp, always shifting between comfort and mockery.

Chapter 28
Will

Will had lived most of his life in a world where corpses get up and walk around, so there weren't many situations he would describe as "unbelievable." The scene back at the truck stop, however, would be one of those.

Nothing made sense. Mike lay on the ground near the fuel pumps, clutching at his face with his one hand, blood gushing out between his fingers. He thrashed around, making sounds that varied between screaming and moaning, but all of which degenerated into bubbling and choking as they forced their way up through the torrent of blood.

Jake knelt next to him, uninjured as far as Will could see. Five corpses were sprawled on the ground near them, all shot in the head. None of them wore the striped shirts, but were bare-chested and filthy. The three lying face up had fresh blood around their mouths. Garrett was rummaging in the back of the wagon.

"Hold him down," Garrett shouted. "He's gonna go into shock soon."

Will held Chris back and they approached more slowly, Will looking around to make sure there were no more attackers. As he got closer, he could see that Mike's free hand had the pinkie and ring finger torn off. What was left of the appendage was twisted around, twitching, blood still flowing out from the wound. His jacket had been pushed up around his armpits, and his stomach and sides were covered with deep gashes, also bleeding profusely. From the amount of blood pouring from his face, Will figured his nose or cheek must've been torn off. The dead often went for the soft parts like that. But now Will could see there was a rope around his ankles. What was that about?

Regardless, Garrett was right—shock would set in any second with that kind of blood loss, and death in just a few minutes. There was no way they could stop all that bleeding, even if they were regular wounds and not infected, fatal bites.

Garrett finally turned from the wagon, approaching them with a clipboard full of papers. He didn't look scared, but definitely shaken and frustrated. "You two—stay put," he shouted as he pushed past Will to get to Mike. "And this time really keep an eye out."

"What the fuck happened?" Chris said. Unlike Garrett, he sounded like he was about to piss himself.

"Shut up. Busy. Jake—I told you to hold him down."

Garrett kneeled down next to the wounded man, holding the clipboard above him. "Mike, Mike, stay with me," he said. "We don't have long. This is the release form. I know we have it on file back at the office, but we need final consent if the person's still conscious, in case someone wants to change their mind at the last minute. It doesn't look like you can sign it, but we'll need some form of consent if your family's gonna get the payment. It can be verbal, but you have to answer the questions. Do you consent to pre-natural termination?"

After another gurgling scream, Mike grew quiet, until he made a sound like, "Yub."

"Okay, just two more. Following termination, do you hereby request corporal harvesting, with the value of such goods harvested to be paid to your estate, at the fair market value to be determined at the time of procurement?"

A moan and what sounded like another affirmative response.

"Okay, last one. You must be aware that all material harvested will be used for any and all purposes, to be solely determined by the City Council of New Sparta, with no further consultation with you or your estate, and no possible retraction of this request for harvesting. Do you understand this and give your full and final consent?"

The answer this time trailed off into what might've been sobs, or maybe just labored breathing.

Garrett stood up. "All right. Jake, step back from him. Mike, we'll give you a couple minutes to get your thoughts together. But we won't let you suffer long. Don't worry. And don't worry about your family. That money will help them out a lot."

Will and the other three moved away from the dying man. "Where the fuck were you two?" Garret said.

"We found some dead chick. It couldn't walk. He wouldn't shoot it," Chris said in an angry, frightened blur.

"What?" Garrett looked between them, seemingly confused. "Fuck it. That doesn't matter now. We just need to get out of here fast once we're done with Mike."

"Done with him?" Will couldn't help but ask. "What happened? I don't know what you're saying."

Garrett shook his head. "We were way over there, by the caps to the fuel tanks. Mike moved to find another one, and he stepped on some kinda snare." Garrett pointed up at the canopy. A rope hung there from a pulley, with the other end attached to a big weight on the ground. "Can you believe that? They had a snare rigged up. Not just digging pits, but pulleys and knots? They're not supposed to be able to do shit like that. Damn thing yanked him up and as he was dangling there five of them jumped out. They were all over him before Jake and I shot them all. Fuck, what a mess."

"This is all his fault," Chris said, pointing at Will. He was really whimpering now, almost on the verge of tears.

"Yeah, new guy acts weird," Jake chimed in. "Never wants to shoot anything. I don't know about him."

"What?" Will said. "I didn't ask to go over there. I didn't do anything wrong."

"Shut the fuck up, all of you," Garrett said. "You're being a fucking pussy," he said, pointing at Chris. "And you," he turned now to Will, "you're just creeping me out. Something not right about you. Take the fucking rifle and finish Mike and let's get out of here."

"Finish him? What're you talking about? You can't just shoot someone."

"Hey, I did it enough before you showed up," Jake said, kicking at the dirt.

"Me too," Chris sniffed. "Well, just the one time, but still."

Garrett glared at Will, taking a step closer. "He consented, and we have to do it now or the body's no good. Think of his family—they won't get paid. Don't you have any compassion for them?"

Will backed away from him, dazed, completely overwhelmed now by what he was saying. "Good for what? What's going on?"

"What do you think? I told you they feed the City Patrol zombies. What'd you think they feed them? Body's worth a lot these days. But it can't be walking around. It's got to be all the way dead. So go shoot him in the head and maybe I won't write you up and you'll still have a job tomorrow."

Will shoved the rifle at Garrett. "No. I don't care. I'm not doing that." He turned and started walking.

"What're you gonna do? Walk back to town?"

"Yes."

"You're fucking crazy. You won't get back until after dark, and they're all over the place out here."

"They don't scare me."

A few seconds later when Will heard the muffled shot, he half wished the bullet had been going into his brain and not Mike's.

Chapter 29
Lucy

The children had done their job well. Lucy expected more dead people to come streaming from the ruined, burning town to attack their group, but as the dust and smoke drifted away, she saw only a few scattered figures, wandering away from them. They moved singly or in pairs, scattering into the fields, disappearing into the woods and over hills. In a few moments, everything was silent, except for the light wind stirring the grass. Lucy couldn't quite decide if the dry, even sound was grating or soothing.

Ben put down the binoculars and started to lead the mob back toward camp. When he picked the large duffel bag back up, Lucy noticed it didn't look empty. Perhaps he hadn't used all the bombs they'd brought, thereby sparing some of the children. It was so hard to judge people in this new place, and Lucy wanted to be away from them, back to Truman, who was so easy to evaluate, so simple in his way. Even Will and Rachel, though they could be annoying, didn't have the awful ambiguity and complexity of both the dead and living around here.

They marched back the way they had come. It was hot and dusty and Lucy again thought of just leaving. But thinking of

Truman's reliability and innocence kept her going. She needed him. She'd have to tell him that if she ever saw him again. Sometimes she was too taciturn, too noncommittal with him. Lucy remembered, almost instinctually, that was how you were supposed to treat a man, but she also felt she'd gone too far sometimes, left too much unsaid. Now she might die out here on the cracked remains of a highway, or back in the camp in a falling-down hovel, and he'd never know what he meant to her, how important and good he was. And even if she got away, what would be out there, anyway? Dead people who set traps that would maim and not quite kill you? More living people with guns who would enslave you, or leer at your broken, emaciated body? No, marching along was still far preferable, and Lucy continued on through the day.

Sometimes Lucy thought she saw wild people following them, or observing them from behind trees or other cover, but she couldn't be sure, and no one came out to offer battle to their group. When they got close to camp, they stopped, and Ben came through the crowd toward Lucy and her two friends.

He smiled at Carole and she again showed her girlish, submissive demeanor. "How are you doing?" he asked.

"Okay, Ben," Carole answered, tilting her head down as she said it. "Tired. Hungry."

Ben set the duffle bag down. "Me too." He unzipped the bag and got out one of the bomb packages. He handed it to Carole, who stuffed it up the front of her striped shirt, then tucked her shirt in to hold it in place. There was still a bulge, but it wasn't too noticeable, since she was skinny to begin with and the garment was so big.

Ben held another one out to Lucy. "You want one, smart, pretty lady?"

Lucy's head swam, she was so confused and aghast at being offered this horrible thing. "No," she said as she shook her head. "Why are you giving me that thing? I hate it. It's bad."

Ben looked from the bomb to her eye and held her gaze a moment, like he was trying to understand her, and trying to formulate a way to make her understand him. "We save bombs, guns, other weapons. Maybe use them on food men soon. But they search us men sometimes," he explained. "They're suspicious. They don't search ladies. Well, almost never. One time one guy did. Lady had hidden a gun we'd found." Ben put his forefinger next to his head, extended his thumb, then dropped it like the hammer of a pistol. "Bang. No more lady. Is that it? You're afraid food men will kill you?"

Lucy narrowed her eye and bared her teeth at him. "Fuck them," she said slowly, drawing out the "F" sound. "And fuck you. I'm not afraid of you or them. I just don't want your stupid bomb. When I kill food men, I'll do it right. With my hands and my teeth."

Ben grinned. "You are a feisty one. I like you, Lucy. If Carole weren't my woman sometimes, I'd want you."

Carole slapped him playfully on the shoulder. "Ben, stop!" she said with a laugh.

"Or maybe I could have you both. Damn, you must've been such a hot one when you were alive."

"Maybe I was," Lucy said quietly. "It doesn't matter now. None of that does. I just don't want that thing."

"Here, let me have it," Christine said, stepping forward and lifting her shirt. "No one's gonna look at my fat, ugly ass or belly."

Ben chuckled as he put the package in the cavity in Christine's middle. He pulled her shirt down over it and patted her hip. "Thanks, Christine. And you're not ugly, either. I'd've gotten with you, too, way back when."

"Yeah, well, that's what you say now. Who knows? Maybe I didn't like black guys. Maybe I didn't even like guys. Maybe you didn't like girls. You ever think of that? How the hell would we even know?"

Ben laughed more loudly. "No, I never thought of that. But I like you now, big girl, either way. Maybe we'll leave it at that. Why do you ladies say such funny things? You all think too much. Especially this new one." He turned to look at Lucy again. "When we fight the food men, you remember what you said. We'll see how you do."

"You make sure you do what you have to," Lucy replied. "You don't need to worry about me."

Ben kissed Carole on the mouth before disappearing back into the crowd to lead them the rest of the way to camp. As he'd predicted, the guards trained their weapons on the returning dead people and had the men remove their shirts before going through the gate. Christine was allowed through immediately, but the guards made Carole and Lucy stop. Shit.

"Which one you think is finer—the tall brunette or the new blonde?" said one of the men from the tower.

"Oh, stop! We got to get them all inside and you're pervin' on your new girlfriend again?"

"Just glad to see her. I was so afraid she might not make it back. Go ahead, you two, show us how much you missed us before we let you in."

The other men groaned and laughed as dead people jostled past Lucy and Carole. Lucy caught her friend's petrified glance. Lucy wasn't scared—only enraged again at the living. Carole followed Lucy's lead in pressing her palm to her lips and blowing the degenerate men a kiss. The whistles and catcalls increased. Carole looked so terrified, Lucy would do anything to take the men's attention from her friend, so she turned her back to them, bent forward slightly, and gave her ass a little shake for their amusement.

"Oh—she did miss us! Look at her! Neither of them has much of a rack, but blondie's ass is the best!"

Lucy took Carole by the shoulder to hustle her into the camp. They let the shambling crowd absorb them and carry them along with it. They found Christine, and she and Carole went into their house, motioning for Lucy to stay outside. They rejoined her in a moment, after hiding the bombs, she supposed. Lucy was surprised they didn't all return to their houses, but remained milling around in the open area near the gate. There must be something more to returning to camp that she didn't know about.

After a while, when it was nearly dark, a truck pulled up outside the gate and men unloaded a metal tub on wheels. The crowd jostled one another, people trying to see over those in front. Inarticulate cries accompanied the truck's arrival, followed by a general moaning of pleasure and anticipation. The gate opened and some of the living men came through with torches, driving the dead people back, as two other men pushed the tub into the yard. Then the living men retreated and closed the gate, leaving the tub behind.

The crowd hung back. Apparently there was some order or ritual to this. Lucy still couldn't see what was in the tub, but she finally caught the scent. Blood. Lots of it, but all polluted and foul. She cringed and nearly gagged. She never thought she could have that reaction to something that would normally be so sensuous and delectable, but this wasn't the good, clean, hot vapors of life, strength, and need. They'd mixed it with other, lesser stuff. It smelled like animals—maybe dogs or pigs, and that gave it such a weak, stale, but penetrating odor. This must be the feeding the women had mentioned before, and what a wretched, debased version it was of real feasting. These stupid, live fuckers could ruin anything.

Ben approached the tub. In the dimness, Lucy could see him point to Carole and gesture her over. He grunted, rather than speaking, since they were so close to the guards in the towers. Carole led Lucy and Christine with her to the feeding trough. The smell got worse. Even though Lucy stopped inhaling, the stench stung her eyes, it was so piercing and intense. Standing next to the tub, she could now see it was full of blood and scraps of flesh. The slurry was dark, almost black. They must've run it through a machine, it was such a soupy and indistinguishable mess. None too fresh, either, by the smell of it, though it was definitely dead and not undead flesh.

The other two women and Ben each dipped a hand into it. They brought these to their mouths and proceeded to slurp and smack their way through the offering, following that with groans of satisfaction and further craving. They plunged their hands back into the stew, this time with more vigor. Lucy slowly extended her hand, easing her fingers into the flesh and blood. Shit—it was icy cold, on top of all its other loathsomeness. How could the others tear into it with such abandon? But Lucy knew. She still remembered eating, and knew she needed it, no matter how awful these people had made it. She would do it, even if she hated it, and hated herself for giving in.

The hideousness was so overwhelming, it limited and contained the hunger, even as the burning need enticed and ensnared her. Lucy drew out her hand, clutching a stringy piece of flesh between her thumb and two fingers. It was tough, sinewy. She rolled it between her fingers till it was a knotty lump, which she placed on the palm of her other hand to consider it a moment. This was hell, when even pleasure was revolting.

Lucy chewed the piece, the flood of energy from it so fleeting compared to the slowly building, diseased simmer it started in her belly. This simultaneously burned and froze her guts, as it compacted and wrenched her soul. As she swallowed, Lucy leaned her head back and looked at one bright star above her. She focused all her despair on that spot of light as she let out a howl that others—living or dead—might mistake for the climax of desire.

Chapter 30
Rachel

Rachel and Shayna were nearly back to their neighborhood when they ran into Ken and another man. "Hey, you two," Ken greeted them as he gave his wife a kiss on the cheek, then bent down to fuss with Aisha.

"Hey, you," Shayna answered. "Hi, Roger," she said to the other man. "Off work early? What're you two up to?"

"Yeah, we couldn't keep working until they got some more materials. They said they'd have them tomorrow. Oh, Rach—this is Roger," Ken continued. "I don't know if you've seen him around the site."

"No, I don't think I have," Rachel said, smiling. "Nice to meet you."

"Same here," Roger said as he shook her hand. He was her age or a bit older, and only a little taller than she was. Small, ordinary-looking white guy with sandy hair. Didn't seem quite as nice as Ken, and definitely not as outgoing, but certainly not as crude as some of the men from work.

Ken held a sheet of paper out to her. "Some kids came by, handing these out," he said.

Rachel took the paper and held it so Shayna could read it too. It proclaimed that, "Tonight Only! At the Dead End—A Show of Discipline and Violence! See the Savage Threat to Mankind Punished! See the Dead Tamed—Even If It Kills Them! Your Curiosity Will Be Satisfied! Justice Will Be Served! Zombies! Pain! Laughter! As Only Doctor Jack Can Present Them! Free Popcorn! (Beer and Wine Available for Purchase with Proper ID)." In smaller print at the bottom it offered, "Adult tickets—buy two get one free—only with this coupon."

"That's nasty," Shayna said, wrinkling her nose. "Why you wanna go see that? Isn't that where they knock that big, ugly zombie down? I heard someone talking about that."

"No. He's there too, but this is different," Roger explained. "Some zombie got a little rambunctious, so they're gonna teach him a lesson. Show him who's boss. I think they use electricity. It should be fun to watch."

"Yeah, we haven't been to anything like that in a while," Ken said, a little more sheepishly than his friend, clearly ready to defer to Shayna if she gave more of an objection. Rachel thought, not for the first time, that he was a guy who was appropriately deferent to his woman, and yet still so manly. Great combination. "I just thought, you know, maybe you'd like to come along, since it'd be free for you anyway. I mean, if you don't mind babysitting, Rach."

"Oh, no, it's fine," Rachel said. "Don't worry." She really didn't mind watching Aisha at all, and the show did sound pretty gross and barbaric. But she couldn't help feeling just a twinge of disappointment, at having to miss some new, unknown experience. It was natural to get curious about something like that. Besides, Will had said they'd taken Truman to the Dead End. Maybe she'd see him while they were going around the displays, and she could put to rest some of her concerns about his well-being—and more importantly, Will's anxieties. Truman never made any trouble, so he probably was just fine, taking people's tickets or making the popcorn or something, and she could tell Will about it and get him to calm down and not worry so much. But, well, she'd have to do it some other day, she supposed.

Shayna patted Rachel on the shoulder. "No, you don't need to, girl," she said. "I don't want to go. Just a couple months ago I saw a kid being whipped for stealing. Don't need to see something like that again for a while."

"You didn't tell me about that," Ken said.

"Well, Aisha was still real little, so when you got home I was probably too tired to remember everything we did that day. We were taking a walk, and we went through the park. They had a black boy tied to a post. It was still cold out, I remember, so I didn't really stop to watch, but just saw them whip him a few times as I walked by. Anyway—I know they have to do stuff like that, but I don't need to see it all the time. Better they just do it and get it over with and leave me out of it, I say. But you could go, Rachel. You should. It's good to see different things."

"You think?" Even though she felt a rush of excitement at the prospect, Rachel started to have all the usual doubts. Would Will be upset about it? He usually didn't get home until much later than she did, so it wasn't like she was wasting time they could spend together—not that he'd been any fun lately, anyway. And it didn't cost anything, so he couldn't complain about that.

"Yeah, come on," coaxed Ken. "It'll be fun. We won't stay long."

"Okay, sure," Rachel agreed. "Just let me run in the house and leave Will a note."

She trotted inside the entryway of her house. As she set her purse down, Rachel considered hiding it in the closet and leaving without it, she was still so scared of losing it or leaving it somewhere. But then she'd have to strap her shoulder holster back on, and she didn't feel like that. So after scribbling a short note, she grabbed the handbag and headed out.

After that brief detour, the three of them started walking. They chatted about the job and what might be built next in the city. Rachel wondered if she'd even be here for the next building project. She'd need to discuss things more with Will. This whole fixation of his with getting out of the city as soon as possible, and his depression with being here—all of it was starting to annoy her. It didn't make sense. If she saw Truman this evening and he was fine, then she'd present that evidence to Will and he'd have to start thinking and acting more reasonably. Rachel didn't want to think about the possibility of leaving him, or even about having a big fight over it, but she had to be practical, had to look out for her own happiness. That was just normal.

They passed through the gate into the Dead End, a tent city just outside the walls of New Sparta. Stepping outside was a bit of a rush, even to Rachel, who hadn't been in the city that long. It wasn't like when she was on the job—there were guards and stuff then. This was more naughty and thrilling—not a place like work that you had to go to, but a place you weren't supposed to, but chose to anyway, even with that knowledge. Once when she was little, her brother had taken her to an abandoned factory near their home, and this place reminded Rachel of that—somewhere forbidden, broken, dangerous, and wrong.

The smells of tobacco and beer were pervasive as they walked among the tents and ramshackle buildings. They were accented with an occasional whiff of urine, gunpowder, and marijuana, all of it swirling into the nastiest but most compelling mixture Rachel could imagine. Every smell and sound drew them to explore further. Roger dropped off some money on zombie blackjack. Ken playfully covered Rachel's eyes, making her laugh, as they walked past a tent proffering the allures of zombie strippers. This was a lot more fun than she'd had in ages, but it also made Rachel angry that Will would probably never consent to come to a place like this.

"Hey—it's getting late," Roger observed. "We don't want to miss the show. Where is that Doctor Jack's tent?"

"Don't know," Ken said. "I haven't been here in forever."

"They should've put a map on the flyer they handed out," Rachel added.

"Yeah. I think it's up here," Roger said. "Let's hurry."

They found the right tent, indicated mostly by the size of the crowd lined up outside it. The two men paid for their tickets, gallantly refusing Rachel's offers of helping to pay. That was just as well, since she'd splurged on the bag, but she felt like she had to be polite. They also offered to buy her a beer when they got two for themselves at a stand outside the tent. Rachel had enjoyed the drink when she had it at Ken and Shayna's house, so she was tempted, but she had to decline this time. As heady and alluring as the scents of the Dead End were, they were starting to get to her a little, making her feel pretty nauseous at the thought of drinking beer. She joined Ken and Roger in laughing at the dead man who gave them their beers, because he was so intent, and seemingly so proud of his ability to pick up a bottle, open it with a metal opener, and hand it to the next customer, repeating the same motions over and over.

The line into the tent snaked past another stand, where a dead man handed them the promised bags of free popcorn. He was dressed in a blue uniform and wore a paper hat. They'd put gloves on him, and no one seemed to mind being served food by a zombie, so Rachel hid her surprise and slight distaste. She didn't want to seem boorish or uncivilized.

The popcorn was cold and too salty, making Rachel's lips sting as she bit into the first handful. But she was really hungry, so she grabbed another handful as she stepped through the entrance of the tent. She was chewing that mouthful when she saw Truman in the center of the tent, strapped to some metal frame.

Rachel choked and could not keep her balance as she realized what was happening. The curiosity she'd felt when first hearing about the show no longer seemed natural or normal, and the pleasure she'd felt earlier in the evening at all the sights now turned into a cold, bitter pain in her stomach. Ken had to grab her to keep her from falling down, as she stumbled into him and began shivering uncontrollably, her popcorn spilling on the ground.

Ken's big arm held her—and although the grip was comfortable and strong, it didn't seem at all reassuring now to Rachel. She managed to rally enough to look at what was going on in the center of the tent. Truman appeared unconscious. She couldn't really tell what the big man in the suit was saying, but he clearly was in charge. He towered over a small black girl. What was she doing in this terrible place?

"What's wrong, girl?" she heard Ken say next to her. It was probably his normal tone, but it sounded petulant and accusatory.

"They can't do that!" she sobbed. "What is that thing? They're electrocuting him?"

"Yeah, too bad we missed most of it," Roger said through mouthfuls of popcorn. "But they'll probably let him come back around and zap him some more. It's still early."

"No!" Rachel shrieked and threw herself at the man in the middle of the tent. She had to punch one guy in the face to get to the larger man, who was turning toward her as she howled and gave him a left to the side of his head. She raked her nails along his nose and cheek, but then the first guy she'd hit, along with another assistant, grabbed her from behind.

"You get outta here!" the big man with the goatee shouted as he and the assistants, joined by others, started pushing Rachel from the tent. "Crazy woman! Upsetting normal people! Now get!"

Rachel had dug in her heels and was thrashing around, screaming the whole time. "No! You can't! Let him go!"

"Look, lady," the man said, "that's just crazy talk. If you have money, that's something we can discuss later. But you're nuts if you think you can come in here and try to make me give you something just because you say so. Now go!"

"He doesn't belong to you! He's not your property!"

"The hell he isn't!"

"Come on, Rach," Ken said, taking hold of her and trying now to shield her from some of the pushing and shoving, but at the same time helping to hustle her from the tent.

"This your woman?" the man in charge said. "You oughta keep her under control. You people on drugs, out here with law-abiding folks?"

"No, she's just—" Ken didn't seem to know how to continue, and he turned toward Rachel. "Rach—you got to calm down. I don't know what's wrong with you. This isn't right."

"Of course this isn't fucking right!" Rachel howled, still swinging with her purse and her fist. "They're torturing someone! What's wrong with you people?"

"Nothing! What's wrong with *you*, crazy bitch?" the man yelled as they finally got her outside the tent. It was drizzling outside. The rain felt good on her face, helped clear her thoughts a bit, though it didn't diminish her anger and frustration at all.

Rachel turned to face him, panting from the exertion. The large man and his assistants stood blocking the entrance to the tent. Rachel ran her tongue around the inside of her lower lip and tasted blood. Must've cut it in the struggle. She was pissed enough and high enough on adrenaline to think of pulling the .38 out of her bag. She knew, of course, that it would accomplish nothing and just get her killed or arrested, but there was a part of her that wanted to see that moment of fear on his face, wanted him to realize that pushing her around might end badly for him.

Ken kept trying to calm her down. Maybe he sensed how close she was to taking it too far. "Come on, Rach," he said again. "You should calm down. We should go."

They were backing away from the tent. "You definitely need to keep that woman under control," the man called to them as he waved dismissively.

Rachel tensed and almost made a move to spring again, but Ken gripped her more firmly. "Stop it," he said in a low voice. It was the first time Rachel had ever heard him sound really angry, and the change was as disappointing as it was unexpected. "Just stop it, or Roger and I will go and leave you here and I don't know what'll happen to you."

Rachel let herself be led farther from the tent, then she turned on Ken. "Go ahead and leave, then," she said, looking from him to Roger and back. "I don't fucking care."

Ken didn't look angry anymore, but more hurt, confused, almost scared. "What's going on with you?" he said. "We were having a good time and you went nuts in there. I don't get it."

"You don't get it? They were torturing him. Did you *get* that? I got to hope he's not dead, or it's my fault." Rachel had to catch herself a moment when she said that last part, or her guilt and grief would overwhelm her anger and she'd break down completely. She was again glad for the rain, as it hid the little sniffle she gave as she peeled the matted hair back from her face.

"What're you talking about?" Ken said. "It was just a zombie. It's just for fun. You're not making sense."

"No, you're not making sense. He's a person, and it's my fault he's in there. I got to make this right. You got money? That big guy wanted money."

"I can't give you money to buy that thing. You got to be crazy."

"Leave her, man," Roger said, trying to pull Ken away from Rachel. "I think she really is nuts. I never seen a woman act like that, hitting people and shit. Maybe she's on drugs, like that guy said."

"Yeah, maybe," Ken said, some of the anger creeping back into his voice, though it still sounded mostly like fright mixed with disappointment, maybe even a hint of feeling betrayed. "And I almost left her alone with Aisha tonight. You got to tell me what's wrong with you, girl, or I'm not letting you near my family again."

"*Let* me?" Rachel's voice rose. God, she'd had everything so ass-backwards for so long. She'd blamed Will for so much, and she'd forgotten what unbelievable pricks other guys could be. "*Let* me? You're not the fucking boss of me. You don't *let* me do anything. And you sure as hell don't tell me to do anything, either.

Or did you get it in your head that I'm your *girl* or your *woman*? Is that what you think?"

"No, no, I didn't mean it that way. Just calm down."

"No. Fuck that all. That shit I just saw in there finally got my head straight. You people sit and watch that stuff? You cheer as you eat your cold popcorn and your bad beer and some poor guy who's better than you has his brains fried? For Christ's sake - you even let a kid in there to see that? I wouldn't care if I didn't know him - I still couldn't watch that. You're sick. You're messed up. Animals don't fucking act like that."

Rachel reached in her purse and pulled out the holster with the .38 still in it. Both men gasped and backed away from her.

"Oh shit," Roger said, hiding behind his friend. Ken had his 9mm on his hip but didn't make a move for it. Roger wasn't even packing. Idiots—both of them.

Rachel threw the handbag at Ken. "God, you two really do think I'm fucking insane," she said as she slipped on the holster. "I'm not gonna shoot you. I just don't want that bag. I don't want anything from you people." She got the holster on all the way and drew her shoulders back. "There. That's how I'm gonna carry my gun from now on. You mind? Anybody mind a girl with her gun out for everyone to see?"

"No, no, it's fine," Ken and Roger both said, backing farther away from her.

Rachel set off from them at a jog, splashing in puddles as she went. God, she really was out of shape, as she was panting after just a little while. The running was making her feel nauseous again, too. But she didn't let up. She kept pushing herself to continue on through the dark streets of the city.

Chapter 31
Truman

Earlier that day, Truman had sat in his cage, waiting for his big show later in the evening. He watched the living people come and go from the tent as they brought in all the various parts to the electrical contraption they would use on him later. He didn't even have the comfort of Ramona; she never sat close to him when they were around. Truman frowned. So much stuff you had to keep from weak, ignorant people, lest they get frightened and kill you.

Late in the afternoon, Doctor Jack approached Truman's cage. "Get up, you," he said. Truman considered disobeying the command, but eventually decided there was no point and acquiesced. He rose and stepped over to face the larger man.

Doctor Jack sized him up again. "You're awfully popular," he said, dragging the "aw" sound out. "I'm giving your friends the night off. It'll be all you tonight, Professor. I sent some kids into the city to hand out flyers for your special show, and they keep coming back and asking for more to give out. I'd think they were throwing them in the trash to get paid more, but they're good kids, like Dalia. So I think you're gonna draw a pretty good crowd. Shouldn't surprise me, I suppose. Haven't had a hanging in years.

Some whippings, and those got huge crowds, but we haven't even had one of those for a couple months. See—smart people learn not to do crazy shit and get in trouble. But not you dumb asses."

He paused and considered Truman some more, nodding. "We don't really kill you folks much anymore, either. Just not as many of you left around, at least not near the city. I guess people are about set for a nice, long show of discipline, punishment, pain—all that good stuff. Makes them feel right. Shows them things work out the way they're supposed to."

Truman examined the torture device in the middle of the tent. As Ramona had said, it looked like a bed—or more precisely, the old wire frame and springs of a mattress. It leaned against the tent support at about a forty-five degree angle. Thick cables ran from the frame to some device with a large crank handle sticking out of it. A few cables also connected to a black box on an old bar stool. Truman thought the whole thing looked strangely appropriate— simple, shoddy, and dirty.

"Yes, sir, the way they're supposed to," Doctor Jack continued. "But not always, not exactly. That's just why folks love things like tonight—makes them believe that way, believe the world is the way it's supposed to be. But things are—messier than all that. Last time we got one of you all and gave him some special training, poor fellow couldn't take it." He shook his head, and Truman might've mistaken his look and tone for real sadness if he hadn't already heard the story from Lou. "Poor kid. Rat boy." He chuckled. "That was some show he put on, though, fighting rats like he did. Can't believe we even thought of that. Some of the boys and I were sitting around, drinking and playing cards, and we kept seeing all these rats running around. Don't know why, in particular, that night. But it made us think one of you all could fight them. Lot easier than catching sharks and keeping a big glass tank from leaking—though whoo-boy! People loved that too, for sure!"

He scowled and looked serious again. "All right, enough of that. What I was saying is that we have here a very blunt instrument. No warranties anymore. You all don't come with any, either. So we do the best we can. We're gonna make tonight bad for you, so you don't go acting up again. I'd rather not finish you off, but don't you think that'll mean it's gonna be easy. No—this is gonna be a long night for you. We're gonna do some other training tonight, too, I think. No sense wasting an opportunity for people to learn. No, that's important."

Shortly after that, people began filling the tent, which had been lit with torches tonight. Doctor Jack was ever the showman—the firelight gave it the foreboding, barbaric look of a dungeon. Some of the spectators would examine Truman for a moment before finding a place to sit. He stood impassively, not really feeling like snarling at them. It all seemed inevitable and he just wanted to get on with it.

Then he saw Dalia over by the entrance. Truman threw himself against the bars, causing the people who were gawking at him to jump back and gasp. How could they let her in for this? Truman cursed himself again, for thinking they might have limits. He should have known better by now.

At the commotion around Truman's cage, Doctor Jack immediately came over and poked at him with a wooden pole. It was about the length and thickness of a broom handle. "Back, you," he said in a loud voice, not quite shouting. "You're in enough trouble as it is." He leaned closer and spoke more softly, so only Truman could hear him. "You think you're a brave little dead fucker, don't you? You don't mind if this goes on longer and hurts more?"

Truman didn't, not a bit. He had only cared for it to hurry up and begin, and now he only cared that they'd subject Dalia to the horrible spectacle.

"Well, how about you think of what she has to see, and how sad it'll make her. You gonna think of that now, and make things easier on everyone—easier on her?"

Now Truman did snarl.

Doctor Jack's eyes sparkled and he smiled. "Oh, yes—a little bit of that will be good for the show! But are you gonna remember that poor little girl and her feelings when we open this cage up and get to business?"

Truman kept his broken teeth bared as he nodded.

The assistants who usually helped with Lou took Truman from his cage and strapped him to the wire frame. The belts were like those on the collar when they'd first taken him prisoner—cold and greasy. He was lucky—Ramona and Lou always had to wear a collar or something on their ankle, while he could move around his cage and didn't always have something touching his skin to remind him that he was tied up like an animal.

Truman closed his eyes and tried to think how maybe this was about his ingratitude: he hadn't been grateful enough for the better treatment he got, compared to the other two wretches in the tent. He should've thought of them, and of Dalia, and behaved himself. He didn't think enough of others.

When the restraints were tight, Truman opened his eyes and strained against the leather. Fuck those thoughts. He'd take all sorts of blame, but not for this shit. He let out a howl and the crowd cheered. Fuck them too. Bunch of fucking animals, they were. He'd give them a show, but why'd they have to bring her here?

"Shut up!" Doctor Jack shouted and gave him a good smack in the ribs with the broom handle. Not too bad, just a little warm up, but the crowd loved it.

Truman turned to see the assistants were now dragging Lou over. What the fuck did they want with him? He was gentle as a kitten. He hadn't done anything wrong. Truman brought his head forward and gave another cry, this one lower and longer.

"Hold him still," Doctor Jack said to the men hauling Lou. "This is for real, so hold on to those chains. That's it. Keep pulling him over here."

Doctor Jack gave Lou the stick across his knees, then the small of his back. The dead man screeched and looked more plaintive than enraged.

"Turn that handle," the living man yelled at Lou. "I know you're not as big a pain as this dumb smart-ass, but you need to show you can still mind!" Doctor Jack struck him two more times—once to his head, once to his shoulder. Lou raised his hands to ward off the blows.

The chains attached to his neck collar went taut as Lou planted his feet and tried to keep them from dragging him forward. Now his look was one of terror as he threw his head back and roared, eyes wide, partly detached jaw flopping side to side. The crowd's cheers nearly drowned out his cries of despair.

Doctor Jack laughed as he kept pummeling the dead men with his stick. "Oh, you're a hoot, Lardo! Didn't put up such a fight when we had you turn the handle for Rat Boy! Is that it? Now you know what the handle does? Ha! You're smarter than I thought, you dumb piss fuck!"

The blows from the stick became more frenzied at this point, and the crowd's sound turned to jeering laughter.

"You actually feel guilty? Is that it? Fuck you! You are! You're guilty as hell! You do everything wrong! Everything is your fault anyway, so just shut the fuck up and do it! Fucking do it!"

They'd succeeded in dragging Lou to the device, but there was nothing more they could do to force him, except beat him over and over. He tilted his head down and caught Truman's gaze. Truman nodded, and after hesitating a moment, Lou's body went limp, the chains going slack as he surrendered. He grabbed the handle and began to turn it, the machinery setting up a whine and then an irregular hum.

"Let's hear it for Lardo, ladies and gentleman!" Doctor Jack shouted. "Give him some positive reinforcement for his good behavior! It's how you train them, you know!"

The crowd gave a combination of applause and some derisive calls of "Fatso!" and "Stupid!"

Doctor Jack walked over to the crowd, gesturing expansively. "Now, while the Great Lardo gets the juice flowing, let me welcome you folks! Sometimes there's positive reinforcement, and sometimes there's negative. I think you all are here for the latter. Am I right?" The crowd sent up a more enthused response to that.

"Now, I'll need a volunteer," he continued, looking over the crowd. "Someone to help inflict this negative reinforcement." Hands shot up at that prospect, as well as shouts. "Good, good. So many people want to help."

Doctor Jack had made his way past much of the crowd and was close to the entrance. "But, you see, it's not just our unfortunate, uncooperative dead friend here who needs to learn," he called out. "So I think the volunteer also should get something out of this." He grabbed Dalia as an assistant shined a spotlight on her. "Here!"

She wasn't here just to observe. No, that would show some restraint or shame on their part. They'd never be satisfied until she was like they were. For a moment Truman strained against his bonds so hard he thought he'd tear his hands off at the wrists. He'd gladly do that, if he could get to them, tear their throats out, taste their blood on this lips, feel their bones snap in his jaws, their flesh tear, hear their screams—not of delight at someone else's pain, but of fear and heartbreak at their own. That's what Lucy would do.

She'd been right about them. Rachel and Will were off doing whatever the merely apathetic and selfish members of their race do with their time—rutting like beasts, or eating dainty foods, or listening to music. Oh, music—would poor Lucy ever get to hear any again? While those two ingrates got what they wanted, he and Lucy were subjected to the degradations dreamed up by those living people who indulged in greater, more imaginative cruelties. Killing them would be a mercy to those among them who hadn't yet become as diseased as the rest.

After this moment of rebellion and despair, however, Truman relaxed. He had to be strong—for Dalia. If he showed all his outrage, disgust, and pain, it would be harder on her. Her anguish at what was happening was not his fault, but he had the power—and therefore, the responsibility—to alleviate it. He'd never forgive himself if he failed at that duty. He'd never forgive the living, regardless.

Dalia struggled a little, but let herself be led over to the black box on the bar stool. When they got there, Truman could hear Doctor Jack speaking to her in angry, low tones.

"You need to learn as much as he does," he was saying.

"No, Doctor Jack," she pleaded, glancing at him, Truman, and the crowd. "I know you have to punish him. But you do it. I don't want to. I can't."

"You can and you will. I won't let you train any more of these things. And I won't be so gentle with them anymore, either. And this one—I might just shoot him tonight when we're done here, and that'd be your fault."

"No!" Her scream was so loud and sudden, it quieted even the raucous crowd for an instant, and there was only the hum of the machinery Lou was turning.

Doctor Jack leaned closer to her. "Yes," he hissed. "Now do it."

Dalia stepped to the box and put her hand on a large dial on one side of it. As he had done with Lou, Truman gave her a tiny nod, but it was more difficult for her to go through with what she had to do. Innocence was as strong as it was fragile—it held up to every assault until it just snapped at a certain point. Truman would witness her moment of loss, but he'd give her the strength to endure it, if he could. They held each other's gaze, her eyes and cheeks wet with tears, as she turned the dial, just a bit.

The first jolt was nothing, less than the beating with the broom handle, even. It tingled was all. Truman gained confidence that he could do this.

"Now, it doesn't do just to give the beast pain," Doctor Jack called to the crowd. "As I said—it's negative reinforcement. He has to associate the pain with some object, so he learns to keep away from that thing."

Doctor Jack came closer to Truman, careful not to touch the metal frame. He rolled the sleeve of his jacket back to the middle of his forearm and extended the limb over Truman's face. "Turn the dial, Dalia," he said, keeping his eye on Truman.

As the tingling increased to a dull ache and burning, Truman didn't look at Doctor Jack or the proffered arm, but stared into Dalia's wet brown eyes, showing as little of the pain as he could.

"You'll have to turn it up more, girl," Doctor Jack shouted. "Tell her, people!"

The crowd roared. Dalia was no longer just standing with tears running down her cheeks, but she was more violently weeping, her body shaking, collapsing down and then coming back up as she took in sobbing breaths. But her eyes stayed on Truman's and he still felt sure they could make it.

The pain was up to a wringing sensation in all Truman's body, a stretching or twisting of every nerve and muscle.

Doctor Jack leaned close, bringing his body in between Truman and Dalia so he couldn't look at her. The son of a bitch. "Look at it, you dumb, hungry bastard," he said in a low voice for Truman, not the crowd. Truman finally looked at the arm above his face. It was thick, like that of the man he'd attacked the day before. Truman knew how bad the blood tasted, how it burned and hurt to swallow. But he knew how much he wanted to make them suffer, and that was all he could think of, all he could imagine or desire— their pain, their loss, their weakness, their wretched, useless pleading.

The electricity made all that moot, of course. Truman's jaw was clamped shut and his neck was bent back, holding his mouth away from the man's arm, regardless of what he wanted to do.

"I see you fuckers sniffing around, so I know you can smell," Doctor Jack continued, grinning. "This must look and smell like juicy porterhouse, hot apple pie, the best fucking bourbon, and the nicest, sweetest pussy you ever could hope to get this close to—all rolled into one!" He didn't take his eyes off Truman as he shouted to Dalia to increase the current. Truman's back arched and his whole body shook. It felt like the vertebrae would just pop out and he'd be a twitching rag doll in a moment. The crowd cheered.

"Now you remember this. Getting this close to live meat is pain. It's bad. You get this close to someone ever again and I'll have her fry you on this thing like a bug under a fucking magnifying glass. How you think that'll make her turn out?"

Doctor Jack stood up and rolled down his sleeve. The crowd applauded the torture and Truman felt the pain decrease.

"No!" Doctor Jack roared. "You stop that, girl! You turn that back up now!" The pain gradually increased back to its previous level. At least Truman could see Dalia again. Her weeping was more controlled now, and she seemed reassured to see him still alert and looking at her. Through the buzzing in his head, Truman thought he could hear rain on the canvas of the tent.

"These two need to learn some more," Doctor Jack continued, standing behind Dalia, his hands on her shoulders. "People can't be friendly with these monsters. It isn't right. So we'll get you two to associate pain with it." He put his hand on top of Dalia's, holding the dial. "Tell him how you feel about him, Dalia. Do that and we'll be able to finish." He made her turn the dial.

"I like him," the girl wailed. The crowd laughed.

"Tell him, not me."

"I like you."

"Tell him more. You've worked together every day. I've seen you. You trust him."

Truman couldn't really say the pain increased at that point. It was sort of past the point where he could note gradations in it. The only added sensation he noticed was a pressure inside his head, like it was going to implode. He wished it would. He didn't know what use his brain was anymore, except to remember and think about hideousness like this, over and over, day after day, night after night.

"I trust you," Dalia said. Oddly, she'd calmed down somewhat. Perhaps Truman had succeeded in hiding any further pain. Though it was nearly impossible to think now, the feeling of triumph at that thought was overwhelming to him.

"And you more than like him. You don't have a daddy. You look at this thing and you love him. You think you can save him, take care of him, make him happy, make him safe. But you can't.

But tell him anyway, so both of you will know what to think of that feeling."

Dalia looked completely calm now to Truman, though it was hard to focus on her, he was shaking so much. And even though the crowd's cheering was louder than before, Truman heard her perfectly as she said, "I love you." He didn't see Doctor Jack turn the dial further, but knew he must've, because the pressure in his head and the thrashing of his body made the whole scene before him into a blur, though the brown smudge of Dalia's face in the middle of it retained some radiance, if not clarity.

Truman did not know he could still lose consciousness. It had never happened in all the years he'd been dead. If it weren't for the pain, it would have been one of the most delightful experiences he could imagine, reminding him of sleep and comfort. He didn't think he closed his eyes, as he was unable to move anything anymore, but his vision slowly closed in around Dalia, then darkened completely. The pain remained constant as this happened, though at the very end it lessened slightly, as he heard other voices, including a woman's. That seemed odd at this point. They sounded like they were arguing.

As the pain decreased, Truman had the most joyous thought that the living people were tearing each other apart, eating each other alive there in the hot, musty darkness. That would be how things were supposed to be, and that idea made Truman the happiest he'd been in days.

Chapter 32
Will

Will had been out in the wilderness enough he could find his way back to the city by cutting through fields and woods instead of keeping to the road. He didn't want to be walking along there as the wagon made its way back. He didn't know what to say to those guys if they caught up with him. What happened to Mike was horrible. But things like that were just part of life. But what they'd discussed doing to him afterward? That was unnatural. That was evil.

Will knew the dead would never know he'd been there, he moved so quietly. His last words to Garrett were not bragging: the dead truly did not scare him. Their presence in the world didn't bother him, didn't present him with dilemmas he couldn't understand or guilt he couldn't assuage. In fact, the hours making his way through the countryside back to New Sparta were about the calmest he'd spent in some time, even though the same thoughts plagued him. Will had gained a certain clarity, focus, and resolve that had been painfully lacking in the last few weeks. He still didn't know exactly how things would work out, but what he would do when he got back to the city and found Rachel had become much clearer to him. They'd get out of that house. Sell all the crap they'd accumulated. They'd sleep on the boat—hell, they were paying for the dockage anyway. They'd sleep out here in the woods if they had to, if there were some stupid law about people not being allowed to sleep on boats at the city dock. But they'd get out of that city now. Rachel could keep working her job and they'd get Truman and Lucy out and be free of this place.

Jumping across a ravine and continuing on through a field, Will wondered if Rachel would go along with that. She had become so different since coming to the city. He wanted her to be happy, of course, but he didn't understand what mattered to her, what made her happy now. He could tell she wasn't as eager to leave as he was—he'd even wondered recently if she wanted to leave at all. When she found out what they did here—how they treated both living and dead—she'd have to see, she'd have to agree.

He loved her so much, and remembered how beautiful and carefree she used to be, both when they were on the boat, and before that, when they lived in their old town. As much as she used to sleep around, there had been a kind of simple, innocent carelessness even about that. Everything about her had been perfect, or he could always see the perfection in it, at least. Now—something was obscured, lost, darkened about her. But he had faith in her, and he knew there was no way she would want to hold on to their comfortable life, once she found out all the horror underneath and around it. There was, quite literally, no way to be carefree in New Sparta. It seemed to Will that the place ran on care and concern, worry and want. He had to get away from it. He'd try his best to convince Rachel of that, but there was no way he was staying there another day.

Later, running in the shade of some woods, he saw a huge crowd of dead people shuffling along the road to the city. They were all dressed in the funny striped shirts. Will kept moving, observing them as he went. Was Lucy in that group? No way he could go down there and find out. Even if they were dead people partly under the control and command of the living, a crowd of a hundred was nothing to fool around with. And what would Lucy be like now, anyway? How much human flesh had she eaten, and what effect had that had on her? Will felt sick when he thought they could be feeding her bits and pieces of Mike tomorrow. If he were growing increasingly confused and confounded by how Rachel acted in the city, how much worse would it be to see what Lucy turned into, under the influence of these people? If he did manage to get her out, would he ever be able to trust her or turn his back on her after this? All her hard work, all her self-control, and maybe they'd turned her back into a monster. Will picked up his pace and determined to get her out, regardless.

Sliding down an embankment that would keep him out of sight of the shambling horde, Will found that he still had the clarity he needed to confront such questions. Rachel was only alive now because Lucy had sacrificed her own safety and happiness. Fuck all of New Sparta's rules about credit and fees and interest and loans: the debt they owed that woman was the only one that had to be repaid, no matter what.

Garrett had been correct about Will not getting back until after dark. But as he walked through the checkpoint at the city gate, his fear increased way beyond what it had been out in the wilderness with dead people all around. The place was noisy and it stank, though the rain that had started falling slightly improved the smell. Will didn't know how he and Rachel had ever tolerated it here, let alone how they could've gotten so used to it, so enamored of all its offerings, so tolerant of all its demands.

Rachel wasn't at the house when he got there. He found a note from her, that she'd gone to the Dead End with Ken and a guy from work. Will tried to think of how to deal with this unforeseen complication. Also, he admitted to himself, he had to restrain his rising anger and jealousy. The jealousy was just him being childish. And the anger? Well, that was more reasonable, since she'd gotten so obsessed with all the fun to be had in the city. But now, he felt sure she'd understand how wrong it was, once he explained what he'd seen happen today. They'd pack what they could carry and be out of there in the morning. There'd doubtless be all kinds of paperwork to fill out, but she'd help him with that ordeal and they could plan on how to get Lucy and Truman back. So he just needed to focus on that, on what he'd tell Rachel when she got home and how they'd clear out the next day.

Will was in the kitchen, shoving cans of food into a duffel bag of clothes when Rachel came in, panting, soaked from the rain. She sounded like she'd been running for some time. She glanced at him, then bent down to grab her thighs as she tried to catch her breath.

"Rachel, where'd you run from?" Will asked, all his other concerns pushed aside once he thought there might be a problem with her. "What's wrong?"

"From—Dead—End," Rachel gasped, separating each word with a pant. "It's—long—ways.—Sorry."

"It's okay. Catch your breath and we'll talk. We've got to talk."

Will gave her a few seconds. As her breathing slowed, she stood up all the way and grabbed his shoulder. "We've got to get out of here," she said.

"What?" Will said. "What happened? I thought you liked it here."

"I did. But I saw Truman. He was in some kind of carnival they have set up there. They were torturing him. Electrocuting him, over and over. God, it was awful, and the people thought it was all fun. Even Ken said it was no big deal, and I used to think he was so nice and thoughtful. I couldn't believe what they were doing. I was sure they were gonna kill him right in front of me and it'd be my fault. I finally ran up and yelled at them to stop, but we have to get him out of there." She grabbed his shoulders. Her eyes were wet, and not just from the rain. "We *have* to. Right away."

"Okay. But it's not your fault. You didn't know."

Rachel sniffled, then lowered her brows. Will had never noticed she looked prettier when she was angry, but he was quite struck by it now. "No, it is," she said in a harsh tone. "I was too stupid and gaga over this place. Please, please, you have to help me get him out of there. And Lucy too. Oh God—I almost forgot about her, and she's probably in a bad place, too. We have to do this. Right away. Tonight. Not waiting around and making plans and talking about it. Just doing it."

"I think I saw Lucy," he said. "I was running back from where we were foraging and I saw a crowd of dead people on patrol. She might've been in there."

"Wait—running? Why were you running back? What happened?" She'd expressed concern for him before, of course, when he'd talk about work, but it sounded so much more passionate and real tonight.

"One of the other guys was bitten, and they wanted me to shoot him. I couldn't, so I just left them out there. I didn't want to have to deal with them and all their craziness anymore."

"That's terrible." Rachel let go of him and seemed to deflate, her shoulders dropping and her sinking. "I'm so sorry," she said in a quieter voice. "God, I've been so stupid. It's my fault all of you are in all these different messes now. I don't know how any of you can forgive me."

"You were sick and we had to take care of you," Will said, touching her shoulder. "That's not your fault. I know."

"No, but everything since is. I was spoiled and wanted to stay. I was comfortable and lazy. I've been such a selfish bitch."

"You didn't know what was going on. They hide the bad stuff. That's why I ran, too." Will paused, biting his lower lip. "They weren't just going to shoot the other guy. I know some people don't want to get up and walk around after they die. You even talked about that, when you were sick. But they wanted the body so they could sell it and feed it to dead people. That was too much for me. They hid those kinds of things from us, or you would've wanted to leave sooner. So don't feel so bad, Rach."

Rachel opened her mouth, and even went as far as heaving a little, before turning and covering her mouth with the back of her hand. When she turned back, she still looked sick and ready to vomit, but some of the anger and determination had returned. "All right," she coughed. "You're packing? We need to do this now."

"Yes. Just food and clothes."

"Good. I don't want anything else from here."

Will still didn't know how this was going to work out, but with that response, his doubts and anxiety about her vanished.

Chapter 33
Lucy

The women shuffled into their home after the feeding, the smell of the blood clinging to them. Even though she'd only had the one piece, it felt to Lucy as though a strand of it was stuck between every one of her teeth, while the rest of it remained a burning lump in her gut. She'd run her tongue all around her mouth, all night, over and over, but always the phantom, wriggling little bits of evil would still be there when she was done. She'd never eat slop like that again. The next time she tasted blood, she was going to make sure it was done right—pure and passionate, like a consecration and not a vile poisoning.

Sometime in the night Lucy heard a light rain falling on the roof. She sat there with Carole and Christine in their usual spots, saying nothing, their individual shame and weakness slowly giving way by morning to the fragile strength of the bond between them.

Lucy walked out front just as the sun rose. It had stopped raining, though there were still puddles on the ground from the night before. She paused to look up at the guard tower and was greeted by a whistle. The one who liked her body so much was still on duty. Yesterday's show hadn't been enough, apparently. No, he'd want something more elaborate and personal before he'd leave her alone. She slowly unbuttoned the big, striped shirt and kind of swayed, as though to music. Of course, in her mind there was music—the fourth movement of Mahler's Ninth Symphony—slow, with only strings at first. She remembered the piece perfectly, vividly. She should, she'd played and listened to it so many times.

With her eye closed, the whole scene didn't even seem so bad, with that internal soundtrack to keep her mind occupied and entranced. Lucy let the shirt fall partly open, careful to keep her maimed left breast covered, and only reveal the firm, round, smooth right one. The morning air felt cool and damp, but the sun was already shining brightly enough that it deliciously warmed her face and bare skin. She cupped her right breast with her hand, sliding her palm up and over it, then slipping it back down to take her nipple between her forefinger and middle finger. She repeated this motion several times, still with her eye closed, as the symphony's movement progressed and picked up pace.

She could've continued this quite pleasantly to the end of the piece, but she heard a snore and a groan and that broke her reverie. It was early enough in the morning that the other men might still be asleep and she couldn't help but think how her unwanted admirer might actually be masturbating to her display. Though Lucy couldn't articulate why that'd be wrong, exactly, she knew instinctively that it was so sufficiently disgusting that no music, no matter how sublime, could drive the thought from her mind, or let her overlook the way she had to degrade herself for their amusement. Lucy turned and bent at the waist, hiking her shirt up, and then hooking her thumb on the top of her pants to push them down a bit. She slowly ran her left hand in circles over her buttocks, then lightly smacked it a couple times. Hopefully, that'd finally be enough to satisfy him, whatever he was doing, so she stood up and continued walking around the corner of the house.

Once she was out of sight of the guard tower, Lucy buttoned her shirt back up. She went around the house, retrieving the pot she'd put under one of the drain spouts. Holding it behind her back, she slinked to the front of the house and returned inside. Thankfully no one stopped her or demanded anything this time.

The light had increased enough that Lucy could see the other two women in the living room. Lucy grabbed a rag as she went over to Carole first. Bending down, she cleaned the woman's face with the wetted rag, wiping off all the blood, scrubbing her chin especially, where the stains were stubborn and caked on. Lucy turned and did the same for Christine, who looked at her more quizzically than Carole had. It was harder with Christine—she was more jowly and the blood had dried thicker in the creases of skin.

Christine grunted and wiped her face on the back of her sleeve. "Huh. When did you get so into being clean?" she asked.

Lucy sat next to her and started wiping around her own mouth, though she suspected there wasn't nearly as much on her. "I don't know," she said. "I just felt like it. The sun's out."

Christine reached for the pot. "Nothing special about that. You want me to do yours?"

"Sure. Do what you can."

Christine helped clean Lucy off and handed the pot back to her. Lucy looked down at the water. It was stained pink from dipping the bloody rag into it. Lucy sniffed, and it still smelled mostly like rain water, fresh and cold. She raised the pot to her lips and sipped. The metallic taste of the blood and the foulness of the rag did little to obscure the sensation of the water's purity. She swirled it in her mouth before swallowing. Her mouth finally felt clean.

"Take," she said, offering it to Christine. "Drink it. It's not bloody."

Christine grunted again. "It'd taste better if it were," she said, but drank anyway. She passed it on to Carole, who took some as well before setting the pot down.

They sat a while longer before Lucy stood up. "Let's go outside," she said. "The sun will feel nice."

They walked outside. The sun did feel very good, but there was some commotion at the gate, with men climbing down the rope ladders they kept stored up in the towers. They boarded a military-looking vehicle that drove away a moment later, as the ladders were raised back up. Only two rifle barrels protruded from the tower now.

Christine pulled her and Carole away from the tower, back around the corner of their house, as more dead people emerged into the yard. "Something's going on," Christine whispered. She raised her shirt. She still had the bomb there. "If something happens, you want this now?"

"What?" Lucy was shocked. Everything always happened too quickly here. You were either sitting around for days, doing nothing, or people were running around asking you to fight and kill and die right then, in the next two minutes. How did they live like this?

"Food men are going away," Carole said. "There must be trouble. Men here might decide to attack. They always talk about it. Never get up the nerve. But if they do, it might be our time to get out of here."

"I thought you said it was easier to stay here?"

"Easier than wandering off by yourself," Christine said. "If men attack, then it's not so easy, 'cause then we can't just stand there and let them be killed. And maybe then we'll all get out. Maybe we'll hurt the bad men. Teach them a lesson. Maybe they won't come looking for us then, if we hurt them bad enough and run away."

"Can't know for sure," Carole said. "Anything could happen."

Christine leaned forward and put her hand on Lucy's shoulder. "We'll stay with you, if you want to stay here. If you want to go and find your man, we'll help you get out of here. It's up to you. But you're faster than me. You could do more with this, if we need to."

"All right," Lucy said quietly. "I'll try. But I'll need a longer string. I'm not just going to stand there like the ch-ch-children. I don't believe in Santa and the Easter Bunny."

Christine smiled and patted her shoulder. "Yeah. I know. We'll go back inside and find some. Then we'll wait. See what happens."

As they came around the corner toward the door, one of the guards shouted. "Hey, you bitches! Get inside! I don't like you sneaking around right now!" It sounded like Lucy's admirer, but his voice seemed nervous and scared. Good. Lucy had her hand halfway up and was extending her middle finger when Christine shoved her from behind and sent her stumbling into their house.

"It's not time yet, honey," Christine said when they were all through the door.

"Yeah. You're right. Thanks."

"No problem."

Lucy stayed in the front room, while the other two women rummaged around for weapons and some string. Lucy could just see the tower through the grimy window. The sick fucker got his rocks off humiliating her, but he couldn't let her out in the sun?

Little shit was all brave, so long as he had a gun and was out of her reach. She'd see what kind of shape he was in by the end of today.

People like Christine and Carole and Truman—she'd do anything for them. Anything. Maybe even Rachel and Will were good enough, in their own imperfect, selfish way. She could still tolerate them. Hell, she was in this cesspool for Rachel's sake: all this shit better be for something worthwhile, so Lucy couldn't bring herself to think the living girl was utterly undeserving. But people like the guard—they should only fear her, and they clearly needed to be reminded of that.

Lucy moved over to the doorway, out of the line of sight of the tower, and looked up at the sun. Its steady, pitiless light had made her task of reckoning quite clear to her now.

Chapter 34
Rachel

"This gate's closed," the guard said. He sat behind a desk, under an awning next to the gate. Different guy than had waved Rachel through the night before, but equally nonchalant. He turned his attention from them, sipped some coffee, and looked through some papers on the desk.

"Why? What's going on?" Will asked. Rachel had forgotten how cute his plaintive voice could be, how that hint of weakness and need added to his attractiveness. But this wasn't a good time for it at all.

"Stiffs acting up in the Dead End," the guard replied without much concern in his voice, looking over toward the tents, back to the two people in front of him, then down to a grainy, black-and-white television screen that showed a section of the city wall. "Happens sometimes. Can't let anyone in. I'm sure it'll be over in a little while."

Rachel sized up the situation. There were some places in the wall where it wouldn't have been too difficult for them to climb over, if the gate didn't work out. It was still early enough in the morning that it would be unlikely they'd be spotted. But, on the other hand, her shoulder and elbow had been painful and stiff all night, and it'd still be risky.

She sauntered up next to Will. "Letting people in isn't the same as letting them out," she said to the guard, smiling, and bending over the desk. She'd changed out of the dumpy skirt from the night before into some tight jeans, but kept the low cut t-shirt, which was still damp and clingy. The guard eyed her boobs as he sipped his coffee. He was a pretty nasty-looking, middle-aged white guy, greasy and unshaven, hair growing out of his ears—he probably had it on his back, too—so giving him a little show wasn't the greatest thrill for Rachel, but it had to be done if they were going to start undoing all the shit she'd set in motion.

"No, I guess it isn't," he said. "But why do you want to go out there anyway?"

"My Aunt Lucy works in one of the shows," Rachel said, improvising. Had to spin it right—little cleavage, now a little sob story. "Snake handler. Real holy roller." That was right on the edge of pushing it too far. You didn't want to lay it on too thick or with too many details, but she'd seen a tent with people doing that, so she just went for it. "We tell her all the time not to stay out there with the zombies, but she says they're the best snake handlers—bitten over and over and they keep going, like the Bible says people can, if they have real faith. So Aunt Lucy says, if God watches over them, He'll watch over her. Long as she survives being bitten by snakes, she says she'll never be bitten by a zombie. Isn't that weird?"

"Yeah, that's pretty weird, I guess."

Rachel needed to wrap this up, both for them to do what they needed, and because the guard licking his lips while he stared at her tits was grossing her out worse than she expected. She put her hand on the desk and left some bills there: sex, sympathy, money—that was about all she could offer this morning, before they'd have to decide whether to retreat and climb the wall, or snap this ugly fucker's neck. The way the hairs flared out and then back into his nostrils as he breathed made Rachel incline toward the latter.

"So, Mom called me this morning and told me to run right out there and check on Aunt Lucy. We'll just go there now, okay? We won't try to get back until everything's clear—right, honey?" she said, turning to Will.

"What? Yeah, of course," Will said. Including him on the charade was probably a mistake, but it felt more awkward, just having him stand there.

The guard looked around, then slid the bills off the desk and into his pocket. "Yeah, sure, whatever," he muttered.

Rachel hustled Will along, feeling a little better at their chances of success this morning.

Chapter 35
Truman

As Doctor Jack had predicted, Truman could, in fact, pick locks. Learning to do so had been a nice distraction from studying the vocabulary books over the last few days. Truman still wasn't very good at it, however, and it didn't help that he was working in the dim light of early morning, with his head still spinning from what they'd done to him the night before. It took him a long time to get the lock off Ramona's ankle and free her. After he did, she shuffled over and helped Lou pull up the stake to which he was chained.

"Help Truman," she said when they were done with that part of the plan. "I'll get my coat and see what other stuff we can take."

Doctor Jack had also been careful about not letting Truman see the combination to one of the locks on his cage, and Truman definitely had not learned how to undo that kind of lock. He thought you were supposed to listen to it as you turned the dial, but he'd already tried that on many previous nights without success, so he didn't try again this morning. Instead, he'd unscrewed some of the bolts that held the bars to the frame of his cage. The cage had not been carefully constructed, and some bolt heads were exposed, especially along the top. But not all of them, so Truman couldn't simply disassemble the whole thing and slip the bars out. There were some bolts along the bottom holding it together, but with Lou's help, he thought he could now wrench and bend the bars out of the way enough that he could slip through. It was taking more time than he'd expected, and was making more noise, too, with the cage rattling and creaking as they worked.

Truman winced and was temporarily blinded by the lights coming on in the tent. Not the torches of the night before, but the regular house lights. He covered his face as he heard Lou groan from the uncomfortably harsh illumination.

"Well, damn," Doctor Jack said, as Truman brought his hands down and saw the man in the middle of the tent. "And here I was, trying to be nice, getting up early to check on you, to see if you were still moving, and you're trying to get away." He had his pistol out. "You are one annoying little fucker, you know that? You just don't learn. Smart as hell and you don't have any common sense— that's your problem. And now you got poor Lardo on your side. You've gone and gotten him in trouble now, too. But that's always how it is with troublemakers, alive or dead. They just drag other folks into their mess and ruin things for everybody. Now we'll have to think of something special for the two of you. Maybe something with fire. Yeah—people always like that. Oh—make you two dumb asses fight while you're on fire! Yeah, that might work. But anyway, once we finish with you two, I'll hardly have a show anymore and I'll have to buy more stock and train them. Well, at least I have Dalia to help me with that, but still—what a mess."

Truman heard a whistle from the other side of the tent. Doctor Jack turned toward the sound just as the cannon went off. The ball hit him, and he flew up and backward, not as far as Lou had when he did it for his show. He landed on his back and lay still. Truman couldn't see the actual wound, but for a moment he watched the bloodstain grow, darkening the right side of his jacket.

"What're you doing?" Truman said as he went back to working on the bars. "People will hear that. We'll be caught now for sure."

Ramona came over and helped Lou pull on the one bar they'd bent the farthest. "Shhh. Just hurry. They'll think they're just practicing. You know how fucking noisy they are all the time. They won't notice one more bang. They'll go back to sleep."

Truman wriggled through the opening. It felt so good to be out of there, even though his whole body ached and his head still buzzed. He heard a moan from Doctor Jack and walked over to him. Truman couldn't tell if the cannonball were still inside him, or if it had gone all the way through. He didn't see it in the hole in the man's stomach, but that was so full of blood it might be in there, maybe behind all the guts and stuff. It didn't matter, of course, but Truman felt strangely curious about it as he knelt down next to the dying man. Funny, too, how people's muscles tensed up, Truman thought, as he had to use both hands to pry the gun out of Jack's hand. Lou and Ramona stood next to him as he worked on getting it loose.

Doctor Jack gave a wet, wheezing chuckle as Ramona knelt down next to Truman. "Ah, women," Jack said. "I should've known you'd be in on it too."

"Yes, you should've," Ramona hissed. Her eyes narrowed and her look frightened even Truman, though he could hardly blame her for her stored-up hatred.

Doctor Jack laughed a little harder. His wound bled more when he did, so Truman pressed down on his shoulder and tried to shush him. "Stop, calm down," Truman said. "You'll make it hurt worse."

"Oh, fuck, you all can talk. Well, then I guess it was just a matter of time before something like this happened."

"Yeah, we can do lots of things," Ramona said. "You just never bothered to find out." Doctor Jack gasped and writhed under Truman's hand as she plunged her fingers into the wound. She held them there a while, blood welling up to the middle of her forearm as she smiled, then she opened her mouth and sighed. "How's it feel, having something moving around in your guts? How'd you like to do that every night while guys laughed and jerked off and called you their 'babe' and their 'bitch'?"

Ramona brought her bloody, dripping hand to her face and considered it a moment, before taking her pinkie and ring fingers into her mouth, up to the second knuckle. Like everything she did, it seemed sensuous and horrible at the same time.

Ramona held her index and middle finger out to Truman. "You want some?" she said, smiling with bloody teeth. "Only nice thing I've ever gotten from him."

"No, thank you," Truman said quietly.

"Lou? You want to reach in there before we go? Liver should be nice," she said before taking the two fingers in her own mouth.

Truman couldn't help but stare as she worked her lips and tongue around the two bloody digits.

"No," Lou replied. "Lou hasn't wanted to eat since he saw Martin with the rats. Never been hungry since."

Doctor Jack rallied for a moment, raising his voice again and pushing up against Truman's hand, finally forcing Truman's attention away from Ramona. "Fuck you all," he said. "You're a bunch of sick, fucked-up monsters, even if you're not as stupid as I thought. So fuck you." He fell to coughing a bit before he wheezed, went slack, and closed his eyes. Truman thought he'd be gone soon, if he weren't already.

"Oh my God!" someone squealed from across the tent. Truman looked to see Dalia there in the entrance, the sunlight framing her tiny body.

Truman and Ramona both stood as the girl came towards them. Dalia stared at the body, then brought her gaze up to Truman's face. She looked shocked, but as they stared at each other, her features grew harder.

"You killed him?" she said, looking back at the body, then up at Truman again. "You killed him because he hurt you? How could you?"

"No," Truman started. "No, he came in this morning. He had his gun out. He was going to shoot us." Truman showed her the gun, but the gesture only seemed to increase her agitation. She cringed from him and screeched.

Ramona, carefully hiding her bloody hand behind her back, took a step toward Dalia, her other hand extended toward the girl. "He was going to shoot them," she said. "So I shot him with the cannon. It was my fault. Don't be mad at him."

Truman made a show of setting the gun beside Doctor Jack's body before taking a step forward. "There—I don't want that," he said. "I'm sorry we hurt him, Dalia. We didn't know what else to do."

Dalia looked at the body, then at each of them, ending with Truman. "You all can talk—not just the Professor? Then you're all smart. You should've known better than to act like this. I was coming here this morning to see if you were all right. I was gonna tell Doctor Jack I didn't want to be his friend anymore, if he was gonna be so mean. But now you're mean, too. I would've helped you escape, if that's what you wanted, and then you wouldn't have had to hurt him. I know Doctor Jack was mean sometimes, but you were always nice. He was mean to hurt you, but you should've been nice and not hurt him back. Why'd you have to go and ruin that?"

Truman looked in her eyes—those beautiful eyes that'd seen so much they shouldn't have. He hung his head. "I'm sorry. Please forgive me, Dalia."

"It's not up to me," she said. "I forgive you, but I can't be your friend anymore. I can't be friends with bad people, even if I feel sorry for them. Now you all should go before more people come and hurt you and you hurt them. More badness." She shook her head.

"What're you going to do?" Truman asked.

"I'll stay here. He'll need to see someone he knows when he gets back up, or else he'll get scared and angry. He was so smart when he was alive. I'm sure I'll be able to teach him some tricks now, but he won't learn if he's all mad and scared."

Truman looked to the body, then to Ramona, who shrugged. "But he might—not be friendly when he gets up," Truman said.

"No, probably not," Dalia continued. "They never are, at first. But I don't think he'll be able to walk, from the looks of him. That'll make teaching him tricks harder, but it means I don't have to run away now."

"Kid's smart," Ramona said.

Truman bent down to retrieve the pistol, which he carefully gave to Dalia, handle first. "All right, but if any more dead people come close, you run back to your mother, and lock yourselves in your house, okay? And take this to her. You all might need it. I think there's going to be some trouble."

"All right," Dalia said, taking the gun.

"Oh, and Dalia, could you tell me one more thing? I heard something about the City Patrols. Do they have a base near here? Where would I find them?"

"Yeah, their base is just a little farther outside the city walls, and closer to the river." She pointed. "You go out of camp that way, and keep going. You should see it before too long."

"Thank you, Dalia," he said. "I'm so sorry we can't be friends anymore."

"Me, too, Professor," she said, nodding. Her features softened a bit. "But I'll pray for you."

"You will?" Truman had never heard anyone say that, and he didn't quite know how he felt about it—touched, but also a little offended. From anyone but Dalia, the gesture would've seemed oddly presumptuous, he thought. And from her, even the harshest, most judgmental comment or action would have a certain irresistible grace, so how could something as generous and innocent as this remark not move and impress him?

"Oh yes. Jesus says to pray even for your enemies." There was just a hint of her impish smile. "But don't worry—you're not my enemy. I just mean I'd pray for you even if you were. You're just a bad man that I can't be friends with. So I'll pray that you not be so bad."

"Oh. Well, thank you. I appreciate that."

Truman looked back at Dalia as he left with Ramona and Lou. The child was sitting where the now undead Doctor Jack could see her, but far enough out of his reach that he couldn't do anything to her except be perturbed or comforted by her presence. Watching the feeble motions of his arms and listening to his moans, Truman wasn't sure which effect it was having on the dead man, but he now trusted in the girl's judgment and quiet strength even more completely than before.

Chapter 36
Will

As they moved into the Dead End, Will looked back nervously, expecting pursuit or an alarm.

"I didn't think we were going to get past the guard," he said as he and Rachel paused to look around and try to get their bearings. "I wish we had more money for bribes. I don't think we have enough. I don't even know if we have enough to buy Truman out of this awful place."

"Wait," Rachel said. "Here." She got out a pretty good-sized wad of bills and peeled it open. She gave him half and stuck the other half back in her own pocket.

"What? Where'd you get this?" Will said, looking down at the brightly colored paper.

"Those plastic cards that kept coming in the mail. I saved them up. When you fell asleep for a couple hours last night, I went out to those machines they have all over the place. What do they call those things? ATVs?"

"No. ATMs, I think."

"Yeah, whatever. I got out what I could."

"Wow. Thanks."

Rachel smiled and leaned closer to him. "No, thank you—for putting up with me. Now let's find Truman."

Rachel led Will by the hand, as he thought how very beautiful her cunning could be.

Chapter 37
Lucy

Lucy still stood in the doorway when the crowd of dead men started toward the gate, sending up an inarticulate chant of grunts and hoots as they advanced. Funny, how they still refused to speak in front of the live humans. Was it just habit, or did they want to keep something secret, even up to their own ends? No telling with people, living or dead.

The dead men huddled behind several large wooden shields, four or five of them behind each shield, occasionally popping out from behind them to throw rocks at the tower. It seemed a precaution, so the guards couldn't really aim at them, but Lucy didn't know how effective the tactic was going to be.

She watched the guards moving around, one of them getting behind the big, fixed machine gun. Lucy could only see two of them, now that the others had left, but it still seemed enough to stop this assault. She thought he could reduce the shields to sticks with that, but he waited. Probably wanted them to get closer.

Christine joined Lucy at the door. "Dumb asses," she said. "What the hell's that gonna do? And what are they gonna do about the gate? Kick at it while they're getting shot to pieces?"

"Yeah," Lucy said. "We got to help them. You found a string for the bomb?"

"Carole, get over here," Christine said toward the back of their house. Carole came up with one of the bombs. She was no longer wearing her striped shirt, but had pulled on a ragged, green sweatshirt with a faded picture of a horse embroidered on the front. She held out two other shirts to Lucy and Christine.

"What? Why?" Lucy said as she started unbuttoning the uniform.

"I figure if we get out, the old shirt won't be much help," Christine said as she undid her own shirt. "They'll probably shoot us anyway, but we won't stick out so much as the dead people who killed guards and broke out. Just an idea. Probably won't work. Besides, I always hated those things."

Lucy took a black sweater from Carole and pulled it on. "No, it's a good idea," she said, smiling at Christine.

Lucy took hold of the explosive. It still made her uneasy, even just the way it felt. Leave it to live humans to transform things as joyous and fulfilling as killing and eating into such grotesque ordeals.

The first burst of machine gun fire made Lucy jump. It was immediately followed by another. Outside, just as she'd predicted, one of the wooden shields had been split in two. That initial flurry of metal had torn the head off one of the dead men as well. Four others were trying now to make for cover, but they fell one by one with their heads smashed open by rifle fire, or completely atomized by the larger machine gun.

"You gonna make it?" Christine asked. "I can try."

Lucy tilted her head and smiled at the other woman. "No offense, but I don't think you'd have much of a chance. I'll do it if I can, if my body cooperates. Throw some bottles at them or something, but don't get yourselves shot."

"You too."

Tucking the bomb under her arm, Lucy waited a moment. She didn't jump as much when the machine gun fired again, and she took that as her signal to go. The guard was tearing up another of the wooden shields as Lucy tottered out and made her way toward the fence. She angled to the right, then turned a little and ran faster to the left, trying to make it a bit harder for them to cut her in two with their weapons.

As she reached the fence, she slid on her side and crammed the package under the barrier, right at the base of the guard tower. Scrambling to her feet, she trotted back, trailing the string behind her. She had reached the end of the cord when a spray of bullets splashed in the puddles next to her.

Lucy turned and slipped, falling to the side as a bullet tore into the left side of her chest. Fuck—if the string had come undone, then she'd just be scrambling around there in the mud until a bullet found her head and ended it. At least it wouldn't take long, and at least she wouldn't have to see her friends killed or worry anymore about Truman. The wound in her chest hurt more than she expected, a burning she didn't think she could feel anymore. She let out a howl of hatred and blame as she twisted on the ground and yanked the string.

The explosion was so loud, it made Lucy wonder if she'd be able to hear again. That'd suck worse than being all the way dead—not knowing what people were saying, not being able to understand them or have warning of danger, not being able to play or hear music. All this raced through her mind as she heard a muffled, groaning sound and screams, followed by the guard tower crashing right next to her, bits of debris hitting her face, dust and dirt stinging her eye.

Lucy got up slowly. Nothing felt broken as she brushed herself off. The wreckage of the tower spread out next to her. Looking back, she saw the fence was torn open, too. Near her, an arm stuck out of the shattered wooden pieces of the tower, and a groaning now came from that direction. Farther away, she saw another limb in the rubble, but that one stayed silent and still. Lucy walked over and cleared the pieces off the nearest body. One of the guards, face down, moving a little. At her mercy. She nudged him with her foot as she growled. This didn't feel like running around with a bomb. This felt right.

He tried to move his hand toward the automatic on his belt, causing Lucy to pounce on him. She bit into his wrist, the blood so hot and sweet on her lips, the scream so high and helpless—all of it perfect and intoxicating to her. She ground her teeth down, feeling the bones crack, and wrenched her head side to side to rend his arm into bloody shreds and jagged bits of bone.

Letting go of his wrist, Lucy wriggled up to lie on top of him. He'd turned his head a bit, so she could see his one terror-stricken, tear-filled eye, and his mud-smeared face. She bent lower. He whimpered and kicked his legs, but couldn't move.

"Don't fucking try to point a gun at me!" she shrieked, and her bloody lips were so close to his face that a pink spray hit his cheek and eye. "You fucking understand me? You'll never hurt me or my friends again—*ever!*"

"I'm sorry! I'm sorry!" he cried before falling into uncontrollable, inarticulate sobs.

Sorry? He thought that was supposed to do something, that was supposed to make up for something? The funny thing was, Lucy felt it did make this whole exchange different, somehow. She licked her lips and savored the taste of blood a little more, but knew all the thrill and joy of it had gone for the moment. Too bad, but she knew it was true. Now she had to proceed more delicately and deliberately.

"Sorry?" she hissed. "You don't want to tell me what a great ass I have? You don't want to see my tit nice and up close now? What's wrong, bay-bee?" She bent closer and drew out the last word deliciously. The guard started squirming so frantically at that, she thought he'd wriggle out from under her, or pass out from breathing so fast and shallow.

"No! No!" he squealed. "That was Bob! Not me! Not me!"

Shit. Just like them to lie, of course. It was second nature to them, even when their lives weren't at stake. And thinking she had a lying little lecherous coward right next to her almost made Lucy tear the back of his neck open with her teeth. Ah, the thrashing he'd make as she tore through the muscles and into the vertebrae. He'd buck under her like they were fucking, shudder and howl at the moment when it was finished. God, that'd feel so damned good. Gripping the back of his head, pressing his face into the dirt, a part of Lucy wanted it so much it nearly overwhelmed her. But as he cried and quivered under her, the flame of that desire gradually subsided in her. She wasn't even sure this was the one who'd tormented her or not. Damn—she should've been more observant, but mostly she'd tried to avoid looking at them. The living usually looked pretty much alike, anyway. Even if it were the right one— what was it she felt needed to be done to him now? She paused and considered again how this should unfold.

Lucy leaned closer. "No? Not you?"

"No! No!" He sniffled, paused. "Wait—you can talk? How?"

"I don't know," she said. "I learned. Twice, I guess. Hard work, too, the second time."

Lucy took her attention from him as she heard the other dead getting closer. Ben was closest, with a large crowd behind and all around, inching toward Lucy and the guard. He twisted, saw them, and started screaming and wriggling under her again.

"No! No!" he screamed. "Please, no! You can talk! You can understand! You're not like them! Save me!"

"Shhh," Lucy said, reaching around to get the automatic out of its holster. "They understand, too, don't worry."

Lucy had watched Will servicing weapons many times—disassembling them, cleaning them. He'd noticed her watching and shown her the basic workings. He was better about sharing information like that than Rachel was, and Lucy again felt herself hoping—almost in spite of herself—that they were all right, too. Lucy racked the slide on the automatic and made sure the safety was off, then lifted the barrel.

"We need a minute here," Lucy said. "You all owe me that."

Ben smiled. "Yeah, we do," he said. He gestured to the others to hold back. "First dibs for our hero, Lucy!" he shouted, laughing. The crowd joined in, with a pained, grumbling sort of guffaw, but after only a moment their look of hunger returned, redoubled, and Lucy knew she'd only have a very little while to transact whatever it was she felt, inchoately, needed to be done there on the ground that morning.

She kept her eye on the crowd, but leaned close to the guard again. "What's your name?" she whispered.

"What? T-T-Tom," he stammered. He was shaking all over now, constantly shivering under her as she leaned her body on his back.

Even though she knew it'd probably terrify him into blubbering incoherence, Lucy couldn't help herself as she licked the back of his neck—a long, raspy raking of her dry, hard tongue up his spine. Soft and greasy, with a nice tickling from the hairs, but a little bitter. He'd put on too much of that smelly stuff. What was it called? Lucy remembered it was called perfume when girls wore it, but she'd forgotten what its name was when guys put it on. Tom squealed and almost seemed to go into convulsions at her touch, but she didn't really blame him for that. He was guilty of a lot of things, whoever he was, but disgust and terror were not under his control and she wouldn't hold those weaknesses against him.

"Quiet, Tom," she said, sitting up more and letting the residual blood in her mouth overpower the bitterness she'd just tasted. "We don't have long. You're going to die in a minute. They'll be quick about it, but it'll hurt a lot, I'm sure."

"No, you can stop them! Please!" he dragged out the last word into a wail.

"I can't. We both know that. I'm not going to lie to you."

He could only sob softly at this.

"My name's Lucy, by the way."

He sniffled and his crying diminished enough for him to say, "Okay."

"I had a name, all those times you humiliated me, degraded me, made me feel like worthless shit."

"No! No, I told you—that wasn't me!" He again fell to crying, this time high pitched and uncontrollable.

"Shh, Tom, don't get so upset. I'm not mad about that. We already said you're going to die now. Really soon. I'm giving you a chance not to have a lie as the last thing you say." She was bluffing, as she still wasn't sure it was him, but it wasn't like any of the guards were nice, so he should come clean, whoever he was, and about whatever he'd been up to.

Pause. "You won't get mad again? You won't hurt me?"

"No, Tom. That's what they're gonna do, and they don't care what you say now. They're not really listening. But I am. If you want to say something, say it. It's totally up to you. This ends the same way, regardless."

Pause. "It was me." Pause. "I didn't know you could feel. I'm sorry."

"Thank you." Lucy ran her hand through his hair. It felt nice. Dead people's hair had gotten so dry and stiff, like straw. And so faded, too. This was deliciously soft, and such a shiny, light brown, like the fur of a frightened, quivering bunny. She could feel his revulsion again at her touch, though it was much less this time, just a barely perceptible tensing under her.

"Tom, they're gonna start soon," Lucy continued after a moment, seeing the crowd jostling one another, hearing their moans and shrieks. "I can put the gun in your hand and you can finish it, if you want. I'd do that for you. I trust you."

He writhed under her and groaned. "I can't move either hand. I couldn't hold it."

"Oh. I'm sorry." She half wished she hadn't bitten his wrist now, but doubted he would've said all that needed to be said if she hadn't.

"I feel cold." Pause. "You do it. Please."

Lucy looked at the gun. Nasty looking thing. It was different when Will handled them. He was so handsome to begin with, and so innocent as well, that he lent a certain peaceful glow even to such evil implements. But Lucy now felt the influence running the other way, like the weapon's cold brutality was infectious and creeping up her arm. She pressed the muzzle to the back of Tom's head and again wondered at how the living could ruin everything, even something as simple and glorious as killing, with their metallic, efficient, noisy tools.

"Are you sure?" she whispered. Some in the crowd started hooting and jumping up and down, seemingly disappointed that their meal would be silent and motionless.

"Yes. Please. Please."

"All right. I'm sorry."

"I know. Thank you. Thank you."

Lucy gritted her teeth and closed her eye against the ugly, loud blast. Her ears still rang and her knees ached as she hauled herself to her feet and handed the gun to Christine. She was glad to feel the metal slip from her hand, though she winced as the tearing and snarling started behind her.

Turning toward the hole in the fence, Lucy thought of how everything that had just occurred seemed to have an odd, inevitable grace about it, perhaps because she'd planned none of it when she first had fallen on the guard. Christine and Carole joined her in shuffling from the compound, and she wondered how many other such moments she hadn't noticed before or since her death.

Chapter 38
Rachel

The Dead End didn't look so mysterious and inviting in the early morning light. It looked mostly dirty and broken. Not even delightfully naughty and dangerous, but pathetic. The smells were decidedly worse in the daytime, too—more putrid and pungent—and Rachel again felt a wave of nausea. She hadn't eaten in nearly a day, and the hunger pangs compounded the discomfort. But there was nothing to be done about it now.

"Damn, the place looks so different in the daylight," she said as they made their way among the displays. "Now I don't know where the tent was where I saw Truman."

Turning down one alley, they were confronted by the most incongruous crowd of undead Rachel had ever seen. Half of them were small children dressed in strange green and red outfits, and the other half were naked young women. The whole crowd was having a good deal of trouble moving because of their footwear. The children had on shoes with long, curved toes, and they kept tripping over one another, while the women wore high heels that made them totter and fall in the mud. None of them seemed particularly to mind, however, but they batted playfully at one another and gave grunts and huffs that sounded something like laughter. It was impossible for Rachel not to be mesmerized by the scene, and then smirk at its harmless absurdity.

Only one dead woman took any notice of the two living newcomers, as she rose from the mass of wrestling undead. She was a corpulent woman with a huge head of auburn hair. A leather corset partly covered her body, though her crotch was bare and her enormous breasts spilled out over the top of her garment. As she stumbled toward them with a growl, Rachel could see someone had trimmed her pubic hair in the shape of a heart—a rather large one, too, the top of which fell just short of her belly button. Though the dead woman bared her teeth and snarled, Rachel couldn't help laughing.

Will pulled Rachel back. "Come on," he said. "We'll go another way."

They'd started down a different path, the leather-clad woman following at a distance, when a dead man emerged from another one of the tents. Though not as funny as the fat woman, he seemed less aggressive or threatening. He kept trying to shuffle some cards as he staggered along. If he dropped a card, he'd slowly bend down to retrieve it before trying again and taking another step. Will and Rachel gave him some room as they continued their retreat and he made no move to attack or follow them.

Just as their surroundings finally started to look familiar to Rachel, a small black girl came out of one tent. The tent where the show had taken place. Rachel also recognized the girl from the night before. The child had a revolver in one hand and a bamboo stick in the other. She calmly considered Rachel and Will, then noticed the dead card dealer and leather-corseted lady.

Without any sign of fear, the girl stepped past Rachel and pointed her stick at the two dead people. "Did they go and let you all out?" she yelled at them. "Willy—you get back to your table. You know how nearsighted you are—there's no way you can walk around out here. And Mistress Titania, you find the other dancing ladies, and you all either go out in the woods and keep running, if that's what you want, or you get yourselves back in your tent. Do you hear me? I'm sure there's gonna be men with guns here soon and I want you all either gone, or behaving yourselves when they get here. Do you understand? I don't want you all hurt."

Surprisingly, the two dead people complied with the orders almost immediately. The girl then turned toward Rachel and Will. "You two better be getting on, too," she said. "I think the Professor and his friends set them all loose, and now they're running around. They don't usually mean any harm, but you never know, especially with strangers."

"You were the girl I saw last night," Rachel said. "In the tent."

The girl appeared to consider her more carefully. "Oh, you were the lady who ran up and hit Doctor Jack and yelled at him," she said. "I remember—you have such pretty hair. That was nice of you to help. I don't know how much more the Professor could have taken. I'm glad you stopped it."

"The dead man—you call him The Professor?" Rachel said.

"Yes, 'cause he's so smart." The girl's face suddenly lit up. "Are you his friend? Is that why you stopped Doctor Jack?"

"Yes," Rachel said. "But I'm sorry you had to go through that." She bit her lower lip to keep from crying at that admission, and didn't know if she could keep talking to the girl without breaking down.

"It's okay. I was mostly worried about the Professor. When you see him, can you tell him I'm sorry I sent him away? I've thought about it and I don't blame him anymore."

Rachel managed to nod and give an "Hm-mmm," but she was on the verge of losing it in the face of such innocent love.

"You sent him away?" Will asked after a pause, holding on to Rachel. "When?"

"Just a little while ago," the girl said. "I thought he was being mean when he and Miss Ramona and the fat man killed Doctor Jack. But I've been sitting and thinking about it, and maybe it wasn't really their fault. He was awful mean to them. Please tell him that."

"We will," Will said. "But do you know where they went?"

"Oh, yes. He asked where the City Patrol base was, and I told him that way." She pointed. "They can't have gotten far, especially if they were stopping to let all these dead people loose. I almost wish they hadn't done that—some of them like Willy really can't get around. But I guess some of them will be happier if they're free. We'll see."

"That's very nice of you to worry about them," Will said.

"You hurry on and find them," the girl said as she moved back to the tent she'd come from. "I'm glad the Professor has friends. I was worried about him already."

The child waved to them, then the tent flap closed behind her. As Will pulled Rachel along, she kept herself from sobbing, but finally let the tears flow freely as they scurried between the tents.

Chapter 39
Truman

Truman had been the one to think of releasing the other dead people, mostly because he felt sorry for them, but also to increase the confusion and give Ramona, Lou, and him a better chance of escape. It was still early enough in the morning that they had no trouble sneaking among the tents and buildings and unlocking cages and chains and collars. Truman felt some concern that the dead people might kill some living person who wasn't so bad, but he hadn't met many of those since coming here. Dalia was the only one he'd be really worried about, and she seemed quite capable of taking care of herself. Truman's concern over the safety of the living people diminished further when he saw that most of the dead people either just sat there when they were released, or they immediately made their way out of the camp and toward the wilderness.

"Shouldn't you have kept the gun, Truman?" Ramona asked as he led her and Lou out of the Dead End and into the surrounding woods, trying to head in the direction Dalia had indicated.

"Maybe," he said. "I thought she might need it. And I hated how it felt, anyway."

"Really? I kind of liked it when I held the cannon. Felt good. And that look on his face."

"Then I'm glad you're the one who used it."

Ramona's bloodthirstiness was a bit unnerving, but not nearly as upsetting to Truman as Dalia's reprimand. Other than that, this morning had gone about as well as he could've expected. He really didn't know if they'd find Lucy, or what would come of this, and his worries now turned to what would happen to him out in the wild—killed by other dead people, or by the living? Just sitting in the cold and heat with nothing to do? Well, it couldn't be worse than what they'd been through. At least they were free, and if death came, it would only be a more radical kind of freedom for them.

From somewhere nearby, Truman heard gunfire. He stopped to listen. It seemed to come from where Dalia had said the City Patrol base was located. Truman's first instinct was to flee from guns, but at the same time he wondered if Lucy might be in danger. He couldn't decide what to do. The gunfire was followed by an explosion, powerful enough to cause ripples in a puddle at Truman's feet. That only further confused and frightened him, and he looked at Ramona with embarrassment. A man was supposed to make decisions and solve problems, but he was powerless at the moment.

Ramona smiled at him, and even took his hand and squeezed it. "It's okay, Truman," she said. "Everybody's scared of being shot. The girl said your woman was that way. We should go. Bad men are shooting. They usually shoot at dead people. We need to help."

Truman now heard a sort of cheer, but it sounded funny, more like a call that dead people would make. This finally shook him from his indecision. "Let's go," he said.

The three of them continued, emerging from among the trees into an open area. A high fence was there, topped by barbed wire. Behind the fence were dilapidated buildings that didn't look fit for habitation, but didn't look fully abandoned either. They weren't overgrown with kudzu or falling down completely, so people must have lived in them, though Truman couldn't imagine how. Farther away, drifting above the buildings, he saw a dust cloud that he assumed was from the explosion.

They followed the fence until Ramona extended her arm and stopped. Three figures were coming toward them. At first, Truman felt terror, that these were guards with guns and everything would be over in a moment. But he and Ramona and Lou weren't fast enough to make it back to the trees anyway, so they just stood there and awaited their fate. As the other people got closer, however, their movements didn't look like those of the living. Good. These were people like him. Perhaps they'd know where Lucy was, though Truman wasn't sure how many dead people could talk or understand. He pushed Ramona and Lou forward toward the strangers.

As they got closer, Truman could not believe it was Lucy, but the cloth across half her face was a pretty distinctive marking. It had to be her, leading two other dead women—one quite broad, the other tall and thin. It seemed to take Lucy a moment longer to recognize Truman, but as her pace increased, he knew she must've realized it was him as well.

"Truman," she said as she threw herself at him. Her voice was the most beautiful thing he'd heard in weeks. Her grip as she held him was even stronger than he remembered.

"I didn't think I was so lucky," he whispered to her. If he'd still been able to shed tears, he would've cried for joy, but all he could do was hold on to her and breathe in her scent.

They only stayed there a moment, before she released him. Truman got a better look at her. He found the blood around her mouth a little disconcerting, but even that added to her beauty.

"These are my friends," Lucy said. "Christine and Carole. This is Truman."

The two dead women acknowledged him with nods. Only after an awkward pause did Truman realize he was supposed to give similar introductions. "Oh, this is Lou and Ramona," he said. He thought Lucy's eye might've flashed as she looked over Ramona, but Truman probably just imagined it.

"I'm glad you found your man," the large woman, Christine, said. "What do you want to do now?"

"I don't know," Lucy said. Truman could only shake his head as he kept staring at her and thinking how happy he was.

"We should get back to the others," Carole said.

"Yeah, we should," Christine agreed. "We need to get them out of there before the food men show up and kill all of them." She turned to Lucy. "But you should go with your man and his friends. Go off into the woods. You can be free of all this shit. You deserve it."

"So do you," Lucy said.

"Maybe we'll find you later," Christine replied. "But we need to get going."

Lucy embraced her two friends, who started back the way they had come. "They're right," Ramona said. "We should get out of here."

"What about Will and Rachel?" Lucy said.

How could she think of them? She was free, with Truman, and they should forget about the people who'd gotten them into all the pain they'd suffered over the last few weeks.

"What about them?" Truman asked, scowling at her for maybe the first time. "We don't need them."

Lucy smiled, in that way Truman always thought was so beautiful, even as he had to admit it looked a little like a snarl. "No, we don't," she said. "But they're our friends."

"We have new friends. People like us. It's better, safer." Truman had only thought of finding her, and he'd been unbelievably lucky to do so. He wasn't about to go traipsing around trying to find those two. "Besides—how would we find them, anyway? We can't get inside the city where they are."

"No, I guess you're right." Truman was shocked at how sad she sounded at that. What was wrong with her? Her strength when she'd held him, together with the blood on her lips, had reminded him of how she really was—savage and powerful—but all this talk about Will and Rachel confused and frightened Truman. It didn't seem natural or right to him.

"People coming," Lou said, pointing back toward the trees. "Truman and ladies should run. Lou can't run as fast. Go."

Truman looked to where two figures were approaching them, then he heard one of them call his name, then Lucy's. Truman looked at Lucy, and saw how excited she was at the appearance of Will and Rachel. Though Lucy's look of joy gave Truman the usual thrill that it always did, he could hardly share her feelings. He knew the two living people would complicate things, as they always did, and he didn't like that at all.

Chapter 40
Will

Will was thrilled and amazed to see Truman and Lucy safe. The other dead people—a tall, beautiful woman, and a big man in overalls with a ruined face—looked peculiar to Will, but not dangerous at all.

"Truman!" Rachel said as they got close. "You're safe. And you found Lucy."

"How did you find us?" Truman asked. Will thought that was an odd greeting, and Truman didn't sound like his usual self. If the abuse were as Rachel had described, it didn't surprise Will to find Truman aloof and suspicious, but it was still a bit of a shock, given how trusting and generous he'd always been.

"The girl back at the tent told us to follow you this way," Rachel said. She also sounded different—a little hurt, it seemed, and contrite.

"How did you know I was in that tent?" Truman sounded even more suspicious with that reply.

"I—" Rachel looked to Will, then Lucy, then back to Truman. "I went there last night. I saw you. I tried to stop them. Then I went and got Will and we knew we had to get you out. God, I'm so sorry we waited. I'm sorry for you, too, Lucy. I didn't know what was going on."

Truman looked away. "You didn't want to know, I think." Will knew he was right, but on the other hand, he didn't want to see Rachel hurt by the accusations. He just wanted to get out of there. It was the last legacy of this place—making them fight and blame one another.

Lucy stepped between them, her hand on Truman's shoulder. "It's all right," she said softly. Then, a little louder, "I said it's all right, Truman."

"If you say so," he replied, but still didn't look at Rachel or Will, only at Lucy.

"We need to leave," Will said. "Rachel and I are going to find the boat and get out of here. You can come with us if you want. I don't think we can get your friends past the guards, though."

Truman looked at the beautiful dead lady in the long, fur coat. She smiled at him. "It's okay, Truman," she said. "I can go with Lou. You stay with your woman and your friends. You talked about your books every night, when you didn't talk about your woman. You go with them. We'll be fine. Right, Lou?"

"Yeah," the big dead man said. "Go somewhere quiet."

The lady started to lead him away. "Definitely," she said. "Or we could make some noise. You think you could fix a car?"

"Maybe. Lou's not real smart, but you can figure things out and help. I think we could."

"I think so too."

"Bye, Truman."

"Bye, Lou," Truman said. "Goodbye, Ramona."

"You take care," she said over her shoulder as she and the one they called Lou walked away. Her eyes weren't as dull as other dead people's, and her smile flashed again. It was a funny thought, but Will couldn't help admiring how Truman got all the prettiest dead ladies to like him. Sometimes being nice did pay off, he supposed, though he wished Truman were being nicer now, like he used to be.

Will rummaged in one of the bags they'd brought. "Guys, I know this isn't nice," he said, "but I think if we're going to get past the guards, it should look like you are restrained. I got some rope, a couple belts. You can put them on loosely. It's just until we get on the boat."

Truman glared at the restraints, but Lucy stepped forward and took them from Will. "Good idea," she said as she put the belt around Truman's neck. He acquiesced to her touch, but still stole angry glances at Rachel, who stood farther away. She was partly turned away from them, but it looked to Will like she was crying.

Lucy turned her back to Truman so he could put the other belt on her. She paused and considered Rachel for a moment.

Lucy turned her attention back to Will. "You got a knife in there?" she said.

"Sure." Will pulled out a thin boning knife with about an eight-inch blade from the bag. "You want it?" This had to be the first time he'd felt better about Lucy having a weapon, rather than Truman.

"Yes," Lucy said as she took it, slipping it under the sleeve of her sweater. She turned to tie Truman's hands together.

Will saw the handle of a Beretta in the bag as well. "You want a gun, too?" he said, offering it to Lucy. Maybe if he showed he trusted Lucy, Truman's mood would soften.

Lucy smiled and extended her hands toward Will, with her wrists together. "No," she said. "Thank you for showing me how to use one before. I needed to know. But I don't want one now. Tie my hands, please. Loose, like you said."

Will stuck the Beretta under his belt in back, then started tying Lucy as she'd asked. He looked up at her as he worked, and she leaned her forehead against his again, as she had when they were on the boat, weeks before. This time it felt cold against his, but still oddly reassuring. They were as ready as they were going to be to try to make it to the boat.

Chapter 41
Lucy

The four of them neared the dock, passing among ruined buildings along the river bank. Lucy walked alongside Rachel, with Will and Truman ahead of them. The two living people held ropes tied like leashes to their dead companions' collars. Will was right—they needed to do at least that, if they were going to pass as tame dead people and get away. But the charade seemed pretty thin, and Lucy didn't put much faith in its success. Ever since she'd seen Rachel and Will coming toward her that morning, however, she knew she wanted to be with them and not wandering in the wilderness.

Truman had been right, of course, when he'd argued for leaving. He was right now, as she saw how angry and full of blame he was for their living friends. But for some reason that morning, those things didn't matter to Lucy. At first it had been an almost aesthetic, sensual response—the two living people were so beautiful and alive, it just felt good to be around them, and an eternity of the dullness of the dead seemed so unappealing and dissatisfying to her now. But then, as she looked in Rachel's eyes when she admitted her guilt to them, Lucy realized something more. She saw that in some way, the city had harmed the girl more than it had Lucy. Lucy could live with all the cruelty and brutality—though she now suspected that it had done much more damage to Truman than it had to her, and she didn't know what to do about those wounds. But Rachel had been subjected to some more insidious contamination, and all Lucy could feel now was a need and a longing to cure her from that, remove the girl from the source of the disease and restore her innocence. That was a much better, more worthy goal than slinking off into the woods, and choosing it gave Lucy only joy and confidence.

Lucy made Rachel hang back a bit, so she could speak without the men hearing. She leaned closer to Rachel, who looked at her with wet eyes but didn't try to pull away.

"Don't mind Truman," Lucy said. "He thinks too much."

"He's right," Rachel said softly, looking down.

"He is, but it's not always about being right."

"I don't understand."

"I know." Lucy blamed herself—she wasn't the right person to offer rationalizations, so she felt a bit foolish to have begun this conversation. "I can't explain it. Just don't feel so bad, is what I mean."

Will shushed them, and Lucy looked and saw a figure up ahead. She pulled away from Rachel and put on more of a pretense of shuffling, as well as trying to look as stupid as possible. As they got closer to the man, she recognized him as the cute one from the boat. He still had a shotgun and looked even more nervous than before.

"What the hell are you doing out with those two things?" he challenged them. "There's all kinds of talk on the radio about trouble. So get the hell outta here."

"We didn't hear anything," Will said. Poor guy was a terrible liar. If Truman hadn't upset Rachel so much, she would've been a lot better at it, Lucy figured, but there was nothing to be done about that now.

"I should call CJ," the cute one said as he reached for a walkie-talkie at his belt. God, he sounded like he was going to cry.

Fuck this. Will should've made a move by now. Lucy remembered CJ was the only one who looked competent in the bunch, anyway, and if he showed up with a couple more, there was no way they'd get to the boat. Lucy shoved past Truman and was on the kid before he could react, batting the shotgun out of the way and knocking him backward to the ground. She had the knife out and was about to give it to him across the neck before he could make a sound, when Truman grabbed her shoulder from behind.

"Don't," Truman said. "He wasn't so bad. The other ones were worse."

The kid's eyes were wide as he stared at the knife. This just wasn't a good day for killing, apparently. Things kept getting in the way. Lucy pressed the blade against his neck anyway, and lowered her face close to his, relishing the look and feel as he squirmed and whimpered under her.

"No?" she said. "What do you want to do with him?"

Will knelt beside her. "Turn him over," he said. "I'll tie him up. We just need for him to stay here a couple minutes while we get away."

As Will tied the kid's hands behind his back, Lucy leaned down closer to him. "Hey," she whispered, breathing heavily in his ear. Unlike the guard earlier that day, this one's revulsion didn't seem to diminish as much when she touched him more. That almost made Lucy angry enough to do something more violent, but she contented herself with touching her teeth to his ear—not enough to break the skin, just enough to make him squeal incoherently. She pulled back a little and let him calm down as Will finished tying him up.

"You can talk," he said finally. "What are you?"

"I'm a person, you dumb ass. And I can do lots of things. Like eat your fucking heart right now. But I didn't. You understand?"

"Yes, yes," he whimpered.

"Remember that the next time you point a gun at someone."

"I will, I will."

They continued after this encounter, Lucy more confident they might pull it off. At the gate to the dock, she saw two of the other guys who'd been there when they first arrived—the one with the big mustache, CJ, and the other young one who had gone off with Truman. They had both seemed like pretty big dicks, and Lucy really didn't feel like sparing either one. Though they eyed her, neither one seemed too scared. Good.

"Hey, it's the hill people again," CJ sneered. "And you got your zombies back. You must've paid a bunch for them."

"Yeah, we did," Will said, making Lucy wish again that their spokesperson were a better liar. "But we got some left. We just want our boat back."

"Oh?" CJ sounded a little more interested and cooperative at the mention of money.

"Yeah. Here. We just want to leave, so we won't need this anymore." He offered some bills.

Taking them, CJ gave the wad a quick inspection, before turning toward Rachel. "What about you, missy?" he said. "You sure look a lot better than when I saw you last. You bring some money, too?"

Rachel handed over some more bills. Lucy didn't like how long this was taking. CJ stepped back, putting all the money in his pocket. "Good," he said. "That's a lot." He smirked. "I got that. Plus all the money I got for you two a few weeks ago—guess I won't get the bonus for you still being in the City Patrol, but this oughta make up for that. Oh, and maybe there's a reward for turning you all in to the cops now. Paid three times for a couple crazy people and their weird pets—isn't that something?"

"Yeah, it sure is," his companion agreed as they both started laughing.

"It's just like I told her—she'd always be somebody's bitch." The two laughed harder.

Truman surprised Lucy by snarling and lunging for CJ at that moment, and it gave her a clearer dive for the other guy. He'd barely raised his shotgun at all, and she had the knife up to the hilt between his ribs. Lucy twisted the blade as she bit into his cheek. The blood running down the knife handle to her arm was hotter than that on her lips, but all of it was sweet and satisfying, the life of some bastard who didn't deserve it, spurting out onto her cold, dry flesh. His shriek turning all wet and gurgly just made it even more delightful, as did that stupid, shocked look in his eyes. Why'd people always look surprised at dying? It was infinitely more unbelievable that anything should be alive in this ugly, fucked-up world. But people overlooked the most obvious things, all the time.

Lucy turned just as she heard the blast of CJ's shotgun. Shit. Truman hadn't been quite fast enough, and he'd gotten shot in the stomach. Lucy lunged now in that direction, but as she brought the knife down into CJ's neck, she saw he had a pistol in his left hand.

Lucy heard the bang and a howl from Truman at the same moment. Oddly, though she keenly felt the knife slashing into the wet flesh and more hot blood on her hand, the impact of the bullet under her chin was nearly imperceptible. Her already imperfect vision shut down immediately, though her other senses drained away much more slowly. She felt more tendons and muscles tearing as she pulled down on the knife with both hands, and a greater, more wondrous flow of blood down both of her arms. Then she felt the man's body falling on top of hers as they both collapsed. Then someone's hands on her face. She assumed they must be Truman's, they felt so cold and rough.

He was the only object of regret and concern for her at that last moment. Everything else had been accomplished, and Lucy felt sure she did not have a shocked look on her face as she died a second time—everything was far too clear and certain for her to look like that. She would've liked to say something to comfort Truman, but her hearing was now gone, and she could not draw in more breath, so she only rasped, "Finished," in a voice she hoped he'd realize contained nothing but joy.

Chapter 42
Rachel

Truman sat by the table in the main cabin. He wasn't reading like he used to. Just sitting and staring. That was pretty much all he'd done since Lucy had killed the guards at the dock, and they'd dragged her body back to the boat.

"Truman?" Rachel said quietly, walking up beside him. He didn't turn or acknowledge her. She put her hand on his shoulder. "Truman?" she tried again. At least he didn't turn away. Rachel hadn't decided what she was going to say, but knew she had to try. She'd betrayed him, left him and Lucy to suffer in that hellhole of inhumanity, put herself ahead of him and Lucy like they were nothing. It didn't matter if he didn't know every detail of it, he knew enough to blame and hate her for it. She knew enough not to fault him for that, too. Rachel knew she didn't deserve his forgiveness and didn't plan on asking for it, but she had to say something to express her regret, admit her guilt, at least. But you couldn't just say that stuff without the other person acknowledging your presence.

"Does it hurt, where you got shot?" Rachel was pretty sure it didn't, and was positive that wasn't what was bothering Truman, but maybe making small talk would help.

Truman drew himself up. If he were still alive he might've taken in a breath at that point, but he just silently lifted his head and squared his shoulders. Then with a speed Rachel had never before seen from him, he grabbed her wrist and yanked her forward. She gave a little yelp, but not enough to alert Will outside at the helm. It was more just an involuntary gasp from being pulled off balance. Truman had pulled her hand across his body and now pressed it against the table, holding her there with her shoulder and arm right in front of his face. By his mouth.

He put his left hand on her shoulder, though his grip there was nowhere near as tight as on her wrist, which was painfully strong and spiteful. He craned his neck a bit, moving his mouth closer to her bare triceps, but still didn't say anything.

Rachel stared at him as the shock wore off. She put her left hand on the table to steady herself, but didn't try to pull away. "Truman," she whispered. "Let go of my arm. You're frightening me."

"Good," he said finally. "People should be frightened. There are lots of scary things in this world."

Rachel's mind raced. Oh God. He'd wigged out and gone feral. They should've known this would happen, especially after the shock and grief of losing Lucy. But he had a hold of her right hand, so going for the .38 at her hip was a non-starter. And besides—this was Truman. Rachel wasn't sure she could draw a weapon on him anyway. He was distraught, and she was partly to blame for it—how could she think of killing him, on top of how she'd already treated him? So they remained there a moment, Rachel staring at Truman but unable to see his eyes or intuit exactly what he was thinking.

"Truman," she started again, "please let me go. We can talk. I know you're upset about Lucy. We all are."

"Don't fucking lie!" Truman said a little louder, but still not loud enough to get Will's attention, Rachel thought. He slammed her hand into the table as he said this and tightened his grip on her shoulder. "You feel nothing for her! Nothing! You people don't know how to feel anything but hate and fear!"

Rachel had never heard cursing from Truman before, and thought it was a pretty sure sign this wasn't going to end well. She expected a tearing, searing pain in her arm at any moment, then the hot, wet blood everywhere, covering everything in defeat and despair. Then she'd scream, Will would come running in and shoot Truman in the head, then a couple days of agony, and then—well, whatever came after that. Stupid oblivion or ravenous madness or just the sad boredom she'd seen in Truman. Whichever it was going to be, it filled her with a frantic longing to live, to whimper and sob and beg for her life.

But Rachel also had that nearly unavoidable reaction a person has when someone else gets angry, especially if that anger is at least partly misplaced: her own wrath and indignation rose in response. "I couldn't fucking help it!" she said in a hoarse voice—and although she was sniffling as the words came out, they sounded more infuriated than pleading. "She scared me. She scared me all the time—I can't help that. But I still feel bad for what happened to her. Don't fucking tell me I don't. You can kill me now if you're that mad at me, Truman, but don't tell me how I feel, or think you know everything."

They again paused, with Rachel's fast, shallow breathing the only sound in the room. Truman's grip relaxed somewhat, but he did not let go of her. "All right," he said more quietly. "She was much faster than me, you know."

"I know, Truman. But why are you telling me this? Why did you grab me?"

"To show you. She could've killed you anytime. And she wanted to. All the time. Every day."

"Yes, I know. That's why I was always scared of her."

"No, you still don't understand." He let go of her arm finally. "I'm not explaining it right."

Rachel slowly pulled her arm back, rubbing her wrist. Now that the danger was past, she was more sick and disgusted with herself, and more in awe of Truman's restraint, even in the midst of his maddening grief. She thought how people always want to apologize without it costing them anything, and how she'd come down here with the same false, cheap assumption. Then for a moment it looked like her fuck-up might cost her something—and that made her feel shocked and scared? How could she even think of killing poor Truman, when he'd done nothing but lash out against her callousness and unfairness?

Part of her wanted to get as far from Truman as possible at that moment, but the better, less rational, more insistent part prevailed. "Scoot down," she said.

"What? Oh." Truman moved down the bench.

Rachel sat beside him—close, with her shoulder touching his. She remembered vividly when her dad had died—it was before all this craziness, when death was just loss and emptiness and pain, when it was confusing for those reasons, and without any of the mess they had now. She remembered how you didn't—you couldn't—really talk about it, but you just needed someone close, a body touching yours, and that was enough, even though it wasn't really enough and you still hurt so much inside you thought you'd die yourself. But words would've just made it worse, putting your empty head more at odds with your overfull heart and tearing you apart even more inside. So they sat there for what seemed a long time without speaking.

"Do you want to try to explain it to me some more?" Rachel finally asked. "I know I'm not good at stuff like that, but I'll try to understand."

Truman took a deep breath. "Thank you for trying. I was saying how badly she wanted to hurt you. Not wanted, like it was something she chose or found pleasurable. It was more of a need, a longing. She'd tell me that on so many nights, how it gnawed at her inside. And we'd talk about it, and every morning she'd tell me how she wasn't going to hurt you. She'd decided not to and she wouldn't, no matter what. Don't you see how hard it was for her?"

Rachel leaned more of her weight against him. "I—I guess I sort of wondered if that's what was going on in her head. I didn't know for sure. And then I'd see her and mostly I'd feel frightened. I'm sorry."

"She was better than you thought. Better than you deserved." Rachel heard the bitterness in those final words, though it didn't make her anxious that Truman might attack again. No, he'd gotten to that point where a person can express his resentment and hurt, even to the person who's wronged him, without it boiling over into rage. He presented it now to Rachel, not to intimidate or blame her, but to ask her help in healing it.

"I'm sorry, Truman. I don't know what else to say. She's gone and I can't trade places with her and I can't make it up to her."

Truman finally turned toward her and they looked in one another's eyes. His were brown and always looked a little sad, though now their anguish gave them the kind of vitality and urgency that Rachel had never seen in another dead person's eye— with the possible exception of Lucy's ethereal blue orb. But that had been different, Rachel thought as she stared at Truman's soulful gaze: Lucy's eye had looked so alive because it seemed so disconnected from her broken, animal body. Truman's eyes right now seemed alive because they knew and felt so intensely the pain of his beloved's death and his own grief.

"No," he said. "You can't make it up to her, and you needn't be sorry. She died for you, and it doesn't matter if I think you deserve it—she thought you did. Now do you understand why she did it?"

Rachel blinked twice. Truman's words seemed right at the edge of making sense, like a riddle she had to answer without him coming out and saying what it meant, for that would ruin everything. And the revelation he was trying to convey to her called for surrender more than reason, so Rachel bowed her head slightly, looking down. "I didn't know she felt that way," she whispered. "I didn't know she could."

"She could. She did. She loved you, in her way. She didn't say it, but she showed it. And now you have to live with that. It's hard."

Rachel felt Truman's fingers in her hair, just lightly brushing it—barely touching it, really. She looked back up.

"I'm sorry I frightened you before," he said. "That was wrong of me. I did it deliberately, too, knowing it was wrong. She would never have done something as mean and bad as that. She was better than all of us. That's what I was trying to explain before."

Rachel nodded. "Yes. Thank you for showing me."

"I hope you'll tell everyone you meet about her."

"What? Well, yes—but you can too. You were closer to her."

"Yes, but you people don't listen to people like me very much. So I leave it to you."

"All right. I'll tell people everywhere about her."

Truman turned and rose from the table. "Rachel," he said, "I think we're going out into more open water. Could you ask Will to look for an island? I'd like to bury her there, away from other people."

Rachel stood. "Of course, Truman, if that's what you want."

"Thank you."

Truman slowly shuffled around, picking up books, looking at them, and arranging them into two piles on the table. Rachel watched him a moment before going up on deck. Will was at the wheel, but she ignored him, going instead to the tightly-wrapped bundle off to the side. Rachel knelt down on the deck, next to where the poor woman's head must be, under the sheets. Rachel put her hands on the fabric, letting them settle around the contours of her nose, brow, and cheeks. She closed her eyes and pictured Lucy's savage beauty and all the powerful mystery behind it.

"You okay, Rach?" she heard Will ask.

"Yeah," she replied. "Just kind of thinking about her. Wondering about stuff. Feeling sad and grateful and happy all at the same time." Rachel didn't think Will would quite understand what she and Truman had talked about—and she was definitely never going to tell him about the arm-grabbing, no matter what—but her description now was accurate, as far as it went. She'd never get over how sleeping with someone meant there were so many things you didn't have to explain, things you could just take for granted, even as that intimacy precluded so many other topics of conversation. Just some more funny stuff to consider, but it gave her a hint of a smile as she sat there holding the face of the one who had saved them.

"Oh." Pause. "How's Truman?"

"He's fine. He wants you to find an island to bury her on."

"That's good. I was worried about what to do with her. You know—a dead body, one that's all the way dead. You can't just let it sit around forever."

Rachel inhaled deeply. There was no odor, just the freshest, clearest air she could imagine. "She won't smell, don't worry."

"Well, if you say so. I still can't believe how fast she was, how she saved us from those jerks."

Rachel leaned down, bringing her forehead closer to the shattered, covered shape before her. "I believe it," she said, and then kept mouthing the first two words silently, over and over.

Chapter 43
Truman

"Please, Truman, please come with us."

Truman looked at Rachel's tear-streaked face as she knelt next to him. She'd been pleading this way for some time, long after Will had given up and loaded the shovels back into the rowboat. She looked prettier than ever. Thinking of the years ahead, sitting on the island alone, Truman considered how feminine beauty might be the one thing he'd miss. Nothing else had much savor anymore for him. All the rest of human interaction or the natural world had faded to a grey, undifferentiated mass of boredom and pain when he'd held Lucy's sweet, shattered head in his hands. But Lucy's beauty, along with that of all the rest of her sex, remained as scintillating and varied as ever, in all its many forms.

Rachel's attractiveness was so different from Lucy's, or Ramona's for that matter—cherubic, wet, overflowing with emotion and with all the strength and weakness of her mortality. It was probably quite different from his wife's charms, if he could remember her. Truman felt so bad for having frightened Rachel. She didn't deserve that. She was young and smart and only averagely selfish: someone like that deserved just a little self-reproach, not a nasty, violent threat from someone who was just as selfish and weak as she was. He'd make that one of the things he contemplated in his exile—his prideful, wicked torment of her.

"No, Rachel," he said quietly. "I told you—I don't think we should be around each other so much, living and dead people. It's not right. Maybe for Lucy, she could, but she was stronger than me. She loved and hated you all so much more, and that sustained her somehow. Me—I just feel angry around living people, now that she's gone. I blame them. They make me feel sick inside, to be frank."

Rachel collapsed in deeper sobs that separated her words from one another and threatened to make her hyperventilate. Such frail things, these living humans: a little too much or too little air and they'd pass out.

"Why—won't—you—forgive—me?" Rachel trailed off into an inarticulate wail that subsided into a moan.

Her head was down, so she couldn't see Truman smiling at her as he ran his hand through her hair—not lightly this time, but luxuriating in the sensuous, thick curls as they snaked around his dry, stiff fingers. She didn't flinch at all, didn't show any sign of mistrust, even after how he'd acted before. He would make that another object of thought and analysis in the days to come—how fully and freely these people could forgive, even forget. It was another quality he knew he didn't share, as much as he longed to.

"I forgive you, Rachel," he whispered. "Don't cry. And you hardly need my forgiveness. But I know how I feel. I know how she felt too. With her, everything came up from so deep inside, as though it started in her stomach. Her feelings had power and authority—over herself, over everyone. Mine don't. They just come from my head, and that's too weak and muddled to stand all the pain and passion that you people bring. But I want you to be happy. I do. She did. So be happy, Rachel, and don't cry."

She looked up, her face florid from the weeping. "Won't there be storms? This island's so tiny—you'll be swept away. Aren't there hurricanes around here, Will?"

Truman looked at Will. He was so charming too, in his way. He'd tried to reason with Truman before, but once he decided it was useless, he just stopped, unlike Rachel. No emotional appeal, no begging. Just rational discourse that came to a measured end when it was no longer useful. Truman wouldn't need to consider

Will and his way of thinking so much, because it was so close to his own, but he'd ponder his generous, simple soul, as well as the mystery that had brought them together, all those months ago.

"I think so," Will said. "We've come pretty far south."

Truman looked over his head at the branches of the tree above him. He had no idea what kind it was, but it had a tall, thick trunk, even though its branches didn't spread out too far. "This tree looks old," he said. "It didn't get swept away. I'll hold on to it if I have to. I'll share its fate."

"What will you do, just sitting here?" Rachel sniffed. Truman was glad she'd calmed down.

He patted the large duffle bag of books next to him. "I have my books. I haven't really felt like reading them since she died, but I think one day I might."

Will held out a tin cup to Truman. "You asked me before if I had one of these you could keep," he said.

Truman took it. "Oh, thank you, Will. You taught Lucy and me to drink water back when we first met. That was so kind of you. I'll let the cup fill when it rains, so I can drink from it and remember you." He moved his hand to Rachel's chin. "And I'll always remember you, Rachel."

She embraced him. Exactly like Lucy, she was unbelievably strong for a woman her size. And it still shocked Truman, how living people were so warm and soft. It was like you were sinking into them when they touched you, as though they'd swallow you up, absorb and crush you into their burning flesh, and you'd be lost in their too-vital selves. It was frightening even as it was exhilarating, but Truman enjoyed it nonetheless and thought the touch of another person was something else he'd deeply miss: and unlike the infinite variety of female beauty, each human embrace was exactly the same in some way, with the same sense of urgency and longing as every other one, from one end of the world to the other, from one age to the next.

Truman leaned back against the tree and watched the rowboat glide across the water, returning Will and Rachel to their ship, and whatever lay in store for them. Truman rested his hand on the bag of books—all those words by men even deader than he, but their ideas sharper and more alive than his dull, clouded mind. And beneath and all around him, her spirit—her driving, consuming spirit of love, surrender, destruction, and rebirth—deliriously throbbed.

Yes, this was where he belonged now. Truman closed his eyes, overcome by the idea that if the mass of dead were always increasing, and if the only thing that survived death were desire, then the total amount of desire in the universe would always continue to grow, whether to infinity or to some unknown upper limit the mind could never reach. Truman would make that another object of contemplation. It was a calculus both terrifying and thrilling to him, and one he felt sure would sustain forever those it did not crush with its threat and promise.

Chapter 44
Will

Will looked back at Rachel, sitting at the stern of the sailboat. He considered her a moment, then followed her gaze across the water to where they'd left Truman. Will couldn't figure either of them out, really, for the last couple days. Well, maybe Truman, a little. He could imagine being so distraught you just sat down and didn't want to deal with anything anymore. He couldn't imagine doing it for very long, though—he was just too anxious, needed activity and distraction too much. Better to throw yourself into some purpose, some job, than just sit there.

And Rachel? First she wanted to stay in the city, then she wanted to go, then she got so upset about leaving Truman behind. She'd always liked and trusted him, but what was it with her and Lucy, before that? She'd knelt over the body so long—first on the ship, then when they laid it on the ground on the island. It wasn't like those two were ever close—quite the opposite. Will was sad about Lucy, too, but it was over, finished, and it didn't make any sense to dwell on it. It wasn't anybody's fault, what happened to her. It was brave of her to do what she did, and they should just accept that and be grateful. So why did Truman want to spend the rest of his days sitting on a little spit of land with no one around and nothing to do? How long would that be, anyway? Years? Maybe even decades, or longer? Sounded pretty hellish to Will. And why was Rachel acting like it was the end of the world? People were weird.

"I'm sorry, Rach," he tried to begin. "I don't know why he wanted to stay there."

"It's okay," she said softly. "He knew what he wanted. But I'll miss him. I was so mean to him."

"No—you just wanted to be happy. It's not your fault."

She turned toward him and raised her voice. "No!" She glared at him. "Stop saying that. It is my fault. I was cruel to two people who were good to me, kind to me, tried to help me. It doesn't matter that they don't still have a pulse—I owed them everything, and instead I hurt them. That city was wrong, it was evil, and I got caught up in it, but it's still my fault."

Rachel got up and walked over to him. She slipped her small, solid frame next to his, her arm around his waist. "It's good we got out of there, if we're going to have kids," she said, then paused a second. "If you still want to."

Will was taken aback by the comment, but didn't hesitate at all. "Of course," he said. What was she so upset about? He still didn't quite get it.

Rachel leaned her head down. "Good. I think I'm pregnant."

Now Will was completely overcome by her words, torn between surprise, joy, and apprehension, and still confused at how she was acting. He grasped her chin to tilt her head up and look in her wet, sparkling eyes. To him, her plaintiveness was as captivating as her anger or cunning, just in a different way. He was shocked she didn't look happy, though. If anything, her expression was a mixture of sorrow and longing.

"That's great," Will said. "What's wrong? You look so sad."

She looked at him very intently, lowering her brows. "I am," she said softly. "This doesn't change that, even if I'm happy at the same time. Being pregnant is just something I have to do, something I'm supposed to do. I've been thinking about it a lot, since she died, and as I got more sure I was pregnant. We owe it to them. It's the only way we're superior to them. But that just makes it another thing we don't deserve. So that's what I'm feeling right now—sad at all the joy I don't deserve. Does that make sense?"

She was acting and talking so weird, though that wasn't quite the right word. Mysterious, was more like it, and it didn't frustrate Will as much as before. He closed his eyes as he leaned down to her. The scent of the soap they'd had in the city—an unnatural smell that was at once too sweet and too acerbic—was nearly gone. Rachel had been pressing her face into Lucy's shroud so long she had that musty odor in her hair, along with some sand from the island—all of it combining into something weedy, salty, and bitter, something frail and irresistible at the same time. Will tilted his head a little to nuzzle her, pressing his forehead instead of his nose into her hair.

"I love you," he whispered. Just as he said it, he was overcome with the thought that the exact spot where Lucy had kissed him was now pressed against Rachel. The thought so overwhelmed him that he didn't actually hear her response, though everything about the moment—her body, her smell, her voice, all the strange things she'd said, the memory of Lucy's unexpected, fated kiss—all of this filled him with a euphoria that he longed to hold on to forever, as well as the strength, he felt sure, to do so.

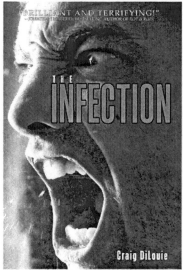

AUTOBIOGRAPHY OF A WEREWOLF HUNTER

After his mother is butchered by a werewolf, Sylvester James is taken in by a Cheyenne mystic. The boy trains to be a werewolf hunter, learning to block out pain, stalk, fight, and kill. As Sylvester sacrifices himself to the hunt, his hatred has become a monster all its own. As he follows his vendetta into the outlands of the occult, he learns it takes more than silver bullets to kill a werewolf.

BY BRIAN P EASTON

ISBN: 978-1934861295

HEART OF SCARS

The Beast has taken just about everything it can from Sylvester Logan James, and for twenty years he has waged his war with silver bullets and a perfect willingness to die. But fighting monsters poses danger beyond death. He contends with not just the ancient werewolf Peter Stubbe, the cannibalistic demon Windigo, and secret cartels, but with his own newfound fear of damnation.

BY BRIAN P EASTON

ISBN: 978-1934861639

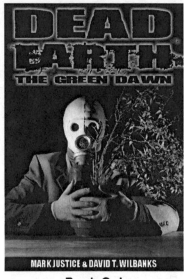

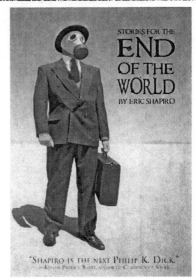

ELEVEN TWENTY-THREE

Layne Prescott meets a strange man in a Shanghai airport and ends up carrying a mysterious briefcase with an attached wrist shackle home with him. Once back in his hometown, Layne's world spirals out of control. Each day at precisely 11:23, the small town erupts into violent chaos. Surrounded by a strict military quarantine, Layne and his friends wait with dread as the clock ticks downward.

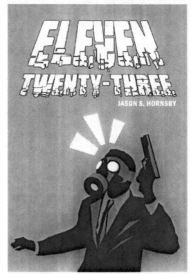

ISBN: 978-1934861349

BY JASON S HORNSBY

VALLEY OF THE DEAD
THE TRUTH BEHIND DANTE'S INFERNO

Using Dante's Inferno to draw out the reality behind the fantasy, author Kim Paffenroth tells the true events... During his lost wanderings, Dante came upon an infestation of the living dead. The unspeakable acts he witnessed —cannibalism, live burnings, evisceration, crucifixion, and dozens more—became the basis of all the horrors described in Inferno. At last, the real story can be told.

THE TRUTH BEHIND DANTE'S INFERNO

VALLEY OF THE DEAD
Kim Paffenroth

ISBN: 978-1934861318

BY KIM PAFFENROTH

MORE DETAILS, EXCERPTS, AND PURCHASE INFORMATION AT
www.permutedpress.com

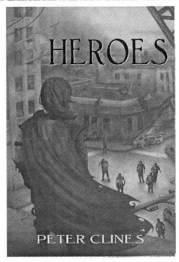
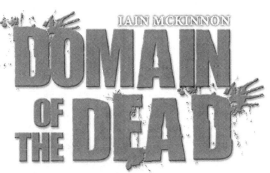

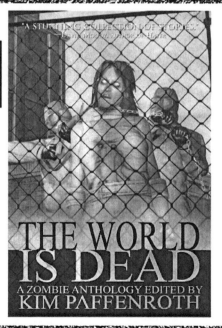

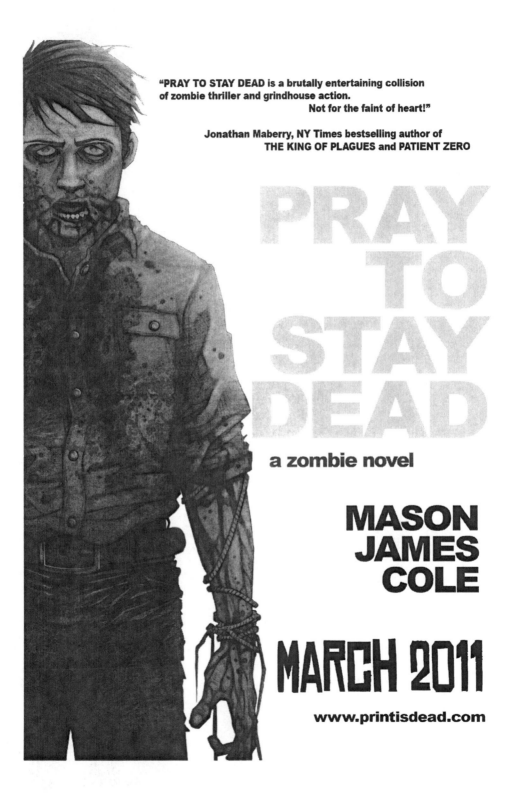

"PRAY TO STAY DEAD is a brutally entertaining collision
of zombie thriller and grindhouse action.
Not for the faint of heart!"

Jonathan Maberry, NY Times bestselling author of
THE KING OF PLAGUES and PATIENT ZERO

PRAY
TO
STAY
DEAD

a zombie novel

MASON
JAMES
COLE

MARCH 2011

www.printisdead.com

CPSIA information can be obtained at www.ICGtesting.com
Printed in the USA
LVOW12s1443111013

356554LV00002B/515/P